Through Shattered Glass

by
David B. Silva

This signed numbered edition of
Through Shattered Glass
is limited to 350 copies.

This is number __77__.

[signature: David B. Silva]

David B. Silva

[signature: Dean Koontz]

Dean Koontz

───── *A Gauntlet Original* ─────

Through Shattered Glass

Through Shattered Glass

David B. Silva

Gauntlet Publications
■ *2001* ■

Limited Edition ISBN 1-887368-41-8
Copyright © 2001 by David B. Silva
Introduction Copyright © 2001 by Dean Koontz
Jacket and Interior Art Copyright © 2001 by Harry O. Morris

This book is a work of fiction. Names, characters, places and incidents are either the products of the author's imagination or are used fictitiously. Any resemblance to actual events or locations or persons, living or dead, is entirely coincidental.

Manufactured in the United States of America

FIRST EDITION

Gauntlet Publications
309 Powell Road, Springfield, PA 19064
Phone: (610) 328-5476
email: gauntlet66@aol.com
Website: http://www.gauntletpress.com

Acknowledgements

"The Calling" copyright © 1990 by David B. Silva.
   From *Borderlands*.
"Dwindling" copyright © 1985 by David B. Silva.
   From *Spectrum Stories*.
"Ice Sculptures" copyright © 1987 by David B. Silva.
   From *Masques II*.
"Dry Whiskey" copyright © 1999 by David B. Silva.
   From *Cemetery Dance*.
"A Time To Every Purpose" copyright © 1993 by David B. Silva.
   From *Amazing Stories*.
"Metanoia" copyright © 1986 by David B. Silva. From *New Blood*.
"The In-Between" copyright by David B. Silva. From *2000*.
"Empty Vessels" copyright © 1994 by David B. Silva.
   From *Love In Vein*.
"The Hollow" copyright © 1990 by David B. Silva.
   From *Cemetery Dance*.
"Nothing As It Seems" copyright © 1999 by David B. Silva.
   From Whitley Strieber's *Aliens*.
"Ice Songs" copyright © 1989 by David B. Silva. From *Pulphouse*.
"Because I Could" copyright © 1993 by David B. Silva.
   From *Pulphouse*.
"Alone of His Kind" copyright © 1991 by David B. Silva.
   From *Obsessions*.
"The Night In Fog" copyright © 1998 by David B. Silva.
   From *Subterranean Press*.
"Metastasis" copyright © 1990 by David B. Silva.
   From *Cemetery Dance*.
"The Song of Sister Rain" copyright © 1995 by David B. Silva.
   From *After Hours*.
"Slipping" copyright © 1991 by David B. Silva.
   From *Borderlands II*.

For Garrett, who sees
his own wonderful stories
through shattered glass

Contents

Dave Silva: Person of Mystery
Introduction by Dean Koontz i

The Calling 1
Dwindling 15
Ice Sculptures 25
Dry Whiskey 37
A Time To Every Purpose 51
Metanonia 69
The In-Between 77
Empty Vessels 87
The Hollow 107
Nothing As It Seems 115
Ice Songs 143
Because I Could 157
Alone of His Kind 169
The Night In Fog 187
Metastasis 215
The Song of Sister Rain 227
Slipping 241

Dave Silva: Person of Mystery

Dean Koontz

I have known David B. Silva for more than fifteen years. This is a long, long, long time by any standard: more than a century in dog years. It's an eternity to any may fly, because may flies live only two days, which is the length of time Dave sometimes takes to get up from his armchair after too much beer and a marathon of Ed Wood videotapes. Cheops—king of Egypt in the 26th century B.C.—built the great pyramid at Giza in but a year, and God created the universe in six days, but after fifteen years of knowing Dave, I'm frustrated to admit that I'm lacking the colorful details needed to create the astonishing and vivid portrait that readers of his work have a right to expect.

Although I have never met him face to face and have no idea what he looks like, I consider Dave a friend. I believe that he considers me a friend, too, because I detect something warm and even affectionate in the violent, wordless spluttering that erupts from him every time he picks up his telephone and hears my voice. And from time to time, I

David B. Silva

receive in the mail a plain white envelope bearing no return address, but which I know comes from Dave because of the Oak Run, California, postmark; inside is always the same and singular thing—a black-ink imprint of Dave's hand, which is his charming way of letting me know that he's thinking about me, his friend.

Dave and I live in the same state, so it seems as though we ought to be able to arrange to meet; however, California is big, a full thousand miles long, and Dave has managed to put a great many of those thousand miles between his house and mine. Occasionally, he goes to a horror or fantasy convention, but I rarely do. When I attended my first—and thus far only—World Fantasy Convention, I asked Dave if he was going. "Are you going?" he asked, and when I answered in the affirmative, he moaned, "Oh, darn, I can't make it." Dismayed, I said, "Gosh, maybe we're fated never to meet," and he said, "That's it exactly. Fate. Damn fate! Oh, how I despise fate, how I loathe fate, the unfairness of it all!" He was so distraught that I offered to skip the World Fantasy Convention and come, instead, to visit him in Oak Run; but fate foiled us once more, because Dave was leaving within the hour to join a search party on a perilous mission to the headwaters of the Amazon, where his kindly missionary uncle had disappeared and was probably being fattened by cannibals who wished to serve him as the main course at their Feast of the Winter Solstice. And his grandmother had died that morning, and his grandfather was on a hijacked airliner over Istanbul, and his dog was having puppies even as we spoke, so it was, you know, a very busy time for him.

I have seen two photographs of Dave Silva, but I am not able to provide you with a vivid physical description of him. Both photographs appeared in genre publications, and both were small. In the first, he is pictured in conversation with another writer, and he is wearing a large hat. The photo is slightly blurry, and the hat shades his face. One cannot discern even his height unless one knows the height of the writer with whom he is pictured, but I have never made this Other writer's acquaintance. (I have written six letters to this Other Writer, inquiring as to his *precise* height, to within a sixteenth of an inch, and politely asking him to inform me if he and Dave were standing on a flat surface or whether one of them was uphill of the other, but I haven't

Through Shattered Glass

yet received the courtesy of a reply—even though the sixth of my six letters was accompanied by a threat.) Anyway, although the first photo reveals little of Dave, the hat is interesting. It is, as I have said, a large hat, and of indeterminate character. Because the photo is slightly blurry and the shadowing is odd, I can't pin down the style: It might be a cowboy hat, an Australian bushman's hat, an oversized fedora, or even a beret to which someone has sewn the brim of sombrero in a hideous, misguided attempt at sartorial innovation. Regardless of the questionable nature of the hat, Dave, being Dave, wears it with flair. The second photo is of Dave alone—the rude and uncommunicative Other Writer nowhere in sight—and although it was evidently taken on a different occasion from the first photo, it is also a very small image, full of shadow, and Dave is again wearing a hat. I believe it is the same strange hat as in the first photo, but I cannot assure you, with confidence, that it is not altogether new headgear. I might go so far as to say that under a magnifying glass, this chapeau almost appears to be a cloche hat with a darling little feather at the base of the crown, but this would call into question Dave's gender, and I remain all but certain that he is male.

Extensive computer analysis of these two photos, employing image-enhancement technology first developed for the United States Department of Defense (Global Intelligence Division, Armageddon Bureau, under the oversight of The-Ruskie-Commie-Bastards-Aren't-Really-Gone Committee, in the Office of Managed Paranoia), revealed less of Dave than I had hoped. Because of the poor quality of the photographs, I can report only that Dave has: at least one eye; something rather like a nose if not, indeed, a nose; one lip and perhaps two; either a beard or a strangely pointy chin; some teeth. The computer enhancement also reveals what appears to be a brooding expression, which may or may not be related to Dave's concern over the possibility that he may be lacking a full complement of facial features, though of course that is purest speculation.

Because Dave is a figure of mystery equaled only by Batman, the Easter Island stone heads, and the Taco Bell Chihuahua (How can a dog talk? How can it possibly eat a burrito bigger than it is? How does it manage to hold a chimichanga with just its forepaws?), I find myself

David B. Silva

speculating about him at odd hours of the day. Just this morning, brushing my teeth, I asked myself, *If Dave had to choose between being eaten alive by a panther or by a pack of rabid squirrels, which death would he choose? What would be the moral, intellectual, and spiritual considerations that resulted in his choice? In his will, has he bequeathed to me his mandolin? Does he even have a mandolin?* He is such a puzzle, this Dave Silva, such an enigma wrapped in a mystery, boxed in a riddle, tied up with a ribbon of conundrum, that speculation of this sort is irresistible, and once one begins to indulge in it, whole days and weeks can pass in a blur.

Although I certainly have days and even weeks to devote to the composition of this introduction, especially if it leads me toward a better understanding of my long-distance friend, I am told by the rather stern-voiced publisher that busy readers will not have time to take such a profound journey into the Heart of Dave. I gather that contemporary readers are a frivolous bunch who would prefer to read the fiction herein, and be entertained, rather than fling themselves, with me, into the intellectual pursuit of the Infinite Possibilities of Dave.

Consequently, putting aside speculation, I will tell you all the important things that I actually know about this man (man, I say, in the assumption that it is not a cloche hat in that photo). He is a fine, sensitive, talented editor who published a landmark magazine; *The Horror Show* was a champion of—and a beacon for—its genre for over seven years, and those of us who read it and wrote for it will miss it always. He is a talented writer of novels and short fiction, who knows where the heart of the story lies, and who deserves a larger audience than he has yet received. When his mom was dying of cancer and, later, his dad of leukemia, he was there for them in a way and to an extent that is unfortunately not common these days. He is a modest man in a profession that generally attracts people with egos larger than Godzilla's morning stool. I have never heard him speak a mean word about anyone. He has a superb sense of humor and a wonderful laugh, and while he takes his work quite seriously, he never takes himself seriously—which, to me, is the primary hallmark of sanity.

It has been my pleasure and my privilege to be a friend of Dave's, by phone and by mail, while nearly 1750 may flies have come and tragically gone. I have shared his keen frustration as Amazon cannibals, Turkish terrorists, pregnant dogs, floods, fires, killer bees, evil extraterrestrials, Big Foot, a crazed Richard Simmons, vampire bats, and so damn many other weird emergencies and catastrophes in his life have prevented him from meeting me face-to-face when the opportunities have arisen, but I am grateful that the post office always gets my letters to him and that every time the monumentally incompetent phone company has changed Dave's number and de-listed it without telling him, I have been able to track it down nonetheless, even if sometimes not by legal means. I remain hopeful, however, that one day we will at last meet and shake hands. I'm confident that modern medicine will find a cure for his peculiar, recently diagnosed condition, and that one day this dear, brave man will be able to enter a room with someone of my blood type and have no fear of spontaneous combustion.

The Calling

It never stops.

The whistle.

The sound is hollow, rising from a cork ball enclosed by red plastic. His mother no longer has the strength to blow hard—the cancer has made certain of that—so the sound comes out as a soft song, like the chirping of a cricket somewhere off in another part of the house, just barely audible. But there. Always unmistakably there.

Blair buries his head beneath his pillow. He feels like a little boy again, trying to close out the world because he just isn't ready to face up to what is out there. Not yet. Maybe never, he thinks. How do you ever face up to something like cancer? It never lets you catch up.

It's nearly three o'clock in the morning now.

And just across the hall . . .

Even with his eyes closed, he has a perfect picture of his mother's room: the lamp on her nightstand casting a sickly gray shadow over her bed, the blankets gathered at her feet. Behind her, leaning against the wall, an old ironing board serves as a makeshift stand for the IV the nurse was never able to get into mother's veins. And the television is on. In his mind, Blair sees it all. Much too clearly.

He wraps himself tighter in the pillow.

The sound from the television is turned down, but he still thinks he can hear a scene from *Starsky and Hutch* squealing from somewhere across the hallway.

Then the whistle.

A thousand times he had heard it calling him . . . at all hours of the night . . . when she is thirsty . . . when she needs to go to the bathroom . . . when she needs to be moved to a new position . . . when she is in pain. A thousand times. He hears the whistle, the whirring call, coming at him from everywhere now. It is the sound of squealing tires from the street outside his bedroom window. It is the high-pitched hum of the dishwasher, of the television set, of the refrigerator when it kicks on at midnight.

Everywhere.

He has grown to hate it.

And he has grown to hate himself for hating it.

An ugly thought comes to mind: *why . . . doesn't she succumb? Why hasn't she died by now?* It's not the first time he's faced himself with this question, but lately it seems to come up more and more often in his mind. Cancer is not an easy thing to watch. It takes a person piece by piece . . .

"My feet are numb."

"Numb?"

"Like walking on sandpaper."

"From the chemo?"

"I don't know."

"Maybe . . . " Blair said naively, "maybe your feet will feel better after the chemo's over." He had honestly believed that it would turn out that way. When the chemo stopped, then so would her nausea and her fatigue and her loss of hair. And the worst of the side effects *had* stopped, for a while. But the numbness in her feet . . . that part had stayed on, an ugly scar left over from a body pumped full of dreadful things with dreadful names like doxorubicin and dacadbazine and vinblastine. Chemicals you couldn't even pronounce. It wasn't long before she began to miss a step here and there, and soon she was having to guide herself down the hallway with one hand pressed against the wall.

"Sometimes I can't even feel them," she once told him, a pained expression etched into the lines of her face.

She knows, Blair had thought at the time. She knows she's never going to dance again. The one thing she loves most in the world, and it's over for her.

The heater kicks on.

There's a vent under the bed where he's trying to sleep. It makes a familiar, almost haunting sound, and for an instant, he can't be sure if he's hearing the soft, high-pitched hum of the whistle. He lifts his head, listens. There's a hush that reminds him of a hot summer night when it's too humid to sleep. But the house seems at peace, he decides.

She's sleeping, he tells himself in a whisper. Finally sleeping.

For too long, the endless nights have haunted him with her cancerous likeness. She is like a butterfly: so incredibly delicate. She's lying in bed, her eyes half closed, her mouth hung open. Five feet, seven inches tall and not quite ninety pounds. The covers are pulled back slightly, her nightgown is unbuttoned and the outline of her ribs resembles a relief map.

She's not the same person he used to call his mother.

It's been ages since he's seen that other person. Before the three surgeries. Before the chemotherapy. Before the radiation treatments. Before he finally locked up his house and moved down state to care for her . . .

She cried the first time she fell. It happened in her bedroom, early one morning while he was making breakfast. He heard a sharp cry, and when he found her, her legs were folded under like broken wings. She didn't have the strength to climb back to her feet. For a moment, her face was frozen behind a mask of complete surprise. Then suddenly she started crying.

"Are you hurt?"

She shook her head, burying her face in her hands.

"Here, let me help you up."

"No." She motioned him away.

He retreated a step, maybe two, staring down at her, studying her, *trying* to put himself in her position. It occurred to him that she wasn't upset because of the fall—that wasn't the reason for the tears—she was crying because suddenly she had realized the ride was coming to an end. The last curve of the roller coaster had been rounded and now it was winding down once and for all. No more corkscrews. No more quick drops. No more three-sixties. Just a slow, steady deceleration until the ride came to a final standstill. Then it would be time to get off. The fall . . . marked the beginning of the end.

It had been a harsh realization for both of them.

He began walking with her after that, guiding her one step at a time from her bedroom to the kitchen, from the kitchen to the living room, from the living room to the bathroom. A week or two later, she was using a four-pronged cane. A week or two after that, she was using a wheelchair.

Everything ran together those few short weeks, a kaleidoscope of forfeitures, one after the other, all blended together until he could hardly recall a time when she had been healthy and whole . . .

She's going to die.

Blair has known this for a long time now.

She's going to die, but . . .

but . . .

how long is it going to take?

It seems like forever.

A car passes by his bedroom window. It's been raining lightly and the slick whine of the tires reminds him of that other sound, the one he's come to hate so much. He hates it because there's nothing he can do now. There's no going back, no making things better. All he can do is watch . . . and wait . . . and try not to lose his sanity to the incessant call of the whistle.

He bought the whistle for her nearly two and a half weeks ago in the sporting goods section of the local Target store. A cheap thing, made of plastic and a small cork ball. She wears it around her neck, dangling from the end of a thin nylon cord. Once, when it became tangled in the pillowcase, she nearly choked on the cord. But he refuses to let her take it off. It's the only way he has of keeping in touch with her at night. Unless he doesn't sleep. But he's already feeling guilty about the morning he found her sleeping on the floor in the living room . . .

When he went to bed—sometime around 1:30 or 2:00 in the morning—she'd been sleeping comfortably on the couch, and it seemed kinder not to disturb her. Seven hours later, after dragging himself out of the first sound night's sleep in weeks, he found her sitting on the floor.
"Jesus, Mom."
She was sitting in an awkward position, her legs folded sideways, one arm propped up on the edge of the couch, serving as a pillow. No blanket. Nothing on her feet to keep them from getting cold. And to think—she had spent the night like that.
He knelt next to her.
"Mom?"
Her eyes opened lazily. It wasn't terribly rational, but he held out a distant hope that she'd been able to sleep through most of the night. "I'm sorry," she said drowsily. "I couldn't get up . . . my legs wouldn't . . . "
"I shouldn't have left you out here all night." He managed to get her legs straightened out, to get her back on the couch, under a warm blanket, with a soft pillow behind her head.
That afternoon, he bought her the whistle.
"When you need me, use the whistle. You got that?"
She nodded.
"Night or day, it doesn't matter. If you need me for something, blow the whistle." He paused, hearing his own words echo through his mind, and a cold, shuddering realization swept over him. He didn't know when it had happened, but somewhere along the line they had swapped roles. He was the parent now, she the child.
"What if I can't?"

"Try it."

Like everything else, her lungs had slowly lost their strength over the past few months, but she was able to put enough air into the whistle to produce a short, high-pitched hum.

"Great."

That was—what?—three weeks ago?

Blair sits up in bed. The streetlight outside his window is casting a murky, blue-gray light through the bedroom curtains. The room is bathed in that light. It feels dark and strangely out of balance. He fluffs both pillows, stuffs them behind him, and leans back against the wall. Across the hall, the light flickers, and he knows the television is still on in his mother's room. It seems as if it's far away.

He shudders.

Let her sleep, he thinks. Let her sleep forever.

Sometimes the house feels like a prison. Just the two of them, caught in their life and death struggle. The ending already predetermined. It feels . . . not lonely, at least not in the traditional sense of the word . . . but . . . *isolated*. Outside these walls, there is nothing but endless black emptiness. But it's in here where life is coming to an end. Right here inside this house, inside these walls.

The television in her room flickers again.

Blair stares absently at the shifting patterns on the bedroom door across the hall. He used to watch that television set while she was in the bathroom. Sometimes as long as an hour, while she changed her colostomy bag . . .

"I'll never be close to a man again," she told him a few months after the doctors had surgically created the opening in the upper end of her sigmoid colon. The stoma was located on the lower left side of her abdomen. "How could anyone be attracted to me with this bag attached to my side? With the foul odor?"

"Someone will come along, and he'll love you for you. The bag won't matter."

A fleeting sigh of hope crossed her face, then she stared at him for a while, and that was that. She hadn't had enough of a chance to let it all out, so she kept it all in. The subject never came up again. And what she did on the other side of the bathroom door became something personal and private to her, something he half decided he didn't want to know about anyway.

If he had a choice.

"How're you doing in there?" he asked her late one night. He'd had to help her out of bed into the wheelchair, and out of the wheelchair onto the toilet. That was all the help she ever wanted. But she'd been in there, mysteriously quiet, for an unusually long time.

"Mom?"

"I'm okay," she whispered.

"Need any help?"

More quiet.

"Mom?"

"What?"

"Do you need any help?"

"I've lost the clip."

"The clip?"

"For the colostomy bag. It's not here."

"You want me to help you look for it?"

"No. See if you can find another one in one of the boxes in the closet."

"What does it look like?"

"It's . . . a little plastic . . . clip."

He found one, the last one, buried at the bottom of a box. It had the appearance of a bobby pin, a little longer, perhaps, and made of clear plastic instead of metal. "Found one."

"Oh, good."

He pulled the sliding pocket door open, more than was necessary if all he had intended to do was hand her the clip. The bathroom was smaller than he remembered it. There was a walker in front of her, for balance if she ever had to stand up, and the toilet had metal supports on each side to help her get up and down. It seemed as if the entire room was filled with aids of one kind or another.

"Is this what you're looking for?"

She was hunched over, leaning heavily against one of the support bars, her nightgown pulled up around her waist. Her face was weighted down with a weariness he'd never seen before and for the first time he understood how taxing this daily—sometimes three or four times a day—process had become for her. When she looked up at him, she seemed confused and disoriented.

"Are you okay?"

"I can't find the clip." She showed him the colostomy pouch for the first time. He couldn't bring himself to see how it was attached to her. Partly because he didn't want to know, and partly because that would have been like checking out her scars after surgery. Some things are better left to the imagination. More important, there was a woman in front of him whose ribs were protruding from her chest, sticklike extensions of her hands; and this woman, looking so much like a stranger, was his mother. God, this was the woman who had given him birth.

"I've got the clip right here."

"Oh." She tried a smile on him, then glanced down at the bag in her hands. The process was slow and deliberate, but after several attempts she was finally able to fold the bottom side of the bag over.

Blair slid the clip across it. "Like this?"

She nodded.

And he realized something that should have occurred to him long before this: it was getting to be too much for her. As simple as emptying the bag might be, it was too confusing for her to work through the procedure now.

"Okay, I think we've got it."

"Oh, good."

"Ready to get out of here?"

"I think so." She whispered the words, and before they were all out, she started to cry.

"Mom?"

She looked up, her eyes as big as he'd ever seen them.

God, I hate this, he thought, taking hold of her hand and feeling completely, despairingly helpless. I hate everything about this.

"I didn't hurt you, did I?"

Her crying seemed to grow louder for a moment.

The Calling

"Mom?"

"I didn't want for you to have to do that."

Lovingly, he squeezed her hand. "I know."

"I'm sorry."

"There's nothing to be sorry about. It's not a big deal." He pulled a couple of squares of toilet paper off the roll and handed them to her. "Things are hard enough. Don't worry about the small stuff. Okay?"

By the time he got her back into bed again, she had stopped crying. But he's never known if it was because of what he had said, or if it was because she didn't want to upset him anymore. They were both bending over backwards trying not to upset each other. There was something crazy about that.

* * * *

The whistle blows.

At least he thinks it's the whistle. Sometimes, it's so damn hard to tell. There's that part of him, that tired, defeated part of him, that doesn't want to hear it anyway. How long can this thing drag on? Outside, all of thirty or forty feet away, a man jogs by with his dog on the end of a leash. People who pass this house don't have the slightest inkling of what's going on behind these walls. A woman's dying in here. And dying right alongside her is her son.

He pulls the covers back, hangs his feet over the edge of the bed.

For several days, she hasn't been able to keep food down. That memory comes horribly clear to him now . . .

"Feel better?"

She shook her head, her eyes closed, her body hunched forward over the bowl. Then suddenly another explosion of undigested soup burst from her mouth.

He held the stainless steel bowl closer; it felt warm in his hands. This had been going on for nearly three days now. It seemed like it might never stop. "You've got to take some Compazine, Mom."

"No."

"I can crush it for you and mix it with orange juice."

No response.

"Mom?"

No response.

"It'll go down easier that way."

"No."

"Christ, Mom, you've got to take something. You can't keep throwing up forever."

"The pills make me sick."

"Sicker than this?"

"They make me sick."

The whistle.

Blair slips a T-shirt over his head, pulls on a pair of Levi's. He tries to convince himself it'll stop. Maybe if he just leaves it alone, the sounds will quietly drift into the background of the television set, and he'll be able to go back to sleep again . . .

"It'll stop on its own," she tried to convince him.

"But if it doesn't, you'll dehydrate."

At last the vomiting appeared to have run its course. At least for the time being. She sat up a little straighter, taking in a deep breath. When she opened her eyes, they were faraway, devoid of that sparkle that used to be so prominent behind her smile.

"Please, just take one Compazine."

"No."

Her skin began to lose its elasticity a few days later. The nausea stopped on its own, just like she'd said it would. But now, the only liquid she was taking was in the form of crushed ice, and there was the very real fear that dehydration might eventually become too painful for her.

"We can try an IV," the visiting nurse told him. "It won't help her live longer, but it'll probably make her more comfortable."

"Her veins aren't in very good shape."

"I've done this before."

They had to lean the ironing board up against the wall behind the headboard of her bed, because they didn't have an IV stand. The nurse hung the solution bag from one of the legs, and it seemed to work well enough. Then she tried to find a vein in his mother's right arm. It wasn't as easy as she'd thought it would be.

After several new entries, he turned away.

His mother began to whimper.

"The needle keeps sliding off." The nurse switched to her left arm, still struggling to find a workable vein, still failing miserably.

"That's enough," he finally said. "Let's just forget it."

"Her veins are so—"

There was a tear running down the cheek of his mother, and her mouth was twisted into a grimace which seemed frozen on her face.

"I'm sorry, Mom. I didn't mean to hurt you."

She rolled over, away from him . . .

He's standing at her bedroom door now, and she's in that same position: with her back turned toward him. He can see the black cord of the whistle tied around her neck, but the whistle itself is out of sight.

"Mom?"

The television flickers, drawing his attention. The scene is from *Starsky and Hutch*, shot inside a dingy, gray-black interrogation room. There's a young man sitting in an uncomfortable chair, Starsky standing over him, badgering him. It seems faraway and unimportant, and Blair's attention drifts easily back to his mother.

"You need anything?"

He moves around the foot of her bed, stops alongside her, the stainless steel bowl on the floor only a few inches away from his feet. "Mom?"

Her eyes are closed. She looks peaceful. Her nightgown is partially open in front. There's a thick tube running up the right side of her body and over her collarbone, running underneath the skin—like an artery—where the doctors had surgically implanted a shunt just a few short weeks earlier. Inside that tube, flowing out of her stomach, up her body, and back into her bloodstream, there's an endless current of cancerous fluid the tumor has been manufacturing for months.

In her left hand, wrapped around a long, thin finger, she's holding the nylon cord. He can almost hear the whistle's high-pitched hum calling to him from somewhere else. Sometimes it sounds as if it's singing his name—*Bl—air*—and he wonders if he'll ever be able to hear his name out loud again without being swept away by the strange concoction of resentment and helplessness that overwhelms him.

He touches her arm.

For a moment, everything is perfect: she's sleeping soundly, the house is quiet, the whistle stilled. Too good to be true.

"Mom?"

He places the palm of his hand over her chest, not believing what's going through his mind now. No intake of breath. No beat of heart. Instead, she feels cool to the touch, and . . . and absolutely . . . motionless.

"Jesus . . ."

"I don' want to talk to anyone."

"You sure?" he asked, holding his hand over the mouthpiece of the phone.

"They'll want to visit."

"Maybe not."

"I don't want anyone to see me like this."

It had happened so gradually: first the phone calls, then the visitors, finally the mail, and before he had realized what had happened, they had isolated themselves from the outside world. It was just the two of them, alone, inside the house, waiting for the cancer to run its course . . .

One more time, he places the palm of his hand ever so lightly across her chest.

"Mom? Please, Mom."

The wall above her bed flickers with the light from the television set, reflecting dully off the underside of the ironing board. He glances up, staring at the IV tube still dangling from the leg of the board, remembering too clearly, too vividly how much pain she went through the night the nurse had struggled to find a good vein in her arms.

"I never should have let her do that to you."

It feels cold inside the house. The room seems darker, smaller, a lonelier place.

The Calling

He stands next to the bed, careful not to disturb her, though somewhere in the back of his mind he's already aware that she's finally at peace now. She's lying near the edge, her legs bent at the knees, her arms bent at the elbows. She looks as if she's praying. For a moment longer, he stares, failing to remember a time when the flesh wasn't pulled taut like a death mask across her face. This is the way he'll always remember her. It's all he has left.

The television draws his attention again, and that tiny distraction is somehow enough to stir him. He turns toward the door, wanting to be out of the room, thinking it can't be over . . . he doesn't want it to be over . . . maybe if he comes back later . . .

Then he hears it again.

The whistle. A soft, echoing sound. Calling him.

Bl—air.

"Mom?"

He expects different when he turns back, but he finds her eyes still closed, her chest still motionless. The nylon cord hangs loosely around her neck, the whistle lost somewhere inside her cotton nightgown. He sits on the edge of the bed, studying her, suddenly feeling like a little boy. It's a lonely feeling.

Bl—air.

It sounds again.

The whistle.

With care, he unwraps her fingers from around the black cord. Then he opens the front of her nightgown and follows the cord down . . . down *there* . . . down to where the whistle is softly blowing, to where the cancer has been growing. The incision from her last surgery is open, the tissue curled back, and inside the cavity—ash gray and darker, pulsing—the cancer is wrapped like a kiss around the mouthpiece of the whistle, exhaling a soft humming song—

Bl—air.

It never stops.

The cancer never stops.

Dwindling

In the summer, just after school let out, the pastures were still green and there was a freshness in the air that wouldn't die until the raw August temperatures broiled it from memory. The wind was tender and breezy then. During the day, the sky was a faint blue. But near sundown, it would open its throat and the blue would turn purple, thick and rich and friendly. It had always been a special time of year for Derrick.

As he scooted off the last bus, making its last stop of the school year, and gazed across the forever fields to the farmhouse, a vague and chilling premonition marched in goose flesh up his arms. The sensation was too difficult to understand to trouble him. But as he kicked stones at his younger brothers and slowly made his way home, he made note of the bitter feeling and how similar it tasted to the bitterness he had experienced the day before Grandma Sanders had died. Then Georgie hit him in the back with a dirt clod and the feeling was put aside.

Six-year-old Tammy folded her hands in front of her, bowed her head, and took a deep breath. "Thank you, Lord, for this food upon our table. Amen."

"Amen."

Hands, small-medium-large, reached for corn-on-the-cob and broth of chicken and fresh green salad made of lettuce and tomato, bell pepper and carrot, celery and onion. There was hot homemade bread and cold unpasteurized milk. Everything and everyone that was important in Derrick's life was all right here. Except for . . .

"Where's Sarah?" he asked as he buttered a slice of bread that warmed the palm of his hand. When no one answered, he asked again, "Where's Sarah?" this time looking directly at his mother. Her eyes seemed tired, as if she were off somewhere faraway in a daydream. A swirl of black hair, singed with the first early signs of gray, fell across her forehead. She brushed it back, absently, apparently still lost in her daydream. "Mom?"

"Hmm?" she said, only half-there.

"I asked where Sarah was?"

"Who?"

"Sarah."

For a moment, there was an eerie pause in the meal. Forks stalled in mid-air. Mouths were closed. Ears were opened. A dozen questioning eyes turned to stare at him. *Who's Sarah?*

Then Tammy grinned. With her mouth full of a thick, cheesy casserole, she said, "Betcha Derr's got a girlfriend."

Derrick felt himself blush, though he had nothing at all to blush about. He was just curious about Sarah, that was all. No big deal. He was sure she was all right; someone would have told him if she weren't. So he smiled uncomfortably and turned back to his plate of vegetables, doing his best to let everyone's attention turn away from him.

The secret behind Sarah would just have to wait.

Derrick didn't breathe another word of her until he was in bed that night. Brian was already asleep in the corner, one of his arms hanging off the edge of the bed, his hand brushing against the floor. Georgie was tossing in the bottom bunk, rocking himself back and forth like he did every night until he would eventually fall asleep. From the upper bunk, Derrick whispered, "Georgie?"

"What?" The light sway of the bunk beds stopped.

"Where's Sarah?"

The rocking started up again.

"Georgie?"

"I don't know."

Derrick leaned over the edge of his bed. "If you don't stop that blessed rocking, I'm gonna slug you."

"I don't even know who she is," his brother whispered.

For a moment, Derrick wasn't sure he could believe his ears. "She's your sister, for crissakes. Your sister! The one who tried to eat the tail right off your kite yesterday."

"That was Tammy," Georgie said quietly. He rolled away from the edge of the bed, his face toward the wall, his back to Derrick, where Derrick could see a luminescent iron-on patch of the Incredible Hulk glowing green in the dark. "Ain't one pesky sister bad enough for you?"

Derrick supposed he could have argued. He could have pointed out a handful of recent incidents when little Sarah had pestered the both of them. Little sisters did things like that. Eventually he knew he could have made Georgie admit that Sarah was missing. But . . .

But somewhere deep inside, gnawing at his gut, Derrick knew there had never really been a Sarah. Her four years of giggling and gurgling and crying—sometimes all night long—had been an odd dream of sorts, an imaginative hiccup, a wistful step outside the boundaries of reality. That's why they had all stared at him with eyes that asked, *Who's Sarah?* Because there was no Sarah. His imagination had played a game inside his head, like it did with everyone, like it did when Tammy played tea party with playmates that weren't really there. A momentary, imaginative hiccup.

That's all it had been.

A momentary, imaginative hiccup.

The summer's first one hundred degree temperature arrived less than a week later, pushing the mercury above the red zone on the

David B. Silva

rusting Orange Crush thermometer that had been tacked to the big oak standing outside the kitchen window.

Pa had allowed them the day down at Miner's Pond. Clad in cut-offs made from an old pair of jeans he'd worn out during the winter, Derrick was busy cleaning the spring weeds out of the little patch of sand that covered the ground between the water and the cliff of rock they used as a diving platform. The others were already in the water, squirming and churning enough to make the pond look like a pot of boiling watercress soup.

Tammy let out a squeal just before Brian dunked her.

Sometimes, like now, when her hair was damp and it closely embraced her thin, almost-hollow cheeks, he would see Sarah looking out from Tammy's laughing eyes. Even though he realized that there had never been a Sarah. And when he remembered those special things she would do, those special things his imagination had made so real for him—like the time she tried to cut her own hair and Ma nearly had to shave her head to make it all even again—after times like those, he wished she had been more than just a daydream.

But she hadn't. He knew that now. She was gone, her dolls were gone, her clothes were gone. There had never been a Sarah.

Derrick collapsed into the soft sand and sifted his strange emptiness from hand to hand in the form of a thousand gritty particles.

"Come on, Derr," one of the others called.

He smiled and shook his head, all of a sudden feeling too old to be splashing carelessly in Miner's Pond. He felt a little sad instead, as if at age twelve he had suddenly realized the time was nearing when he would have to give up some of those cherished things that stood between being a boy and being a man. Perhaps the joy of Miner's Pond. Perhaps some other never-to-be-forgotten place or time or person.

That's what his parents had done. Over the years, they had somehow given up their happiness for something else, something he wasn't sure he understood. And maybe that was what growing up was all about. Giving away those things you liked most about yourself.

If so, it didn't seem fair.

"Derr, come on!"

It didn't seem fair at all.

Dwindling

Derrick wiped the sand from the butt of his cut-offs, and with a laughter he wasn't ready to surrender yet, he did a painful belly flop into the circle of his brothers and sister.
It felt great.

They played away the afternoon, exploring creek rocks for crawdads, building a miniature dam to house minnows, diving off the cliff, playing tag up and down the creek's banks until their feet were sore and their bodies were bright pink from too much sun.
Now it was getting time to head back home again.
Derrick gathered up the towels they had brought along, and the lunch bags which Ma would want to use again. The others were down the creek a ways. He could hear their laughter whistling through the paw-like leaves of the oak trees.
"Gotta go!" he yelled as he shook the sand out of the towels. He liked being big brother, the one they looked up to and depended upon. Sometimes, he felt more like their father than their brother.
"Let's go!" he called again.
The boys came busting through the bushes. Brian collapsed in the sand. "Beat ya," he said, lying flat on his back.
"Did not," Georgie cried. His arms were braced on his legs as he collected a breath. His eyes kept looking to Brian, as if he knew he had been beaten and wondered if his younger brother might make too big a deal out of it.
"Where's Tammy?" Derrick asked. "Pa's gonna be real upset if we don't get ourselves back by supper time."
Brian dragged himself to his feet. "I beat ya," he said again, pushing Georgie up the side of the short bank. When they had made it to the top, they stopped and turned back to their older brother. "Thought you were in a hurry," Brian said.
"What about Tammy?"
There was a short pause that seemed to last forever. His brothers exchanged a curious glance. A chill wound up Derrick's spine as he recognized their familiar bewilderment. He didn't inquire a third time. The story was still fresh in his mind. *Who's Tammy?* Just another hiccup, that's all. No need to ask further, just fill in the blanks. *There*

is no Tammy. There never has been. She was just a product of the same game, the same hiccup of imagination, that birthed Sarah. And now they were both gone. An imaginative quirk, that's all it was.

"Derr, it's getting late."

He glanced up at the voice and wondered, almost casually, if the two boys who had been his brothers for almost every minute of his life, if they too, were mere hiccups. The thought scared him.

"Derr . . ."

"Yeah," he said, flipping the towels over his shoulder. "Coming."

Tammy never returned. He knew she wouldn't. The same as his parents and his brothers, he never asked about her.

That night, Brian went off to sleep in his own room, the room that Derrick's imagination had leant to Sarah and Tammy. It seemed lonelier without Brian sleeping in the corner, without his arm hung over the edge of the bed, brushing a hand against the floor. He leaned over the edge of the bed and stared down at Georgie. At least Georgie was here. At least he still had the comfort of Georgie's rocking, the comfort of the bunk bed swaying back and forth like it had always swayed at night, as long as he could remember. At least that hadn't been taken from him.

Summer lost its magic after that. The days became too hot, Miner's Pond too cold. The beautiful yellows and greens around the farm shriveled, becoming deadly browns. The laughter that had so often swept around the dinner table, became a whisper, a cough of its past joy. Everything changed, and somewhere along the line, memories of yesterdays gradually became more and more difficult to call up again, as if pieces of his life were somehow being consumed. The magic of summertime had been lost and everything was suddenly different.

Even his parents seemed somehow different, somehow changed. Although he wasn't sure exactly what the difference was, and he caught himself wondering if perhaps it was merely his imagination at play again.

"Remember before?" Derrick heard his mother ask his father one night. They were outside on the front porch, casually gliding back and forth on the porch swing, allowing themselves to be overheard by the evening stars and by Derrick himself. He was upstairs in the attic,

Dwindling

poking through old boxes of toys, searching for a game of *Coodie* which he hadn't seen in years. Just a bored-night impulse, that was the only reason he was there.

"Before what?" Pa said.

The arthritic squeaking of metal to rusting metal filled the moment of silence and drew Derrick curiously closer to the window.

"Before we got married," she said. "Remember how we used to walk along Dogwood Creek at night and the breeze would rustle through the trees, sounding like God himself was trying to talk to us? And how we always knew we'd get married and live out the rest of our lives together. How it was never gonna change?"

Pa chuckled. "I remember."

"I miss those times," she told him.

"Guess I do, as well."

"They were *good* times."

"The best," his Pa agreed.

"I want to go back." The rhythmic squeaking paused for a breath, then started up again. "I want it to be like it was then, without the worries and the fears, without the kids and the farm to look after."

Pa didn't say so much as "Hmm."

"Mind ya, I'm not unhappy," she said. "But it's all slipping by so quickly. I want to do it all again. I want to court and marry and make babies all over again, like it was the first time."

"Been feeling this way all summer, have you?"

Derrick couldn't see them on the porch, they were sitting almost right underneath him, but he imagined her nodding her head. He stepped back from the window, suddenly feeling a strange sense of shame from his eavesdropping, realizing his ears had crossed the path of something they were never meant to hear. But they *had* heard, and Ma *had* been different all summer. Perhaps that was the only trick of his imagination that hadn't really been a trick. She *had* been different. The whole summer had been different.

He left the attic without ever finding the game of *Coodie*.

Brian blinked out of his life two days later. Derrick woke up to find the bottom bunk empty and when he went searching for Georgie, he found the ten year old in Brian's room where Brian should have been, rocking Brian's bed the way he used to rock the bunk beds.

"What are you doing in here?" he asked. "Where's Brian?"

Through sleepy eyes, Georgie expressed his puzzlement, that same puzzlement that had surfaced after each of Derrick's summer-long inquiries, after each loss that had seemingly slipped away unnoticed. And Derrick knew, he knew and he understood and he felt the emptiness devour another portion of his life. Georgie was all he had left, and what would happen after his last brother slipped away?

What would happen then?

It was early August all too soon. The fields were dry and dusty. Miner's Pond had dipped so low that a soul couldn't dive off the cliffs without meeting the bottom head first. His mom was looking different by the day. His father was too. As if the summer hadn't withered them like everything else it had touched. As if they had somehow thrived on the heat and the dirt and the peace that had shadowed the farm. That's what it was — peace. Too much for Derrick's liking. The meals were too quiet, the days too empty.

He stayed close to Georgie whenever he could, whenever he wasn't off tending to chores or running errands or sleeping in his own bed, a wall away from his little brother.

But it happened just the same.

He woke up one morning and he was the last, all his brothers and all his sisters were finally gone. He was all that remained. He imagined his parents breathing a heavy sigh, relieved that at last the inevitable moment was near, that moment when their oldest child would finally slip away like the others.

There were days now, unlike past summers, when he wished he had never been the oldest, the last to go. How much easier it would have been to have simply slipped away like Sarah, right at the beginning, never having to watch as the others were taken one-by-one, never having to feel each loss. How much easier.

Each day painfully dwindled away, seconds feeling like minutes, minutes like hours.

Dwindling

Then one night, the sky black without the moon as its companion, as he lay in bed, his mother came to visit. The window was open, inviting the slight breeze inside to chase away the godawful heat. It was like a thousand other summer nights, yet unlike any that had come his way before. From the top bunk, with his arms folded behind his neck, he gazed out the window to the darkness of the universe and wondered where it ended, wondered if he would float out there after . . .

"Derr?" A shaft of hall light sectioned his darkness, and his mother's silhouette filled the doorway. "How you doing?"

"Okay." He didn't want to look at her, kept his watch on the universe instead. It would be easier that way. But she crept into the darkness anyway, right up next to his bed. She stood over him, a shaft of light falling across her face. It was the first time, as he finally forced himself to look at her, that he had fully realized just how much she had changed over the summer.

"Is it too hot for you?"

The singe of gray that had danced like a wind-blown scarf through her hair was no longer there.

"I'm comfortable."

And her eyes had come alive again, they had a sparkle in them that he hadn't noticed in years.

"You sure?" She brushed the hair away from his forehead, then held his hand in hers. "You know I love you."

Derrick glanced out the bedroom window at the watching universe. He wanted to tell her he still loved her, but knew he wouldn't be able to find a way to say the words.

"Remember that," she said. "Remember I love you." Then all too quickly, she turned and started out of the room.

"Ma," he said, still looking away. "Are you sorry I'm your son? Are you and Pa sorry you ever had me?"

She paused, a wisp of shadow in the doorway. "Of course not. You're our son, our flesh and blood. You're part of us. We'll always love you."

"Even if I have to go away?"

Her eyes were hidden in a checkerboard pattern of black and white, but the long silence answered his question for her. He knew then that she didn't understand what she had done, that it had all been done innocently, out of ignorance of the consequences of her wishing. *I want to court and marry and make babies all over again, like it was the first time.*

"I still love you, Ma," he told her. "Even if I have to go away."

"There's nowhere to go," she said. "Nowhere at all. This is where you belong."

The bedroom door closed.

Darkness rushed in through the open window.

Derrick rolled over, away from his doorway to the windowed universe, until he was nestled safely in the wings of his blankets. Then a single tear tumbled down his cheek, a tear not for himself, but for his mother.

Ice Sculptures

I thought I'd forgotten.

Spring, summer, and autumn have each since come and gone, and I guess it was easy to fool myself into believing the past was finally something left to cold impossible yesterdays. Out of season, out of mind. Unfortunately, things unfinished have a way of hovering around the edges of your life until you can't ignore them any longer. I guess that's why I had to get the film developed. I guess that's why I'm not surprised by the photograph I always knew would be there.

Yesterdays never really let go of your soul. They just pretend they've gone away until they're ready to return again . . .

Eagle Peak in the summertime was a soft white cloud hanging mid-universe somewhere between heaven and earth. Swallow up the air, it would chill your soul. Cup your hands and sip the water from its lake, it would remind you how alive you really were. Each breath was the incense of fresh cut pine, each glance a bright and bountiful rainbow of alpine flowers.

David B. Silva

It's that summer aliveness I've tried to remember about Eagle Peak. But it's the winter I can't seem to forget.

It's such a cold queer season, winter. Of dark dreams and hibernations. Of snow that floats gently from heaven-to-earth like white milky butterflies, deceivingly turning marrow to ice, painting summer as a vague and distant memory. Spellbinding. Let it once lull you to sleep, it'll take you to death. Touch its tapered icicles—hanging stalactite-like from tree and rock, sometimes dripping, sometimes not—and before you're aware, the pellucid ice turns red with your blood.

Mother Nature at her wickedest is winter.

Mother Nature at her wickedest.

When we first established camp at Eagle Peak, it was late in the summer of '80, a year that had no autumn. One September day was all blue skies and tee-shirts, the next was gray gloom and parkas. That same year, in fact only a few months before, Mount St. Helens had explosively erupted, sending a plume of ash as high as fifteen miles into the atmosphere. Meteorologists were already warning that the ash might have a significant influence on weather patterns. For some parts of the country, they were forecasting what they called a small Nuclear Winter.

But who listened to meteorologists?

Stairway To Heaven was what we called our little commune at Eagle Peak. Esoteric and self-important, perhaps, but that's the way of the artist. A government grant had brought us together, a small group of strangers, each an artist setting out to illuminate the four seasons through his or her own unique artistic medium. (And yes, it's true. The National Endowment For The Arts does, in fact, fund projects that don't have anything to do with bodily functions or sacrilegious interpretations.)

There were twelve of us, all previous strangers, all on separate paths of artistic endeavor — wood carving, leather craft, oils, sculpting, acting, photography, etc. I was the Hemingway of group. As much as possible, we were each supposed to integrate the resources of nature into our work. Paints were made from berries and saps and chalk-like rocks, leather from animal hides, wood carved fresh from fallen trees, etc.

Creativity ran rampant, you could say.

We established our little Stairway in a small valley—a cliff of rock

Ice Sculptures

to the north to protect us from the northerners that sometimes swept through the park, and an open lane to the south where we hoped the southern sun would keep us warm on those cold January days when the skies were cloudless.

As the lone writer, I suspect my presence at the Stairway was more for the purpose of recording the experience than anything else. The grant wasn't terribly explicit in this area, and the coordinator had emphasized that each of us were to interpret our experiences individually so that the canvas would be of the broadest, most varied nature. My own personal goal (which has long since been abandoned), was to compile a book of the folklore and mystique that I felt would inevitably grow out of our back-to-nature experience.

I gave up that goal when I was no longer able to comprehend exactly what was taking place at the Stairway.

There were two of us who matched up as outsiders right from day one. Margo McKennen was a photographer, full of f-stops and shutter-speeds, wide-angles and zooms. In a way, she and I were each observers more than creators. Sometimes I think that fine distinction was what kept us a cold breath apart from the others. On the artistic social ladder, Margo and I each had one foot on the bottom rung and one foot dangling free. I think there must have been an unwritten rule (naturally it would be unwritten) about the dirtier the hands in the creation of one's art, the higher up the ladder one stood. Margo and I, we were just doing our best to keep aboard.

When I first met her, her camera was always busy *whirr-clicking* this and that with a nervous energy that never seemed satiated. In some ways, I imagined that camera as an extension of her. She saw the world—for all its ugliness, and all its splendor—through an open shutter, almost as if she were afraid to put the camera down for fear she might miss something that shouldn't be missed.

"Blink once, and a piece of the world goes scampering by unnoticed," she would say. "Blink twice . . . and there's nothing left to see."

When she first used that line, I thought it had something to do with her own sense of being one of life's non-participators. But now, when I think back to the sadness that sometimes darkened her eyes at such times, I wonder if perhaps it was the blindness of death she was warning me about.

Blink twice . . . and there's nothing left to see.

It was September 16th when the first snowflake came fluttering down from the heavens, melting against the ground of Eagle Peak. Then another flake came whispering out of the sky, and another, and it was only a short time before they quit melting as they kissed the earth.

Two days later, a park ranger—all yellow-jacketed and puffing out great breaths of hot air—came snow-mobiling up the trail. They were closing the park (something usually reserved for shortly after the Thanksgiving weekend), and he wanted to know if there were any . . . "last requests" is how he put it. I remember how he was trying his best to keep warm, clapping his hands together and scratching at the snow like a great elk trying to uncover the skeleton of a buried shrub. Beneath his words, there was a poorly-disguised contempt. *Goddam fools!*, he was saying. *This ain't no place to be. Not this winter. Not here.*

They officially closed the park on September 20th, 1980.

And that began the longest winter I've ever experienced.

During those first winter days, Margo and I were detached observers, more or less keeping a wide eye on our fellow artists, and a curious eye on the strange weather. She was fascinated with the bitter cold of the early snow storm. And I guess that's what I found so attractive about her, that wonderful child-like curiosity, always wanting to watch, to be patient, to wait to see what would happen.

Together—for we became almost inseparable after awhile—we watched as our artistic cohorts slowly lost their facelessness and became real people, whole and eccentric and Jekyll-and-Hyde-ish each in some personal way. It was during those early winter days, when Margo and I were standing just at the fringe of the Stairway experience, left alone to take our little notes—both visual and written—that I enjoyed the most.

Of the lot, Billy Dayton, our resident sculptor, was the oddest. He was a man out of his time, a lost child of the Sixties. He wore his hair long, tied in a ponytail with a strap of fur taken from a rabbit. His face was hidden behind a full beard with touches of gray that made him look older than his age. His eyes were as dark as a moonless night, always seeming to hide something uneasy going on inside him.

I met him one late-summer day about a mile from camp. He was kneeling at the base of a monolithic slab of volcanic rock, chipping at it with a chisel made of granite.

"What is it?" I asked, in all innocence of the answer.

"The revolution of nature," he answered with a voice soft and fragile, the kind of voice that makes you believe every muttered syllable even though you knew it was nonsense. That was Billy Dayton, always talking nonsense and making it sound right. At least that's the way I saw it at the time. Now . . . well, now I'm not so sure. Perhaps it wasn't nonsense at all.

"Catchy title," I said.

Then Margo came along, *whirr-clicking* away at everything that found its way into her camera frame. When she saw Billy's monolith, she snapped off four or five shots, then paused with her camera clutched in her hands. "What is it?" she asked.

"The revolution of nature," I answered.

She didn't giggle, at least not out loud.

But something hit Dayton wrong, because he turned on his knees and caught eyes with her, as if he were reading her mind. I remember, for just a moment, thinking his eyes were afire with liquid mercury. Then Margo shivered, and I could see the joy shriveling up inside of her, the way a child's joy sometimes shrivels when an adult walks into the room. "Let's go," she said, giving my arm a tug. Her hand was ice-cold, as if the blood had drained out of her body.

I followed along, while Billy turned back to his *revolution*. When we were out of ear shot, I asked Margo why the sudden escape.

"Just a feeling," she said. Then her camera came up and she was *whirr-clicking* first this tree, then that one. And that was the first time I realized Margo's camera wasn't just a window to the world, but was also her way of closing off the things she didn't want to see.

Out of frame, out of mind.

As winter nights grew colder, the Stairway slowly divided into smaller and smaller groups, each with its own self-interest. Inside this tent, a great debate on craft versus art, and which is the soul of creativity. Inside that tent, a sharing of berry-paint recipes and ten great uses for volcanic rock. Inside our tent, Margo and I—once strangers, now friends—safely sharing tiny, protected pieces of ourselves.

"Perspective is the greatest gift we can give the world," she said on one of those cold nights. She was bundled warmly in a mummy bag, the flickering light of the fire reflecting brightly in her eyes. "Outside, you see the bleakness of a harsh winter, I see ice castles and snow fairies. We look at the same thing, yet see it differently. That perspective—yours unique to you, mine unique to me—is our greatest gift to the world."

I thought I could understand that. "Take the same idea for a story," I said. "Give it to fifty different writers and you'll get fifty different stories. Each with its own personality. Each as individual as its writer."

"Yes!" she shouted excitedly, teacher to student. "And from where do we draw our unique perspectives, you yours, me mine?"

"From yesterdays and todays! From childhood delights and adolescent nightmares! From staring monkey-like at the mirror! From growing up so fast we never quit feeling like we're still children!"

"And from the smells we smell!" she said, raising up on one elbow and spitting out the words as fast as they'd come. "And the sounds we hear, the roughs and smooths and squares and rounds we touch! From what makes us sad, and what makes us happy! From our beliefs about the world and the universe, about birth and death, about promises and lies! From all of it!"

She took up a great breath, held it, smiled through it, and let it all out in a white cloud that filled up the tent. She had said so much more than she realized at that moment. Because I think that's what happened to Dayton. He had a perspective all his own, and somehow it got loose.

"I want you to see this," she told me one late-January day. The sun was shining free over Eagle Peak, and the white snow on the ground was nearly blinding as she tugged at me. "It's beauty at its ugliest."

"That's a contradiction in terms. It must have something to do with Dayton," I said.

Ice Sculptures

"Who else?"

"Another revolution?"

"Of sorts, I suppose." She stopped to snap off a few quick pictures of some deer tracks in the snow. "Take a guess at what the man has done this time. Make it the wildest, most bizarre guess you can come up with."

"He's built his own stairway to heaven," I said.

Margo lowered her camera, then shared the oddest smile with me, as if she were giving actual thought to the possibility. "I wonder," she said softly. Then the camera went up again, and she said, "Guess again."

"I give up. The man's too unpredictable for a writer's imagination."

"He's sculpting in ice."

"Sculpting what?"

"A self-portrait."

There were three sculptures cut in the ice, each slightly different in a not-so-subtle way I still find difficult to describe. A progression of some sort—young, old, older, first came to mind. The first, a marvelous likeness of Dayton himself. The second, a little less recognizable. The third, Picasso-like, only softer, less sharp in line and cut. Perhaps *digression* might better describe the three since each appeared less distinct, more oblique than the one to its left.

"That's a self-portrait?" I asked. There was an odd sense of *imbalance* about the work, something that seemed to say: *the wiser the man, the more self-destructive.* And that was Dayton himself, wise and self-destructive.

"What else can it be?" Margo answered.

Dayton damned all twelve of us that winter. Each of us became one of his ice-cut similitudes done in three distinct digressions—born, living, dead—as if the breath of death had slowly shriveled the ice. All twelve of us, he cut and shaped and sculpted. Sally at 7,000 feet, near Eagle Lake. Hampton at 7,500 feet near Goat Head Pass. The others hidden in places we were never able to locate.

At the completion of the last sculptured likeness, sometime in mid-April when the snow at the lower elevations was already beginning to turn to water, Dayton disappeared inside his tent and never came out again.

We didn't know it at the time, but the "revolution" was on its way.

It arrived near the end of April. The sun was shining almost summer-like in the southern skies. And the spring thaw was slowly lending life to an endless number of trickles and runnels and fountains, sculpting deeper into mountainsides, and here and there rearranging the topographical anatomy.

Eagle's Peak was finally coming back to life after its long winter hibernation. And I for one, could hardly wait for the day when I could let out a warm sigh and not see it mushrooming before me in the cold air.

As much as I thought of myself as nature's victim, I suspect Dayton thought of himself as nature's messiah. Perhaps that was truly what he was — Mother Nature's messenger. It had been two weeks since anyone had seen him poke his nose outside his tent flaps, so Margo—her wondrous curiosity piqued—convinced me we should try poking our noses inside for a glimpse.

"This isn't the time to be taking photographs," I whispered to her. We stood outside Dayton's tent, Margo with both hands on her camera, me with both hands on the canvas flaps.

"Just one," she said with a sparkle in her eye. "Go on."

I pulled back the flaps.

Margo snapped off two or three quick shots.

And we both stood silent for the longest breath, Margo's camera dropping numbly back to her side (a sight I'll never forget, because it was the first time I had ever seen her come face-to-face with something horrible and not try to hide herself behind the lens of a camera).

What was left of Dayton was on the floor, partially hidden beneath some clothing and that strap of rabbit fur he always used to tie back his hair. I nudged a foot against the pile, heard the eerie clicking of bone-against-bone, saw the jelly-like substance ooze outward a little further, and tried to keep my stomach from heaving.

Ice Sculptures

Dayton-the-messiah had delivered his message.
Something in Mother Nature was out of balance.

Stairway To Heaven disbanded the next day, partially because of what had happened to Dayton, partially because the long winter months had finally taken their toll on our collective state of mind. Even in the face of spring, it had become too easy to see things as forever cold and frozen and hopeless.

Sally and Hampton left early the next morning for Mount St. Helens. Some of the others went home, some went south where the weather was warmer, some drifted out of camp without saying a word. Margo and I stayed on.

We were curious, I guess. And maybe that's what had set us apart from the others right from the beginning. I think Margo felt somehow responsible for what had happened to Dayton, though we both tried to label it as a fluke of nature, something like spontaneous combustion, something better left unquestioned. Still, she wanted to keep taking photographs until (through the eyes of her camera) it somehow made sense. And for myself, well, I wanted to write more about Dayton and how he seemed so different from the rest of us, and maybe how things at the Stairway might have been different if we'd tried to understand him a little better.

We both felt compelled to remain at Eagle Peak a little longer.

The twenty-first day of May was my last day there.

I was sitting on the ground, leaning back against a rock, soaking up some sunshine, and scribbling stray ideas into my notebook. I couldn't escape the thought that somehow Dayton and Mount St. Helens and the ice sculptures were all intertwined in some strange malevolent way that had brought about Dayton's death. Then Margo quietly appeared from the mouth of a small valley that fed into a single-file trail leading upward toward Eagle Peak's 12,000 foot summit. Her camera was resting at her side. Her steps were nearly staggering, and I remember my first thought being that she must have tried to hike to the top of the mountain. She was glistening in the mid-day sun, her hair was damp against her forehead, her face and arms and legs were alive with reflected sunlight. And her eyes were glassy and ice-like, as pure as the crystal-like agates I used to play marbles with as a child.

"Margo?" I had her rest against the rock, knelt next to her, and noticed for the first time, the blood coming from her head. "My God, what happened?"

She handed me a roll of film—the touch of her hand was cold, like a mountain stream in early May—then another, and another. And when she tried to smile it was a sad smile she couldn't hold. "You're still up there," she whispered. "I couldn't reach you, but you're there."

I brushed the hair away from where she was bleeding. There was a dark, red hole where her left ear should have been. "Oh, Margo . . ."

"I found my ice sculpture," she said, between small, fought-for breaths. "Thought maybe if I shattered it . . ."

"Dayton's likeness of you?"

She nodded. "Yours, too. Another thousand feet up. Near the summit."

There was a long, breath-held silence. I sat next to her. She curled herself into my arms. "I'm dying," she said, and it was as innocent and honest a statement as one of her photographs. "And there's nothing I can do."

She leaned into me. I whispered, "I love you," and pulled her closer. She felt soft, too soft, like a worn pillow or a balloon losing its air. Her skin was moist and cold and slick to the touch, wax-like in some ways, ice-like in others. I knew I was going to lose her.

I held her till the sun went down, till I couldn't see in the darkness any longer, because I wanted to remember what she looked like before the flesh began sliding off her arms and legs and face, before the tissue and muscle and cartilage turned jelly-like and puddled beneath her. When there was only a distant, hazy moonlight overhead, I listened to the final clattering of her bones, and felt the last of her form melt beneath our embrace the way the last of her ice sculpture was melting beneath the May sky two thousand feet higher up the mountain . . .

It's raining outside.
I've left the windows open and the heat off, and still I can't help

Ice Sculptures

feeling too hot on this winter day. I know what's happening to me, though that doesn't make it any less painful, any less hideous.

In the photograph, taken from a distance, I can see where my ice-sculptured likeness is sitting proud just a few hundred feet below the Eagle Peak summit. Low enough to be warmed by three season's of sun, high enough to somehow resist the melting.

And I feel like an icicle in the late afternoon of an overcast day, moist to the touch, dripping here and there just a bit, but ever so grateful for the first chill of the coming cold night.

Dry Whiskey

When I was a boy, I would look at my father and see everything right with the world. He seemed bigger, then. At the end of the day, he would come in from the fields with his shirt slung over his shoulder and the sun at his back, and every muscle in his body would be perfectly defined. I had looked up to him back then, like most boys looked up to their fathers. And I had wanted to grow up to be the same man that he was.

The rub of it is . . . time has a way of changing the order of things.

My father had started drinking nearly twelve years ago, not long after my mother had died of ovarian cancer. At first, though I was only eleven at the time, I thought I had understood: anything to help forget that bone-thin skeleton, that rictus smile that she had become just before her death. It was an image that haunted me for a long time afterward. And it was an image that had never stopped haunting my father.

Now, I was sitting in the truck, staring at the house, wondering how things could change so much in just ten or twelve short years. It was mid-morning. The sun was already high in the sky, and there was a dark shadow enclosing the front porch. I stared a while longer, then climbed out of the truck and closed the door.

By the time I made it to the front steps, my father had come out of the house, dragging himself across the porch like a man who had been ill for a long time now. The screen door bounced off the jamb behind him. He fell into one of the rattan chairs my mother had bought, hawked up a wad of phlegm and sent it flying over the porch railing. "What're you doing here?" he asked.

"Just thought I'd come by and see how you're doing. That's all."

"Yeah?" He scratched at the stubble on his chin, which had been growing for better than a week by the look of it. It hadn't been all that long ago that the first signs of gray had begun to sneak in. Now, it was almost *all* gray. "Well, I'm doing okay. Anything else?"

"Heard you were in town last night."

"Believe I was."

"Heard you got booted out of the Forty-Niner."

"Did I?"

"That's what Len Dozier says."

My father nodded slightly, as if that sounded close enough to the truth to suit him. Then he buried his face in his hands and let out a slow breath of air that seemed like an effort to control something inside that he found frightening. When he looked up again, I was reminded of the fact that this was the morning after. His coloring was ashy, his eyes bloodshot. "I might have," he said. "I don't exactly remember."

"How'd you get home?"

"Drove."

He thought maybe he had taken Buzzard Roost Road, which was the long way home no matter how you figured it. But he really couldn't be certain. He might have gone down Old Forty-Four and across. To be honest, he finally confessed, he couldn't recall much of anything about last night. "Things get a little fuzzy after I stopped at the Forty-Niner."

He stared down at his hands then, silently, with that look of shame that I'd seen cross his face a thousand times before.

"Have you eaten breakfast yet?"

Dry Whiskey

"Uh-uh."

"Then let's get some food in you, okay?" I cooked him up some eggs and bacon and poured him a cup of strong, black coffee. We sat at the table in the kitchen. For a while we talked about the drought that had settled over the state the past four years, wondering how much longer it was going to go on. It hadn't proved to be as bad as the '77-'78 drought yet—*that* one had been the worst in the state's history—but summer was here now and it was going to be a long time before we were likely to see any new storms move through.

After breakfast, I cleared the dishes off the table, and placed them in the sink. "I've gotta be going, Pa."

"You working today?"

"Len Dozier needs a hand repairing his tractor."

"Well, you go on, then."

"Are you gonna be all right?"

"I'll be fine."

He walked me to the front porch, the suspenders hanging loosely around his waist, his gait a bit shorter, a bit slower than it generally was when he had had a belly full of whiskey to move him along. Outside, there were shimmering waves of heat rising off the bed of my father's old pickup, and in the distance, you could see a mirage in the crease between two brown hills. It looked a little like a pond. But there hadn't been a pond there in nearly five years now. Not since before the drought.

My father had let the farm go to hell after my mother had died. It had always been a small farm: four, fifty-acre parcels, about two hundred acres altogether. It sat near the base of the foothills, with South Cow Creek flowing lazily along its southern border. He leased out two of the parcels: one for grazing, the other for bee hives in the winter months when the bees were dormant and there wasn't much call for pollinating. He had his own small herd, too, about twenty head of cattle, and that was pretty much it.

I stopped at the foot of the steps, wanting to be on my way and feeling a little guilty for it.

"You looked yet?" he asked me.

"No, Pa."

"You gonna?"

"Sure." I didn't know when this routine had first started. Like everything else, I suppose it was around the time that my mother had died. Definitely sometime after he had started drinking. I was use to it by now, and I guess because nothing had ever come of it, it seemed more like a routine than a real concern. But I gave the front end of his truck an honest look anyway.

He drove an old Chevy flatbed with aluminum running boards and an unpainted, right front fender. The fender had been replaced several summers back after he'd clipped a fence post—trying to avoid a jackrabbit, he claimed. The rest of the truck was in fairly decent shape, considering its age.

Something was wrong with the front end, though. I noticed that almost immediately. The bumper, which was second-hand scrap he had brought home from the junkyard and painted off-white, had been smashed up against the front grille. It looked as if someone had taken a sledge hammer to it. And just above the bumper, the lens of the headlight was broken, its mounting ring dangling loosely off to one side. If that weren't enough, there was also a good-size depression in the top of the left fender, where it looked as if the metal had been crimped at a weak spot almost directly over the wheel well.

Last night, on his way home, my father had hit something. "Jesus."

"What is it?" he asked.

I ran my fingers across the bumper. There was a dark stain that looked as if something had spilled over the top edge and had run down the white paint. It was shaped something like a waterfall, with a mix of thick-and-thin lines flowing unevenly, top to bottom. At first thought, it looked like a kid might have taken a black Magic Marker to it. But when I looked closer, I realized the color was brownish-red, and it hadn't been done by any Magic Marker. Because it was a blood stain. "Oh, God."

"What?"

"You did it, Pa. You finally did it." I looked up at him, and he was standing at the edge of the porch with an arm wrapped around the post like it was the only thing holding him up. His face had turned ashen, and for the first time this morning, there was a hint of sobriety behind his eyes. "The bumper's smashed, and there's some blood, Pa. You hit something last night."

I spent most of that afternoon at Len Dozier's place, working on his tractor. We got it up and running some time around four, so I stopped by the market in Kingston Mills, picked up a couple of steaks, some potatoes, a 64 ouncer of Coke, and headed back to my father's place. When I had left, he had been sitting at the kitchen table, staring vacantly into his half-empty cup of coffee. It was only a matter of time, I figured, before the coffee was replaced by whiskey, and if that had already happened, it was a good bet I was going to find him passed out cold on the living room couch.

But that's not where I found him.

He was sitting on the front porch, next to a pile of plastic bags filled with bottles and cans. I climbed out of the truck with the grocery bag in one arm, and as I closed the door, I watched him toss an empty whiskey bottle into the air. It sailed a good fifteen or twenty feet, landed smack-dab in the middle of a feeding trough with loomix stenciled across the side, and then shattered with the harsh sound of a bottle landing in a recycling bin.

"What are you doing, Pa?"

He didn't bother to look up. As I went through the gate, he popped the tab off a can of Budweiser, dumped the contents out through an opening between the porch slats, then crushed the can and tossed it in the direction of another pile only a few feet away. It fell short, making almost no sound at all.

"Pa?"

When he finally did look up, his face was drawn and haggard, and though I had seen him like this before, this time was different. This was not a man who had hung one on while I had been gone. It was a man who had looked at himself in the mirror and had been frightened by what he had found.

"Pa, what's the matter?"

He stared at me a moment, something apparently aching silently inside him. "You ever meet Lloyd's kid?"

David B. Silva

"Joey Egan?"

He nodded.

"Yeah, a couple of years ago, I think. When I was helping with 4H."

"He died last night," my father said mechanically. He took a bottle of Johnnie Walker Black Label out of the plastic bag next to him, gazed fondly at the label, then unscrewed the top and emptied out the whiskey. "It was a hit and run, off Buzzard Roost Road. He was on his way home after a school dance."

"Are you sure?"

"It was in this morning's paper," he said. Then he sent the empty bottle sailing across the yard, end over end. A spattering of sunlight glittered off the glass just before the neck of the bottle landed against the side of the trough and fell apart before my eyes. I'm not sure I even heard the sound it made. It seemed a thousand miles away just then.

"Maybe it wasn't you," I suggested.

"You're forgetting the blood on the bumper, Will."

"Yeah, but . . . Jesus, don't you remember anything from last night?"

"Not after I left the bar." He pulled another bottle out of the bag, poured the liquid down an opening between the slats, and flung it in the direction of the front gate this time. It landed short, in a soft mound of dirt where my mother had once planted a bed of wild violets and Shasta daisies, even some brown-eyed susans. *Just because we live on a farm*, she had said, *doesn't mean we can't have a little color around the place*. The bottle kicked up a cloud of dust that lazily drifted away on the evening breeze.

I plopped down in a chair next to him. "So what now?"

"You can join me if you want." He handed over a six pack of beer.

The farm sat at the west end of a valley. It was a little past five now, the last week of May. The shadows from the hills were beginning to lengthen, and I could feel the coolness of evening coming on. I popped the top off the first of the cans, poured out the contents, and began my participation in a ritual that took nearly an hour before it was finished.

We never discussed calling the police. I suppose we should have at least discussed it. But what was the point? It wasn't going to change the fact that there was blood on the front end of my father's pickup. And it wasn't going to bring little Joey Egan back, either.

In a strange way, though, what had happened had already started to bring my father back. He had been hiding inside a bottle for a long, long time, but suddenly it looked as if he might at last come out and show himself. If he did, I didn't want to risk losing him again.

We barbecued the steaks on an old grill out back that night. We had planned to eat outside at the picnic table under the dogwoods, but the mayflies were swarming, so we ended up inside at the kitchen table instead. It wasn't until we had finished the meal, and I had poured him a cup of coffee that I noticed his hands were shaking.

"Are you all right?"

He nodded, appearing unaffected. "The booze is wearing off. That's all."

"You sure?" He looked warm, and a little haggard. Though I had seen him looking much worse after an all-night bend.

"I'll be fine."

"You want me to stay tonight?"

"No, you go on home. I'll be all right."

I stacked the dishes in the sink, wiped my hands off on a kitchen towel, then turned around and stared at him. When you're a kid, you never think about your father as being old. I wasn't a kid anymore, of course. But I had thought of him as an old man for a good many years now, and I wondered briefly when it was that *I* had become the father, and he the son. And I wondered how much longer he was going to be with me.

"I'll come by in the morning," I said.

"No need."

"Just to check to see how you're doing."

"If that's what you want."

Joey Egan's funeral was held three days later. He was buried in a family plot in the Black Oak Cemetery on the outskirts of town, next to his mother, who had died of pneumonia the year before. After the services, I drove my father home and stayed with him that night, because I was afraid that he might start drinking again. He hadn't shed a tear since the day my mother had died. But in the truck, on our way out of Black Oak, he had broken down and started a long, painful crying jag.

More than just his drinking, I guess I worried about him doing something crazy that night.

The next morning, my father woke up with a hangover.

He came dragging into the kitchen sometime around nine, his eyes bloodshot, his brain apparently pounding unmercifully at the inside of his skull. He stopped at the sink, shading his eyes against the morning sun, and took a drink of water right out of the faucet. It was the one-hundred-and-seventeenth straight day without rain, and while the well hadn't gone dry, it sometimes took a while before anything came out of the spout.

"How's bacon and eggs sound?" I asked.

He shook his head guardedly. "Nothing for me, thanks."

"You gotta eat something." I had already tossed some bacon in the skillet. He hadn't been eating much of anything since the accident, and I had promised myself not to let him get away with it again. But he looked like the man of old this morning, like a man coming out of a stupor: ragged and foul and slightly out of touch with his surroundings. I didn't think he was going to be able to keep his food down even if he tried. "Christ, you didn't go on another drunk last night, did you?"

He looked up at me, his lips dry and chapped, his face expressionless. "You know I didn't. You were here all night, weren't you?"

"Then what the hell's the matter with you?"

"It's a dry drunk," he whispered hoarsely. He wiped his hands across the front of his undershirt, where one strap of his overalls was unfastened and hanging loosely.

"It happens sometimes," he said. "When you've been drinking as long as I have."

"All the more reason to get some food in your stomach."

"Maybe." He shut off the faucet and moved to the table, where he sat down a little gingerly, and let out a half-hearted sigh. "I saw Joey Egan last night," he said.

"Joey's dead, Pa."

"He came into my room and stood over my bed. There was a mess of cuts and scratches all over his face. Looked like some fool had taken the business end of a pitchfork to him. And I think his left arm was broken. It looked that way at least."

"It was a dream, Pa."

"No, it wasn't no dream. He knew how your ma died."

"Everyone knows she had cancer. That's no secret."

"But the cancer ain't what killed her, Will."

"What?" We had never talked about my mother's death, but she had been sick for a good many months before she died. For a long time afterward, my father had always said that it was the consumption that got her. I guess it was less painful for him to think of it that way. It took a long time before he was ever able to use the word *cancer*.

"I couldn't stand to watch her suffer," he said.

"What did you do, Pa?" He looked up at me, a man whose rounded shoulders reflected the heavy weight they had been carrying, and suddenly I understood everything. All the nights at the Forty-Niner. The way he had pulled back from me after she had died. The way he had pulled back from everyone. I understood it all. "You killed her, didn't you?"

"I . . . I placed a pillow over her face," he said softly.

"Jesus."

"She was in so much pain . . ."

And then my father broke down and cried for the second time in less than a week. I sat next to him, with my arm draped over his shoulders, feeling helpless. Guilt carried a heavy price, and my father, I suspected, had been paying a hefty markup for a long, long time.

After a while, he caught himself and took in a deep breath. "I'm all right," he said uncertainly. He stared out the kitchen window, off to the distance, where a small twister had kicked up and was swirling the dust across the open field like a child swirling finger paints across a paper canvas. I had never noticed the burden in his face quite the way I noticed it just then. Here was a man who had been killing himself for years with booze, and now he was killing himself without it. I wondered if I had ever really known my father, if anyone had ever really known him.

"Things'll be all right once the booze wears off," I said weakly. "You hear?"

He nodded.

I gave him a pat on the back. "You sure you don't want anything to eat?"

"Later," he said.

I left him around eleven that morning. He was sitting in a chair on the front porch, staring out across the barren terrain, his mind a million miles away. I had gotten myself a six-week stint up in Oregon, hauling trees out of a private co-op that was selectively logging its land, and I reminded him about the job.

"I'll be back in six weeks. Okay, Pa?"

"I ain't going nowhere," he said.

"Six weeks," I repeated. As I drove out the dirt driveway, I caught a glimpse of him in my rearview mirror. There was something standing next to him, something I couldn't quite make out. And the man, himself, was hardly recognizable. A man so completely different from the man of my early childhood that I felt a little rattle of uneasiness run through me. What had happened to him? What had happened to the man who had been as strong as an ox, who had put up the barn by himself one summer, using a block-and-tackle, who had been able to stack a hundred bales of hay in a day and still have the energy to shoot some hoops out back under the last vestiges of twilight? What the hell had happened to that man?

He had grown old, I wanted to tell myself.

He had grown old and alone and empty.

But there was more to it than that.

He had also grown frightened.

I called him twice while I away was in Oregon. Under the circumstances, I guess I should have called more often. But that picture of him in my rearview mirror had been haunting me like a ghost. I kept thinking that I had caught a glimpse of little Joey Egan, standing next to him on the porch. That Joey had been that *something* I couldn't quite recognize, and that he had had one hand on my father's shoulder as if he were trying to hold him down.

The first time I called, the phone rang relentlessly, maybe as many as a dozen times, before my father finally picked it up. "No more," he said sharply. "You hear me? You call me one more time and I swear I'll come out to Black Oak myself and dig up your goddamn remains. You hear me? I'll feed 'em to the damn buzzards and that'll be the end of it."

"Pa, it's me."

There was a sudden, surprised silence on the other end. Then, quietly: "Will?"

"Yes."

"Oh, Christ. Will? That really you? Where are you?"

"I'm in Oregon, Pa. What's going on there? What's all the shouting about?"

"Oregon ..." he mumbled, in nearly a whisper. And for a moment, I thought he had gone back to the bottle again. In fact, I was certain that was exactly what he had done.

"You've been on a drunk, haven't you, Pa?"

"What's my boy doing in Oregon?"

"Listen to me. You've been drinking again, haven't you?"

Then the line went dead.

I called him back within seconds, my hands shaking almost uncontrollably as I fumbled with the phone. What the hell was going on? He had sounded like a man on the verge of self-destruction. I couldn't even be certain he had recognized me. Maybe he wasn't drinking again, but if it wasn't the booze I had heard, I hated to think what it might have been.

The phone rang thirty, maybe forty times without an answer. Eventually, I hung up and tried to convince myself that I had probably disturbed his sleep, that I must have caught him in the middle of a bad dream, and that there was nothing to worry about. He had been tired, was all. The call had wakened him and *that's* why he had sounded so crazy, because he'd still been half-asleep.

I wasn't able to get hold of him again until nearly three weeks later. It was the night before I was due to head back to Kingston Mills.

I'm not sure what I expected him to sound like after that first call. Still a little crazy, I guess. But he didn't sound crazy, and he didn't sound like a man who would be dead in a few short hours. He sounded like a man who had finally forgiven himself.

"Is everything all right there?" I asked.

"I'm finally dry," he said serenely.

"What?" I thought I could hear something in the background that sounded dry and brittle, something that made me think of autumn leaves and sand through an hourglass. And then he chuckled.

"I think the booze is wearing off," he said. "My head's clearing up. It's been a long time since I've seen things this clearly."

"Look, Pa, I'm coming home tomorrow. Are you gonna to be all right till then?"

"Fine," he said. "I'm gonna be just fine."

I don't remember what I said in return. But I remember holding the phone in my hand after he had hung up, and being overwhelmed with a strange jumble of emotions. It had been years since I had felt close to my father, and suddenly I was terrified that I might never have a chance to feel close to him again.

Early the next morning, I left Oregon, arriving at the farm shortly after one o'clock in the afternoon. His pickup was parked out front, in the same spot it had been parked the day I had discovered the blood on the bumper. There was a layer of dust a quarter of an inch thick across the hood, and it was nearly impossible to see through the windshield into the cab. The pickup had sat there like a dinosaur for nearly two months now. In the back of my mind, I suppose I knew it would eventually be buried under that dust like an old desert ghost town. But at the time, I didn't give it much of a thought.

The front door to the house was unlocked. It had been left slightly ajar, and just inside there was a strange wind-cut pattern of sand and dust scattered across the hardwood floor. Kingston Mills had gone a hundred-and-fifty-nine days without rain, and the dust, it seemed, was no longer content to stay outside.

"Pa?"

In the kitchen, I discovered a pyramid-shaped pile of dirt in the sink, maybe five or six inches high. One of the faucet handles had been

Dry Whiskey

broken off. It was lying on the lip of the drain, partially buried by the dirt. I took hold of the other handle, turned it, and watched a slow, steady stream of dirt sift lazily out of the spout.

"Pa?"

I found him, or some general semblance of him, in his bedroom at the back of the house. He was lying in bed, on top of the sheets, his hands folded peacefully across his stomach. He was dressed in the same clothes he had worn nearly everyday of his life since my mother had died: an old pair of work boots worn at the heels, a pair of blue-jean overalls with one unfastened strap hanging loosely at his side, and of course, the long johns he always wore come hell or high water.

Underneath, there was very little left of the man I remembered. Something had happened to him in the few short weeks that I had been gone, something I didn't think I was ever going to be able to understand. Maybe it had something to do with the drought—after all, the well *had* gone dry. Or maybe it had something to do with all those damn bottles he had tossed off the front porch the night he went dry. The booze had kept him going for a good many years. Maybe without it, the well of his soul had gone dry, too. I don't know. All I know is that the man I discovered at the back of the house was all dust and bones.

He looked as if he had been dead a very long time. I had spoken with him last night, but here he was now, less than twenty-four hours later: his skeletal hands peeking out from beneath his shirt-sleeves, his teeth bared in a dreadful, lipless grin, his eyes no more than dark, empty sockets.

Like the flowers my mother had planted out front, after an unquenchable thirst, my father had simply shriveled up and died.

There's a prayer from The Book of Common Prayer that reads: *Earth to earth, ashes to ashes, dust to dust, in sure and certain hope of the Resurrection unto eternal life.* I find myself often thinking back to these words.

My father was buried in the Black Oak Cemetery, two rows over from Joey Egan. A bunch of the guys from the Forty-Niner came by the house afterward, drank a little beer, and talked about the good times they'd had together. Mostly, though, they seemed to stare off into the distance, reflecting on things that I suppose I will never be privy to.

Late in the afternoon, Lloyd Egan pulled me aside and told me about a man they had locked up in Sparks, Nevada. They had caught him robbing a small Mom and Pop liquor store and during the interrogation, he had confessed to Joey's hit-and-run. He had leaned across the seat to roll down the passenger window, he had said, and his car had drifted onto the shoulder, and . . . and there was Joey, turning around, his eyes bright and surprised, just as the car made impact. The man had stopped and got out and realized that the boy was dead, and then he had got back into the car and had driven off. It had apparently been haunting him ever since.

Lloyd took a swig of his beer, and gazed off into nothingness, looking like he was on the verge of tears. I put my arm around him, tried to comfort him, and then led him back into the kitchen, where someone was telling a story about the time my father had had a few too many and had gone home and tried to shoe one of the steers.

Several days later, a storm moved in off the Pacific and dropped nearly five inches of much needed rain across the north state. It was the beginning of the end of the drought. But it had come too late for my father.

To this day, I don't know what it was he hit coming home from the bar that night. It could have been a deer or a cow, I suppose. But it wasn't Joey Egan, and I'm grateful for that, grateful beyond description.

I still think back to those times when I was a boy and he would come in from the fields with his shirt slung over his shoulder and every muscle of his body taut and perfectly defined. And like most boys, there are still the times when I wish I could have grown up to be that man.

The shame of it is . . . I don't think I ever really got to know who he was.

A Time To Every Purpose

After the summer we had both graduated from junior high and he had moved away with his mother, I had never expected to hear from Jeremy Taft again. We had been friends of a sort that summer. Not so much because I liked him or he liked me, but because we shared the kind of secret that binds two people together, whether they like it or not.

That was the summer Andy Bale reportedly fell off the edge of Dead Man's Lookout and landed, nearly unrecognizable, at the bottom of the cliffs.

It was the summer Melissa Jenkins disappeared for four days and came back with a hollow, faraway gaze behind her eyes.

And toward the end, during the bristling hot days of August, it became the summer Jeremy Taft and his mother finally moved back to the mid-west somewhere, much to my delight.

I suppose over the years I had fooled myself into thinking that I had put that summer behind me. Twenty-some-odd years had passed since then. I was married now, with two kids, one eight, the other six. My hair was beginning to thin. There was an extra fifteen pounds around my mid-section. And though I had recently given up my Pall Malls, the last time I had gone hiking with Ellen and the kids, I had been the one bringing up the rear.

That other summer, just after junior high, belonged to a different person, from a different time. Some things, though, no matter how far toward the back of the file they're buried, have a way of working themselves to the front again.

The call from Jeremy came in a little after nine. "I need to see the place this afternoon, Dave. Sometime before three. That a problem?" If he hadn't introduced himself first, I'm not sure I would have recognized his voice. In school, Jeremy had been the invisible boy, sitting at the back of the class, silent except for those few times when Mrs. Crawford had specifically called on him. That was not something that happened often. I think after a time, teachers learn instinctively which kids are worth their while and which are best not to tangle with.

"You're back," I said, trying not to sound as uneasy with the idea as I felt.

"Just for a few hours," he said. "I've got some business at the house, then I'll be on my way again."

The "house" was an old Victorian two-story off Tule Elk Road on the other side of the river. Before they had moved, his mother had made arrangements with Banner Realty to handle the rental and upkeep. It had only been a year or so since Fred Endore had retired and I had been asked to take over the property. And it had been less than six months now since Jeremy's mother had written and asked us to give notice to the current renters. She wanted to make certain the house was vacant this summer.

"It's empty, isn't it?" Jeremy asked.

"As of three weeks ago."

"What time can you be there?"

I had a walk-through at eleven-thirty, a young couple from out of town had expressed interest in seeing the duplex off Sutter Street. And after that . . . "How about one o'clock?"

A Time To Every Purpose

There was a short silence on the other end, as he gave it some consideration. "Can you make it a little closer to two?"

"Sure, that's no problem."

"I appreciate this, Dave."

"No trouble."

"Meet you there, then?"

"Two o'clock," I said. I hung up, and sat at my desk for a while, staring numbly out the window at the traffic going by. Not much had changed since Jeremy had left. The town was a little larger now, but not much. They had built a new middle school next to Leighland Park in the early eighties, and Southern Pacific came through only once a day now, usually late at night when the town was sleeping soundly. Most of the kids I had grown up with had moved away long ago. A few of them were still around, though, trying to raise their own kids the way they had been raised. I suppose you could argue that time had stood still here.

Outside, a delivery truck rolled by. Across the street, eleven-year-old Brian Aickman was trading shoulder-slugs with one of his friends. They were laughing, so it all must have been in good fun. Then Brian motioned that he had to get going, and without even a glance over his shoulder, he darted out into the street. A white Ford van skidded to miss him, leaving a couple of black streaks in the pavement and a cloudy exhaust of burnt rubber in the air. For a moment, it brought it all back again . . .

And I felt a shudder tear through me, because it had been so close to what had happened to . . .

To Andy Bale, I thought coldly. I had spent the past twenty-odd years trying to forget, and for the most part, I guess I had done a fairly decent job. No matter how deep you bury a corpse, though, eventually the smell finds its way back to the surface.

Andy Bale.

He had been twelve years old the day he died.

It had happened on an overcast afternoon, less than a week after school had let out for the summer. Mom was visiting her sister in Tucson that day. I remember because she brought back a poster of a skull bone of a cow leaning up against a wagon wheel. Underneath it said: Rest Stop. She thought it was the funniest thing she had ever seen, and for several years I kept it pinned to the wall over my bed.

Dad was working at the lumber mill in Kingston Mills that summer. He came home late most of the time, usually well after I had gone to bed. And he was usually gone in the mornings by the time I came down for breakfast. But sometimes I could smell the damp, pulpy odor of sawdust still lingering in the kitchen, and it was almost as if he were still somewhere in the house.

That morning, the morning of the day that Andy Bale died, the faint odor of my father had still been in the air when I came down for breakfast. Though I had nearly forgotten about it by the time I accidentally met up with Jeremy at the rail yards.

Jeremy stepped out between two box cars in front of me, his thoughts faraway, a look of surprise crossing his face when he looked up to notice me. We had never spoken in class, but for some reason I guess I'll never understand, he called out my name as if we were the best of friends. "What're you doing down here?"

I shrugged uneasily and looked past him, both of us feeling a little uncomfortable by the surprise encounter. "Nothing much."

"Yeah, me neither," he said. "Been looking for railroad spikes. Not much luck, though."

I remember thinking he didn't seem like such a bad guy after all. His hair was kinda long, especially in the back, and he was wearing an old khaki shirt that looked like it had come from the Army Surplus shop next to the Chevron on Placer Street. Still he seemed friendly enough, and somehow we ended up sitting on the edge of a flatbed, talking about how boring summer could be and how he hoped he'd get to see his father before school started again and how we both thought Melissa Jenkins was the best looking girl in class.

For awhile, I suppose I thought we might actually become friends, me and Jeremy.

But then Andy Bale showed up and everything changed.

I don't know what he was doing down at the rail yards, either. Probably just kicking around like we were, killing time on a boring summer afternoon. It was Jeremy who saw him first. He tapped me on the shoulder and pointed across the tracks at Andy, who seemed lost in

A Time To Every Purpose

his own world, playing hopscotch or some other damnable thing on the railroad ties.

"Wanna have a little fun?" Jeremy asked.

I took a good look at Andy, and thought how small he looked. He was one grade behind us. His father worked over at the mill in Kingston Mills like most of the fathers in town, and we had played together on occasion, mostly at back yard picnics and such. He was an okay kid.

"Come on," Jeremy said, sliding down off the flatbed. I followed him down the tracks, where we crossed behind a box car and circled around, maybe thirty yards behind the kid. The sun had finally burned its way through the overcast, and there were shimmering waves of heat rising off the ties. Somewhere behind us, I could hear the faint rumble of the five o'clock freight train to Oregon.

"What are you going to do?" I asked.

Jeremy looked at me, that coldness I had always seen in class suddenly back. "Just scare him a little, that's all."

"Let's just leave him alone, all right?"

"I won't hurt him." He picked up a rock from next to the tracks.

Andy was still lost somewhere in his own world of thoughts, unaware, as far as I could tell, that we were even there. And I guess that took some of the fun out of it for Jeremy. I think he wanted to be able to look into the kid's eyes and see the fear there. I think that was the real thrill for him.

"Hey, Bale!" Jeremy called.

The kid turned around, unconcerned at first, and then a slow recognition crossed his face and that expression of fear that Jeremy had been looking for, was suddenly shining brightly from behind the kid's eyes. He had picked up what looked like an old rivet, but his fingers went slack and it slipped out of his hand and fell to the ground, kicking up a small cloud of dust. For maybe another five or six seconds, everyone stood motionless, and then without a word, Andy Bale took off running.

Jeremy laughed and took off after him. "Come on!"

There's something about being left behind, even when you never wanted to go along in the first place. Somewhere behind me, I heard the rumble of the freight train again, like a nudge back to reality. But I watched Jeremy running after the kid, and all I remember was that I didn't want to get left behind. I didn't want to be left standing alone on the tracks.

Jeremy laughed again, and tossed a rock that skipped off a tie, struck the tracks, and dug into the dirt. He was running a good thirty yards in front of me now.

I thought if I cut across the tracks I might be able to catch them before they entered the woods. But that was only assuming the kid remained headed in that direction. He might just as easily cut off toward the station, and try to lose us in the confusion of people and buildings.

From behind me, I heard the rumble of the train again. The sound had grown into a near roar by now, and only distantly at first, I realized it was right on my heels. I glanced back, startled to find myself in the growing shadow of the huge black mass.

A whistle blew.

Jeremy screamed something at the kid, something I couldn't hear, then tossed another rock.

Andy Bale looked over his shoulder, his eyes red and shining back a terror like I'd never seen before, and in that instant, like some sort of clairvoyance, I knew exactly what he was going to do. He was going to cut across the tracks in front of the train. I suppose I would have done the same thing if our roles had been reversed and I had been the one in front, running for his life. It was a decent bet, by the looks of it. The train didn't stop here. It went right on through to Kingston Mills, hauling seventy or eighty cars behind it. If he made it, Andy Bale would have himself a good five minute head start before we even got a glimpse of the caboose.

Jeremy screamed again: "What's the rush, Bale!"

To this day, I'm not sure if he knew the train was coming or not.

Andy knew it, though. He glanced back at Jeremy, then made a break across the tracks.

I heard the train's whistle blow, and the screech of brakes, and though I couldn't be certain, I thought I also heard the sound of impact. There was the commotion of black shadows beneath the belly of the engine, and the long, almost endless slide of the train down the tracks, its wheels locked and screaming. My mind, I suppose, filled in most of the rest.

After the train came to a stop, I looked to Jeremy, who was standing motionless not far from where he had let go of that last rock. His face was pale, his lips trembling. He stared, dark-eyed, at the place in the tracks where Andy Bale had tried to out run the train. Then Jeremy fell to his knees, his hands curled into a fist, his eyes closed tightly, his mouth open wide with one, long, defiant sound: "Noooooooo!"

For a moment, I felt caught between hating him and feeling sorry for him. Then he raised his head, and I could see the darkness behind his eyes, and all I could feel was a cold shiver rattle through me.

It might have been an accident.

Or it might have been on purpose.

I guess I'll never know for sure.

But I know this: even though Andy Bale died that day, they didn't find his body for another week. And when they did find it, it wasn't packed under the belly of a freight train. It was lying at the bottom of the cliff at Dead Man's Lookout.

No one ever knew the difference, I suppose. No one except me and Jeremy. The engineer got out and hunted around for nearly half-an-hour before deciding he hadn't hit the kid after all.

But I knew.

Jeremy Taft had sent Andy Bale on a little excursion through space and time. And by the time Andy had arrived at his final destination it was some six or seven days later and a good twelve miles up the line.

I knew.

And so did Jeremy Taft.

I put away my thoughts of Andy as I turned into the gravel driveway of the old Victorian. Jeremy Taft, now an adult, was sitting on the steps of the front porch, his back against the handrail. He had changed over the years, as I guess we all had. But I would have recognized him anywhere. It was the eyes that gave him away. Those dark, impassive eyes. His hair had thinned a bit, though not much, and he was wearing glasses now — thick wire rims. He looked as if he had grown into his perfect weight, just under six feet tall and maybe a hundred-and-seventy pounds. He waved, without a smile.

"Hope I'm not late," I said as I climbed out of the car. It was hot out, close to ninety-five by the feel of it, though it was blessedly dry and not too humid.

Jeremy checked his watch. "Nope. Looks like you're on the early side."

"Good. I hate waiting for people, and I hate making people wait for me."

"Me, too," he said. "Sometimes, though, we don't have much choice, do we? Whether we like it or not."

We shook hands, the grip firm, like two young kids, each trying to hold his own in a test of nerves. In a way, I guess that's exactly what we were doing. Each trying to hold his own.

"It's been a while," he said, with a smile that was empty.

"Yeah, I guess it has."

"You're looking good."

"A little weight here, a little balding there, but I feel good." I looked up at the house, wanting to escape his gaze as much as anything. "You wanna have a look at her?"

Jeremy checked his watch again. "Sure. Why not?"

Even with the succession of renters, the house had been well kept. I had only been inside once, shortly after the most recent couple had vacated. The original furnishings had stayed with the house after Jeremy and his mother had moved away. Though the realty company had had to replace the curtains upstairs, as well as the mattress in the guest room. Everything else had held up rather well, I thought.

Jeremy stood in the entryway and glanced toward the living room, an unreadable expression cut into his face. "It looks . . . smaller," he said, rather quietly.

"Does it?"

"Yes." He ran his fingers across the top of a pine chest that stood against the foyer wall, leaving a thin line in the dust that he hardly seemed to notice. "I always loved the feel of this house. It was the only place that ever really felt like home."

A Time To Every Purpose

I followed him across a patterned throw rug, past the fireplace, and around a corner that led into the kitchen. The house was furnished modestly in a style that you might call country or farmhouse. The kitchen, which opened to a family dining area, looked cluttered and chaotic at first glance. But if you looked closer, gradually you realized that everything had a place and it was all fairly-well organized. There was an open-faced china cabinet in one corner, empty now, though the family living here most recently had lined it with a set of Danish stoneware, as well as a beautiful collection of ceramic goblets.

Jeremy paused next to the tile-lined sink, and stared out the window into the back yard. "You never came by to visit when we were kids, did you?" he asked absently.

"No, I don't think I ever did."

"You remember Melissa Jenkins?"

"Sure."

"She came by once," he said. He seemed melancholy all of a sudden, and that seemed completely out of character with the Jeremy Taft I remembered from my childhood. "Is she still around?"

I tried to recall the last time I had seen her. It had been years ago now, not long after I had graduated from high school. She had been coming out of Morgan's Five & Dime with her mother, and I had nearly knocked her over in my hurry to get to my summer job at the Rexall soda fountain. I apologized. She looked away, a hint of fear crossing her face. And I remember thinking what an odd duck she had become. She had never fully recovered from that summer, I imagined, when she had disappeared for those four days.

"I think she moved upstate somewhere," I said to Jeremy. "Sometime around '85."

"Oh." He sounded disappointed.

We followed the layout of the house, through the kitchen and a small utility area where there was a washing machine and a dryer. There was a small family room on the other side, and beyond that the entryway at the bottom of the staircase where we had started the tour.

Jeremy stopped and glanced at his watch again. It was about twenty minutes after two now. He sat down on the bottom step, buried his head in his hands a moment, then sighed and looked up at me. It was the first time we had made direct eye contact, and I turned away almost immediately.

"Still scared of me?" he asked.

Maybe not scared, I thought. *Maybe just uneasy.* Fear has a way of inflating itself if you don't keep a check on it, and I suppose I had spent the last twenty-odd years trying to pretend it didn't really exist. But a trace of it was back now, like Jeremy Taft himself, and I felt like a little boy again. I hated myself for it, but I felt like a frightened little boy.

"I'm not the same person," he said. "I know what I was like back then, but things change. We all grow up, Dave. We all have regrets."

"Is that why you're back? Regrets?"

He checked his watch again. "In a way, I suppose. Partly that, and partly to fix things that should have been fixed a long time ago."

"Things like what?" For the first time, I began to feel the stuffiness inside the house. It had been closed up all summer, and the air was thick and hot. I wiped a bead of sweat from my forehead, hating the idea of being middle-aged, especially when it showed itself so easily.

"Just . . . things," he said with a thoughtful pause. Then he looked up at me, his eyes not quite as dark, but still serious, still very serious. "You ever think about that kid . . . Andy? The one at the rail yards that summer?"

"Yeah. Sometimes."

"Me, too. I don't think I've ever been as scared in my life as I was that day," he said. "I never meant to hurt him. Not really."

"Yes, you did."

Jeremy looked up at me, as surprised as I was by what I had said. "Not seriously. Not like that. I just wanted to scare him, that's all."

"Well, you did that."

"Yeah, I guess I did," he said regretfully.

"Is that why you came back? To make peace with Andy Bale?"

He shook his head. "No, not with Andy. With Melissa."

"Melissa?"

"I told you she came by once, didn't I?"

"Yeah, but . . ." But it had seemed like a casual, almost unimportant comment at the time. Now, though, I realized there had been nothing casual about it. It had been a comment designed to solicit information.

Jeremy looked away again, staring out the big picture window in the living room, staring out beyond the front yard somewhere. "Christ," he said, fighting somewhere inside himself. "I don't know where to start, Dave. I've been looking for an explanation all my life. Why it was me. Why not you or that Andy kid or the kid down the block. What was it that made me so different from everyone else? For a long time I wanted to blame it on my mother. She was all caught up in the drug scene in the sixties, and I guess I thought, well, maybe . . ."

He caught himself and fell silent, and I had the feeling he had gone round and round with it a thousand times before. Then he checked his watch again. "Getting close to two-thirty," he said.

"What's supposed to happen at two-thirty, Jeremy?"

"A trip down memory lane, I'm afraid." He stood up, brushed some dust away from his jeans, and started up the stairs. "Coming?"

I had come this far, hadn't I? It wasn't because I had wanted to, at least not initially. But now that I was here, I found myself wondering about the past again. What was it about the past that had always kept me looking back? And wasn't it getting time to start looking forward again? I had come this far. I had stared into the great black gullet of my memories of Jeremy Taft, and what I had found was a man not that much different from myself, a man uneasy with who he was, uncertain with who he is.

I followed.

"The first time it happened," he said at the top of the stairs, "it scared the holy hell out of me. I had just turned thirteen, and I was playing in the backyard with our neighbor's cat. Roughhousing, I guess you would have called it. Anyway, I got a little rough, and I was holding the cat tight with both hands around its neck when it panicked and scratched me across the face. I didn't drop it, like you might expect. Instead, I closed my eyes and I thought the cat away. I wanted it somewhere else, in some other time, and I couldn't stop my hands from squeezing down against its throat."

"You wanted to kill it?"

"I suppose, in that moment, that's exactly what I wanted."

David B. Silva

"Because it had scratched you and now you were angry?"

Jeremy stopped and looked at me, a trace of shame in his expression. "I was always angry back then. Always. It felt like I was standing on one side of the fence and everyone else was on the other side. Me against the world."

"Did you kill it?"

"I think so. I think I did to that cat what I did to Andy Bale. Because when I opened my eyes again, the cat was gone. For a couple of days, I thought my rage must have been so intense that I had somehow made the cat disappear. All I could remember was the instant anger that had exploded out of me, and the image of the cat lying in the bottom of the garbage can with its neck broken." Jeremy looked away again, the memory apparently as fresh as ever in his mind. "Then my Mom asked me to empty the trash one night . . ."

He didn't need to finish the sentence, because we both knew where it was going. He had found the neighbor's cat, dead, in the bottom of the trash can, its neck twisted and badly misshapen.

"You'd think I would have felt like the most powerful person in the world, and I guess I'd be lying if I told you any different. But that wasn't the all of it, because it had scared me something awful. Not only scared me, but made me realize that I wasn't like everyone else. I was like that guy who killed all those nurses that one night."

"Richard Speck?"

Jeremy nodded. "Like him and like Manson and the Zodiac."

There was an open landing at the top of the stairs. Across the opening, the bedroom door was slightly ajar and I could see the leaves and branches of a dogwood tree through the window at the far end of the room.

"I don't think I'll ever know for sure if I killed Andy Bale or if the train killed him," Jeremy said quietly. He followed my glance toward the master bedroom, then turned his attention down the short hallway to our right. "This way."

I followed him down the hallway to the far end, where there was a foldaway stepladder built into the ceiling. A rope dangled freely from an eye hook screwed into the base of the facing material. Above us was the attic.

A Time To Every Purpose

"Melissa Jenkins came by one afternoon when my Mom was away at work," Jeremy said. He gave the rope a pull, the ceiling opened up and the stepladder descended. He checked his watch again, then started up.

I hesitated at the bottom, looking up into the attic where it seemed the afternoon sun had rarely come to visit. I had come this far, and somehow the journey had become our journey, a little of Jeremy's, a little of mine. I still didn't fully understand what it was all about. But I thought it had something to do with putting the past to rest, and that was something we both needed to do. "What are you looking for, Jeremy?"

"The same thing we're all looking for," he said. "A little peace of mind, that's all."

The attic was three or four inches short of headroom. It had been used mostly for storage over the years, and though it was empty now, I could see faint outlines in the dust where old boxes full of clothing and used toys had once sat. Off to one side, there was a stack of two-by-fours, some R-19 fiberglass insulation, and half a panel of sheetrock.

Jeremy, resting at the top of the ladder on bent knees, took a long look around the room. "It looks smaller than I remember."

"Things from childhood usually do," I said.

"No, not like that. It looks . . ." He paused, appearing mildly confused.

"They added a wall," I said.

"What?"

"The last renters. They built an insulating wall across the north side. To save on the heating bills."

"Oh, Christ." Jeremy glanced at his watch, then took a quick look around the room, this time nearly in a panic. "We've got to break through that wall," he said.

"I don't understand."

"She's going to end up behind the wall."

"Who?"

"Melissa."

He made his way across the dust-covered floor, to the stack of two-by-fours, and found one near the top that was maybe three feet in length. "Grab yourself something you can use to knock out a hole," he said.

I didn't move for a moment. "Jesus, Jeremy, what's going on?"

And then I heard it.

We both heard it.

A scream from the other side of the north wall.

"Oh, my God."

"It's Melissa," Jeremy said. He was at the wall now, his ear pressed up against the sheetrock. The scream had suddenly cut off, and now you could hear the faint sound of someone crying on the other side. "Shhh, we'll get you out of there. Just hold on."

"Hurry," she said. "Please hurry."

Jeremy's face was still pale as he raised the stick of lumber and brought it down against the panel of sheetrock. I had never seen panic on his face before. Even at the moment that Andy Bale had darted across the tracks in front of the train. Jeremy had appeared upset then, the way a little boy who's caught doing something wrong might get upset. But this was different. This was genuine anguish, I thought.

Another scream exploded from behind the wall.

Jeremy had made a small indentation in the sheetrock, offset to one side. He raised the two-by-four again, brought it down again, and the indentation grew into a small hole.

I had watched this, captivated, unable to move, not completely understanding what was going on. And then suddenly I was next to him, in concert, beating a stick of pine against the wall like an old lineman pounding a spike into the dry, brittle earth. Whatever it was that was happening would have to be sorted out later.

The screaming had melted into sobbing now.

"I'm sorry," Jeremy said through a ragged breath. "I thought I had it worked out."

We had broken a hole into the sheetrock big enough to get our hands through now. Jeremy dropped his two-by-four and began to tug at the panel, trying to pull it away from the studs. It didn't come away as easily as I would have expected, but gradually it did come away.

And there on the other side, pinned between the insulating wall and a window frame, was Melissa Jenkins.
Thirteen-year-old Melissa Jenkins.
She was still alive. Still sobbing, but still alive.
Jeremy helped her out of the tight space. She appeared dazed, and somewhat disoriented. For a moment, all she could do was glance back and forth between us, as if she were trying to put names to our faces but couldn't quite make the right connections. Then she stared down at the front of her dress, where a strap had been badly torn.
"I'm sorry," Jeremy said again, this time to Melissa. He tied the two ends of the strap together, as gentle and as loving as I had ever seen a man. Then he closed his eyes, and in an instant, Melissa Jenkins was gone.
I suppose I already had a fairly decent idea of what had just happened. It had happened to Andy Bale some twenty-odd years ago. And it had happened to a neighbor's cat sometime before that. Still, I asked the question anyway. "What did you do?"
"I sent her back," Jeremy said.
"Four days later?"
He nodded.
I stared, somewhat numbly, at the hole in the sheetrock, wondering what we had just done. "You know she'll never be the same."
"I know." He brushed back his hair, wiped the white dust off the front of his pants, and looked at me with all the darkness gone out of his eyes. "If I could have gone back and fixed things myself, I would have. It just doesn't work that way."
"You nearly raped her, didn't you? Then you panicked, and that's why she ended up here, back in the attic of the old house, some twenty years later. This was where it happened, isn't it?"
"She was beautiful," he said quietly. "And when it got out of hand, she started screaming, and …"
Jeremy didn't need to finish. We both knew what had happened next. In that way of his, that way of moving someone from here to there, from this time to some other time, he had willed her from that day to this. And today he had returned for the purpose of willing her back.

"That was the last time, though," he added, almost as an appeal. "At least until today."

Maybe the oddest thing of all was that I believed him.

Downstairs, I locked the front door and dropped the key back into my pocket. Jeremy stood at the edge of the porch, looking out across the yard, somewhere faraway in his thoughts.

"You don't have to be scared of me anymore, you know," he said.

I knew that was only partially true. He was trying, that much was obvious. But I didn't think the struggle was ever going to end for Jeremy, and how long it might be before the rage slipped through again was anyone's guess. "I wish I could believe that," I said.

"I came back, didn't I?"

"Yes."

"I didn't have to."

"No, I don't suppose you did."

"I just wanted to make things right," he said, turning to me as if he were hoping I would give him my approval.

I shrugged. "Why? I mean . . . why now?"

"I don't know. I guess because I had to."

He gazed off into the distance again, without saying anything for a time, and when he looked back, I could see the toll that time had taken on this man. It was different from the toll that time had taken on me, though it wasn't so different that I didn't recognize it. Something happens as the years begin to slip away. I'm not sure I fully understand it, but I think it's a bit like one of the bad dreams we all have as children. As much as it scares us, we're always a bit saddened when it's over, because part of us wants to go back and see if we can make it turn out differently. I think a part of Jeremy wanted to go back, too. To see if he could make things turn out differently. Only it was too late for that now.

"There was a turning point," he said quietly. "Not long after what had happened with Melissa. I had gotten into an argument with my mother. I don't even remember what it was about now. Probably something stupid. But it was enough to stir things up inside me. I remember looking at her, and thinking how much I wanted to see her

A Time To Every Purpose

dead. I mean, kids think that kind of stuff all the time. You know that. They may not want to admit it, but it's there just the same.

"Anyway, I remember looking at her, wishing this terrible thing, and seeing a godawful look come into her eyes. It was the same thing I had seen in Melissa's eyes just before I had sent her away, and it stopped me right there, cold, realizing how close I was coming to doing it again."

Jeremy was looking through me now, the toll still showing on his face. "That was the first time, Dave, that I was able to stop it. And I haven't let it overtake me since then."

"I'm sorry," I whispered. The fear that had come with me this afternoon was gone now, replaced by something far more sympathetic. Jeremy Taft, of that long-ago, childhood summer, was a changed man. It had been a struggle for him, as I guess it was a struggle for all of us trying to make our way through adolescence and into adulthood. But his was a struggle that would always be with him. Silently, I wished him luck.

We didn't say much else after that. I stood on the porch and watched him drive away—headed where, I didn't know, because I didn't ask—and I felt a strange heaviness raise off my shoulders. I don't know if it was the fear I had been carrying all those years. Or if maybe it was the guilt about what had happened to Andy Bale that summer. But it lifted and I felt ready to get on with my life.

Much later, I tracked down Melissa in a small town set back in the mountains near the Oregon border. I kept remembering that time I had bumped into her outside the Morgan Five & Dime. She had been afraid of me that day. She had recognized me and she had been afraid. I wish I would have known it at the time.

She was living in a small group home, along with three other adults who were apparently having trouble adapting to the outside world. I gave it a good deal of thought before deciding to leave her to her own life. If she had seen me again, if I had frightened her, I'm not sure I could have lived with myself. So I left her alone, knowing that like Jeremy, she would be struggling with those long-ago demons for the rest of her life.

And maybe the hardest part for me that day was knowing that in her eyes, I would always be one of those demons.

Metatonia

The afternoon waves break cold and powerful against the fine sandy beach. In the distance, sixty-three year old Clayton Saunders can see the curve of Monterey Bay, the long piers of Fisherman's Wharf. The wind is blowing gently, whispering his wife's name in his ear. *Ella.* And the sun is hovering above the horizon like a giant eye, watching him the way Ella watches him. *Don't blink an eye, Ella! Keep a watch on me! I'm depending on you!*

Clayton kicks one foot at the sand, feels the wind blow the gritty crystals back at his face, and laughs. He feels alive again, the way it was when he was a child and the ocean sang songs to him, the way it is with Ella at his side—*Look at the seagulls, Clayton! White and gray and as free as angels up there in the heavens! Can you imagine such a thing, Clay? Gliding against the breeze, feeling the wind ruffle your feathers? Can you, Clay?*

He can.

When Ella's with him.

"You with me, Ella? You watching over me, with eyes that don't miss a trick, not the scurry of a sand crab or the sparkle of sunlight off a chip of abalone shell? You keeping a close eye on me?"

She laughs, and points to a lonely fishing boat on the horizon. "The ocean's calm today," she says. "*Cheryl's Pride* is sitting as still as an anchor out there."

"And what about the sailboats, Ella? Tell me about the sailboats."

"No sailboats today, Clay. The wind's too soft, the afternoon's too late. The adventurous have already sailed their endless seas and returned home again. No sailboats today."

He stops, and leaning forward on the strength of a cane, he fills his lungs with the fresh ocean air. There's something cleansing about the breath of ocean, something that reminds him of those long ago days—before the sardines disappeared—when he worked in the canneries. The sardines have returned now. The ocean has a way of protecting its own, he thinks. The way a husband and wife look out for one another.

He can feel the warmth of the sun against his face, the warmth of the sand beneath his feet. And when he touches his tongue to the afternoon air, he can taste the ocean salt.

Everything's so alive.

They stop suddenly, Ella guiding him to his knees. "It's a sand castle, Clay. A beautiful castle made of seaweed and driftwood, with a moat and a drawbridge and a tower on each corner."

And he knows she's thinking back to childhood sand castles of her own, castles with imaginary knights, and maidens in distress. He touches the castle, feels the warm sand tickle his palm, the cold sand chill his soul.

"It feels so real," he says.

"Doesn't it, though."

And they're walking again, feeling the cold ocean water underfoot, hearing the song of the breaking waves sing to them. These are his favorite times of life, these walks along the beach. And he wonders, only briefly, what he would do without his wife of thirty-six years at his side. Life would be empty, he thinks. And too lonely to imagine.

He tightens his grip on Ella, sending a silent message which he hopes she can read. *I love you, woman. You're my breath, my life, my only sense of yesterdays and tomorrows. And you're right here with me, where you belong. How can I ask for anything more?*

Children come racing by, laughing at the wind and the sea and the gulls. Their voices are younger than their faces, their faces are younger than their wisdom. They stop for a moment, and stare in silence until one asks, "Where you going, old man?"

"Nowhere," Clayton answers. "From here to there and back again. Nowhere."

"That's a long walk."

"Only if you're alone," Ella says.

"We're collecting," Clayton adds.

The boy kneels to closer watch the wet sand squeeze through his curled toes. He giggles at the feel of it. "Collecting what?"

"Memories ... the ones we somehow left behind."

"Oh," he says, and it sounds as if he doesn't quite understand. How does one go about collecting memories? Then a new smile comes to him, and he asks, "Did you see our castle?"

"As real as the real thing?" Clayton says. "With walls thick enough to fight back the ocean, and a mote with alligators and crocodiles to snap their jaws at enemy soldiers? Is that one yours?"

"Yes, that's it!" the boy nearly shouts. "That's *my* memory, the one I'll keep with me until I'm as old as you. You don't have to leave memories behind, do you? Because when I think back to these days on this beach, I don't ever want to forget that sand castle. Not ever!"

Ella smiles. "You won't forget," she says. "You never forget the things that are most important to you."

"Not ever," says Clayton.

And the boy is off again, running stallion-like down the beach with his friends, kicking up sand and splashes of ocean and seagulls.

"Wasn't he cute?" Ella asks.

"So young and so wise, wasn't he?"

The sun is dropping lower on the horizon, just beginning to dip below the line where ocean meets sky. And a breeze has risen from somewhere unseen, whispering louder of its presence.

They stop where the beach turns rocky. There's the sharp smell of kelp in the air, and on a faraway breeze, they can hear the voices of children giggling through a game of blind man's bluff.

"Can you hear them?" Clayton asks.

"I hear."

"Johnny or Debbie or Billy or Sue!"

"It's just a child's game, Clay."

"I know."

They kneel where a small tide pool is nestled in the rocks. The water's cold and clear. And beneath its surface are black mussel shells clinging to rocks, and hermit crabs comically staggering across the sandy bottom. It's another world, there beneath the surface.

Ella grabs up a hermit crab and places it in Clay's palm. It shyly hides for a moment, then legs appear out of nowhere and they tickle when the crab tries to walk.

"He must feel lost," Clay says. "Suddenly swept out of his world and into ours. Suddenly walking on an earth of aging flesh instead fine, moist sand. Perhaps he's frightened?"

"Perhaps," says Ella. She takes the crab from his hand and returns it to the tide pool where it clumsily tries to make an escape. "Do you remember this place?" she asks then. "The first time we came here?"

"A memory left behind?"

"Not for me," she says. "It was 1951, before Hyatt came along and plopped itself down in the middle of the beach, even before the sardines went away and Cannery Row dried up. Monterey was still small town back then. I remember. As if it were yesterday, I remember."

Clay sits back against a rock, leans his cane against a neighboring rock. "This is it? This very spot? The very first place I brought you when we came to Monterey? The place where I knelt and held your hand and asked for your love? This is it? Where we set out on life together? Right here?"

"You weren't such a shy man then."

"And you weren't such a shy woman," he insists with a smile. He takes up his cane again, holds it in his lap where it feels more comfortable. "We'll come here again, won't we? Maybe tomorrow? When the sun is higher and the day is warmer?"

"If you'd like."

"Yes," he says. He stands and stretches and looks out to where the sun is half-buried by the horizon. "It helps when we visit old places."

"I know."

A wave breaks, and the ocean slides and weaves between rock walls until the tide pool next to where they're sitting is all foamy and white and twice as deep. A splash of seawater splatters their clothing.

Clay laughs, because it makes him feel younger than his years. "You think it's a hint?" he asks.

"Nothing so subtle as a hint," Ella answers. "It's getting dark. The sun's setting, the Monterey lights are beginning to reflect off the ocean, the seagulls are folding up their wings for the night. Perhaps we should do the same?"

"It seems so soon that a good day ends

"I know."

In the dark-orange evening, the beach reflects back the sinking sunlight and brightens their journey home. *There is no finer time of day*, thinks Clayton. *These few fleeting moments—just an eye wink between evening and dark—are the times I love the most.*

"A time for putting the day all in order," says Ella. "Isn't it?"

"Just my thought."

He takes up her hand and they walk quietly along the beach, well above the tide line. There are voices and laughter coming from inside the Hyatt as they pass by unnoticed. And across the bay, they can see the outline of the wharf lights against the darkness. It seems later than it is.

Home is a salt-eaten one bedroom house, painted white where the wood doesn't show through. Once, long ago, it was well protected from the ocean by an acre of sand and ice plant. Now, the ocean waits at its back gate, sometimes only a high tide away.

There is a long series of steps leading up from the beach to the back door of the house. An overhead light shines a white circlet over the area where the back porch is waiting. Clayton carefully works his way up the stairway, one step at a time, stopping to catch a breath every so often. Ella is as patient as ever with his snail's pace.

At the top of the landing, he stops and turns back to the ocean. In the distance, where the city lights can't reach, he remembers again of that time in their youth when he had proposed. It seems so long ago, yet almost yesterday. And he wonders how that can be. "Again tomorrow?"

"Would you like that?"

"Yes," he says. "Very much."

"Then of course!"

He fumbles in his pocket until he finds the key to the door, and with a jingle-jangle of key and lock, the door swings open to home. "Hurry on," he says, as if it has been Ella lagging behind, and he closes the door behind her. "Home again, home again."

Every square inch of this house he knows by heart. Every warped board and curled rug corner, every scar in the plaster, every chip in the paint. Thirty-four years of knowing, it's been.

He stops at the chair sitting next to the door and hooks his white cane over the headrest. "A game of blind man's bluff, Ella?"

"Like the children on the beach tonight?"

"Makes me wonder why not," he says. "If them, why not us?"

"Perhaps another night," she says, and she sounds tired.

"I understand. A long walk wakens the mind, and puts the body to sleep. I'm a bit tired myself. Blind man's bluff can wait another day." He yawns, and shuffles across the living room floor to stand next to the fireplace mantle. There is a line of seashells displayed there—conch and cowries and cockleshell—and behind them a mirror that reflects his smile back at him. "Why didn't you tell me I looked so tired?" he asks.

"Because you look fine," Ella answers.

"If old and tired is fine, I look fine," he grumbles. In his hand, he holds the glass vial he's been carrying since morning. In the clear liquid alcohol of the vial, two bright blue eyes—one atop the other—float like bobbers. He uncaps the vial, dips a finger into the liquid, pulls out the top orb and gently places it into an eyecup at the corner of the mantle.

"I see you," Ella teases.

Then Clayton fingers out the remaining eye and places it alongside the first. He adds a few drops of alcohol to the cups, and smiles. "Better?"

"Thank you," Ella says

"My pleasure." He slips off his jacket and blindly hangs it on the corner of the mantle where he knows it will be waiting for him the next morning. "It was a lovely day, Ella."

"Sand castles and children, hermit crabs and memories. Why, it *was* a lovely day, wasn't it?"

Another yawn slips out of him, and he stretches his arms in the air. "Again tomorrow?" he asks. "Back to where the tide pool still fills and empties like it did all those years ago when I proposed marriage? I like it there most of all."

"Then that's where we'll go."

"Wonderful!" He turns toward the bedroom, almost naturally, because it's been years since he's lost his eyesight. "And you'll watch over me, Ella? Like you always have. Be my eyes when smell and sound and taste won't do? Show me the burning orange of the sunset and the ice-blue of the ocean, as if your eyes were mine? You'll keep a watch over me, won't you?"

"I'll never let you out of sight," she says.

Clayton smiles. "I love you, Ella."

"I know," she says.

As Clayton Saunders sleeps, he dreams of endless oceans and sandy white beaches and his wife's deep blue eyes.

And he dreams them all in living color.

The In-Between

The Inside

Sometimes when he closes his eyes, he can imagine the outside—the bright blue sky with a puff of white clouds just above the horizon, a flock of Canadian geese in silhouette heading south. The house in this imaginary picture sits in the middle of a long suburban block. Two and three bedroom homes, all perfectly manicured and freshly-painted. Sports cars parked in the driveways. He can imagine dew on the morning lawn, the smell of the damp earth, the feel of gravel under his naked feet. He imagines feeling small.

His name is Cody.

He is eleven years old.

His room sits on the second floor, above the living room. The window is shuttered from the outside, barred on the inside, and though it happens so rarely that he usually thinks of it as something of a miracle, a sliver of sunlight sometimes finds its way through and slices across the darkness like an angel in the night. He can see his hands on those rare occasions. A little boy's hands, with long, thin fingers and nails chewed down to the quick.

When the Mother comes home, he can always tell it is her and not the Father. She parks inside the garage and when she comes through the downstairs' door, she locks it behind her. Her footsteps are whispers, even across the tile in the kitchen, even when she wears high-heels. She drops her keys and her purse on the counter, next to the cookie jar, then she heads to the refrigerator and pulls something out to hold her over until the Father arrives home. They always eat dinner together, in the dining room, with the hollow sound of their knives and forks against the good china echoing through the tomblike house like the rattling of bones.

Cody knows all this because he listens.

The Father rarely arrives home before the Mother. He drives a little sports car, something with an engine that purrs like a cat. The car has never been inside the garage. He parks it in the driveway, under the hot summer sun, in the brutal winter cold. It doesn't matter. All that matters to the Father is that the neighbors never forget what he is driving.

He loves his car.

Maybe as much as he loves the Mother.

Certainly more than either of them love Cody.

When the rain is coming down in torrents, the Father closes the driver's side door with the kind of loving gentleness most people reserve for the door to the baby's room. Then, with the comfort of routine, he snatches up the newspaper off the walkway and falls through the front door with an audible sigh, as if he were on the last leg of a long journey and the end is finally in sight.

His briefcase goes on the floor to the right of the entry.

His jacket goes on the coat rack.

The living room television goes on, and he sits alone, reading the newspaper, the sound of the pages crumpling and expanding, fighting and surrendering as he ventures through the sports section to the entertainment section, and finally the headlines, a lonely warrior trying to "unwind after his long day at the salt mines," as he often jokingly refers to it.

The In-Between

Afterwards, he meets the Mother in the kitchen, and they prepare dinner together, talking back and forth in muted whispers, like children sharing secrets. The Mother shows off some new piece of jewelry she has bought, the Father asks if they can get away this weekend, maybe go over to the coast and spend some time at that hotel on the beach.

"What about the boy?" the Mother asks.

"He'll be fine," says the Father. "He always is."

And that is the end of that.

Sometimes the talk is about their investment portfolio or moving to a better neighborhood. Sometimes it's about a promotion at work or where they are going to go on vacation this year. Sometimes it's about his golf game or her next craft fair, where the Mother likes to look for porcelain dolls to add to her collection. ("They're like little people," she is fond of saying. "Precious little people.")

Cody knows all this, because he listens. When he presses his ear against the vent in the floor, their voices rise up through the ducting as clear and as sharp as if they are standing in the room with him.

Those are the times, when the voices seem nearby, when he almost feels like a member of the family.

Cody walks the edges of the room and stops at the window. He slips his hands through the space between the bars and flattens his palms against the glass. It feels warm. The sun is out today. First day in nearly a week.

There was a time when he could stand next to the window like this and hear the sounds of children's voices on the other side, rising and falling as they played freeze tag or kickball in the street below. Cody puts his ear against the wall, listens, and hears nothing. It's been a long time since the children last played. He misses their laughter.

In their place this day, he hears the Mother drive up outside. Beneath him, the floor vibrates as the garage door opens and she parks the car inside.

The garage door closes.

The engine shuts off.

The car door slams.

Cody moves around the edge of the room to the adjacent wall and listens against the panel of unpainted sheetrock. The Mother drops her

79

keys and purse on the counter and goes to the refrigerator. She does not remove any food. Instead, she places something on the glass shelf near the top. Tonight, like many nights, she has brought something home for dinner.

He falls to his knees and listens through the floor vent as she puts on a pot of coffee and sits down at the kitchen table with a sigh. She's tired, he imagines as he hears the snap of a rubber band and imagines further that she is going through the mail.

The coffee begins to percolate.

The Mother climbs out of her seat, crosses the kitchen, and takes a cup from the cupboard. She stands over the stove, drumming her fingernails against the ceramic top in a patter that sounds something like a soft rain against the roof.

The coffee finishes percolating.

The Mother fills her cup, then moves out of the kitchen, across the living room, and starts up the stairway. Her footsteps turn to soft whispers on the carpet, and he hears her hum a tune that he has never heard before.

Cody raises himself off the floor and hurries across the room to the door. He listens as the soft whispers and humming pass by, his splayed fingers pressed against the cool surface of the wood.

"Hi, Cody," she says wearily.

Weakly, almost to himself, he says, "Hi."

But there is no response.

The Mother opens her bedroom door, enters, and closes the door behind her. A moment later, Cody hears the bath water go on, like it does nearly every evening after the Mother has disappeared into her own private world. Like an hour glass, the water begins to fill the tub.

Cody heads into his own bathroom, what was once a closet, lifts the lid of the toilet, pees, then wanders back into the room in time to hear the Father drive up outside. He listens at the window as the car pulls into the driveway and purrs a moment before the engine shuts off. The Father climbs out, dragging his briefcase with him, then closes the door and starts up the walkway to the front door.

He drops his briefcase on the floor to the right of the entry.

He hangs his jacket on the coat rack.

The In-Between

Cody moves to his left, following the sounds around the edges of the room until he can hear the Father turn on the television set in the living room. He hears the squeal of the chair as the Father sits down, the crinkling of the paper as he unfolds the pages, searching for the sports section.

There is the running water coming from the master bathroom, the crinkling of paper from downstairs, and he knows it will be this way for a time now. He stretches across the bed, his hands clasped behind his head, and his eyes close. The moment takes him drifting past the walls, beyond the darkness, where he doesn't feel so alone, where his dreams have a way of painting pretty pictures.

The water stops running in the master bath.

The Father folds up the newspaper and puts it away. He climbs out of his chair with another squeal from the leather, and moves into the kitchen. He takes a coffee cup down from the second shelf of the cabinets, fills it, adds milk from the refrigerator, then sits at the counter and sips his drink.

Across the hall, the master bedroom door opens. The Mother moves down the hall, then down the stairway, wearing shoes now that don't make a whisper against the carpet.

Cody's eyes open. He falls off the bed, crawls across the floor, and plants his ear to the heating vent.

"How was your day?" the Father asks.

"Brackton dumped the quarterly report on me. He had to go home early because his oldest girl—I think her name is Nancy—got arrested for shoplifting from the Penneys at the mall."

"You're kidding. How old is she now?"

"Fifteen."

"Isn't she the one who ran away from home last summer?"

"No, that was the boy—Leaf."

"Glad they aren't my kids,"

"Me, too, "the Mother says.

"Hungry?"

"You forgot, didn't you?"

"What?"

"The party at the Hendersons."

"That's tonight?"

"In less than half-an-hour. Pot luck. I bought some chicken and potato salad."

"What about the boy?"

"He'll be all right by himself. He always is."

"How long has it been since we last saw the Hendersons?" the Father asks, putting an effective end to the previous line of conversation.

"Months," says the Mother. "There's never enough time anymore. I still need to work on the flyers for next week's used book sale at the library."

The Father says something else, something Cody can't hear, and then the sound of him climbing the stairs vibrates through the floor. Cody leans back against the wall. He hears the master bedroom door open and the Father rummage through the closet, changing out of his business suit and his dress shoes, taking several minutes to run the electric shaver over his five o'clock shadow, then emerging from the room again and tromping back down the stairs.

The front door opens.

Cody raises his head and listens.

The voices are muffled, the conversation indecipherable. They spend a moment at the door, debating something, then the door closes and Cody can feel the draft of cool night air slip under his bedroom door like a whisper calling him from outside.

He leans back against the wall and looks across the room at the silhouette of the boy on the bed. Evening shadows, like shrouded ghosts have taken their places around the silhouette, but already he knows the boy's features by heart. The arms that are crossed over the boy's chest. The sallow, emaciated body. The sunken eyes and the smell of death.

He knows all of these things. He has made their acquaintance before and they are not strangers.

Not strangers at all.

The In-Between

It was only a matter of time.

Cody sits against the wall, watching, and he can see the boy's

The In-Between

chest expand with a new breath that fights its way into the tiny lungs, then quickly collapses again. The breaths are fewer now, coming farther apart.

It was only a matter of time.

Cody climbs to his feet, and the shadows resemble shrouded ghosts oh so much sharper as he crosses the room. He stops at the bed, both fascinated and saddened by the placid face looking up at him. It is his own face, of course. They are near peace now, both him and this other incarnation.

It was only a matter of time.

The soul needs its nourishment.

The boy struggles to draw another breath, this one so shallow it's barely discernible. A burning sensation settles into Cody's chest with the weight of a bad flu or an early case of pneumonia. He coughs, then realizes the boy is no longer struggling for one more breath. The struggle is over now.

It was only a matter of time.

No longer can these walls keep him prisoner.

No longer can this darkness keep him blind.

Cody leans over the dead body and kisses the boy on the lips.

"Good-bye," he whispers. Even after years of torment, years of being the invisible, unwanted boy, there is a sense of sickening loss at having to leave behind the only life he has ever known.

But the time has come now.

The house is quiet, and the quiet, with all its mystery, is calling him.

He goes to the door and passes through its hollow core as effortlessly as if it were a gaping threshold drawing him into another universe. It has been a long, long time since he has been on the other side. He looks across the hallway at the slightly-open door to the master bedroom, and turns to the stairs on his right.

The stairwell is lined with photographs: the Father as a boy in his Little League uniform, the Mother receiving an award of appreciation for her work with the library, a photo of them on their wedding day, another of them on vacation at a ski resort in the Sierras. There's a handwritten note beneath this last photo that says: our first vacation

away, alone, since Cody's birth. They are smiling joyously, snuggled arm-in-arm, a beautiful snowcapped peak their only backdrop.
There are other photographs as well.
Though none of them include Cody.
Downstairs, in the living room, he drags his fingers over the keys of the piano, listens to the sounds and smiles appreciatively. He wonders why he can't remember anyone ever playing the piano, and wonders if in some strange way the piano is to the Mother the way the car is to the Father.
The case, behind the music stand, is lined with the Mother's porcelain dolls. Each doll, each "little person" as the Mother likes to call them, is perfect. Not a wrinkle in the clothing. Not a smudge of dirt or a speck of dust. Not a frown or even a hint of anything suggesting displeasure. Just perfect little people who are there when she needs to show them and out of the way when the showing is done.
Cody takes a doll in his hands. It is a boy, with a broad white collar over a black jacket, with black shoes and huge brass buckles, with a round black-rimmed hat that sits flat atop its head. It smells of attics and steamer trunks, and the porcelain is cool and smooth to the touch.
He puts it back where it belongs, where it will be safe.
Across the room, the trophy case, made of rich, dark mahogany that shows the powerful grain of the wood, stands in the corner, floor to ceiling. For the most part, it holds the Father's golfing trophies, though there are a few from the Father's high school days in track and field, and a solitary trophy at the back for something called The Houghton Award For Excellence In Team Management.
Cody stares at the trophies for a long time, fascinated by the wood and brass, by the depiction of men in motion. It has grown dark outside, and the shadows have made their way across the white living room carpeting from one wall to the other now. He looks up and sees a streetlight go on through the curtains at the front of the house, then wanders into the kitchen.
Beneath a mailbox magnet, a calendar is pinned to the refrigerator door. The month is October. The last day is circled, with a note about dinner at the Henderson's handwritten into the tiny box in red ink. There is another note above this, printed in black. It says: Halloween.

The In-Between

He sounds the word out slowly, one syllable at a time. *Hal—low—een*. And when his cheeks fill with air, he grins happily. It's a good word. *Halloween*. It's a word that nudges at him like a playful friend, familiar somehow. He touches the calendar, unable to put a meaning to the word, then drifts out of the kitchen the same way he came in.

Next to the huge windows in the living room, he stops on the Spanish tiles that serve as the foyer. There is an uneasiness rolling in his stomach. Before him stands the ornately-carved double doors the Mother was so excited about when they were installed last winter. The carvings are of serpents and naked women, of plants and vines and leaves.

Cody passes his hand through the door near the spot where one of the women is reaching out toward a snake, and he can instantly feel the cool night air on the other side. It is the first time in longer than he can remember that he has felt so alive.

He steps through the door.

The Outside

The porch light is on, and its bright cast falls like a halo over a huge bowl of candy sitting on the concrete landing. There are Snickers and M&Ms and Butterfingers filled to the brim of the bowl, all undisturbed.

He steps out into the front yard, stands on the cool, damp lawn, and looks down the long line of streetlights that mark this little piece of the suburbs. There are no cars in the driveways. The parents are all gone. There are no voices in the evening air. The children are all hidden.

There are no masquerades

—he remembers now, the meaning of Halloween: ghosts and goblins, masks and capes, children and candy, trick or treat—

there are no masquerades roaming in small groups, laughter as their companion, faces painted, pillow cases bulging with the evening's take of candy.

There is none of that.

But they are beginning to emerge from the houses now, one after another, all up and down the street, children like Cody himself, ghosts, too long invisible, too long ignored because there aren't enough hours in a day. They pour from the houses, a hundred other young souls, left unnurtured when what they needed most was nurturing, and the street is as cold and as empty and as lifeless as any street without laughter and children, and the bowls of candy are left untouched, and the Mothers and the Fathers will hardly notice when they arrive back home, and they will hardly notice tomorrow when they get up and there's no laughter in the streets, no children playing in the front yards. But eventually ... *eventually* ... they will come to notice.

And it will be too late by then.

And they will mourn not for themselves but for the children they never knew, for all their wasted hours with porcelain dolls and business over golf games, for all those things they once had thought important but now realize were not important at all.

And it will be too late by then.

Empty Vessels

First off, I guess I should let you know right up front that my mother was not a woman you'd consider for sainthood. When I was a boy, she referred to herself as a lady of the evening. It wasn't until the fifth grade, when Paul Whittaker called her a whore that I first began to understand the true meaning of her self-reference. I had always assumed that the night was her playground, that she liked the full moon and the darkness and the dim streetlights, that she was like a cat, nocturnal in her nature, sleeping during the day, out prowling at night. And all that was true, I suppose. Just not in the way that I understood it.

But Paul Whittaker straightened me out.

Whore.

My mother the whore.

I never could bring myself to use that word—*whore*. It was not the way I would have described her. Though looking back now, I doubt I would have described her as a lady of the evening, either. She was neither of those, and she was both of them.

David B. Silva

Beyond the semantics, though, was this: there wasn't an eleven year old alive that wanted to hear his mother was a whore. Or that his father was a stranger, a man who had driven out of the night in an old pickup, done his business, then disappeared again, never to return. Or to know that as much as his mother loved him, he had been a surprise to her. Given the choice, she would have preferred not to have been a mother at all.

My mother did love me, though, as much as she could, and I confess I would have liked to have had more time with her.

I was eleven—going on thirty-three, as she liked to say—the night my mother's soul was taken. It was a school night. I had gone to bed around nine, after finishing my homework and watching an hour or so of television. Mom had been "out"—something else she liked to say. Exactly when she had returned, I'm not sure, but it was a little after eleven when something stirred me out of my sleep. I sat up, listening intently, feeling the cool night air against my skin. Outside, there was the soft whistle of wind through the branches of the walnut tree in the back yard. Inside, it was as if the house were holding its breath; everything had fallen under the spell of a hush.

"Mom?"

It had been raining on and off for several days. Through the curtains, I saw the sky above the tenement across the way light up with a flash of lightning. The darkness in my bedroom scurried back under the bed and into the corners, and I found myself counting out the seconds—almost five—before the thunder hit. It hit with the crack of a whip, followed closely by a long, low grumbling noise that sounded a little like Grandpa Edmonds when he was fussing about a sales clerk or a waitress.

And then I heard a cry.

It was like nothing I had ever heard before. Not a shriek or a scream, but a whimper that sounded oddly submissive. And it had come from my mother's room.

I had heard noises from that end of the house before, strange sounds that I had mostly chosen to ignore. I guess I'd always had a general idea of what was going on when she brought men home, though maybe not the specifics. Maybe not the reasons why. But I knew it was something to be kept behind closed doors, away from a young boy's curiosity. My mother might have brought home lots of guys, but she had never been ugly about it. She had always been discreet. She had always tried to shield me.

But this was different.

"Mom?"

It came again—softer this time—as I made my way down the hall. Outside her door, I pressed my ear against the cool surface and held my breath. It was quiet on the other side, so quiet I could hear my heart pounding in my chest. It was something I had never done before, but finally I reached out and tried the knob. My hands were shaking. The latch slipped. The door swung silently open an inch, maybe two, and suddenly there was just enough of an opening that I could see into the darkness.

There was a soft glow pouring in through the window from a street light. I could see the block-like silhouette of my mother's bed, the sheets rumpled, the pillows out of place. For a moment, I thought she hadn't come home yet. Everything was dark and perfectly still. Then a flash of lightning exploded outside. The room brightened, and I saw the light gray form of a man rise up off the bed. He arched his back, threw back his head, and drew in a huge uninterrupted breath.

I shrank back.

"Jesus, Blaine."

That was my mother, talking to the stranger. There was a mix of anger and unease in her voice, something I had heard only once before, after she had come home all swollen and bleeding from a beating some john had given her. She had kept the curtains drawn, the house dark, for nearly a week after that. And for a while longer, she had even insisted that she'd finally had enough, that she was ready to make some major changes in her life. She had said that before and like all the other times, there had been no change, things had continued merrily on their way. And now, as I listened, it sounded faintly as if they had brought her back full circle.

The stranger whispered something in response, something I couldn't quite hear, then he lowered himself back into the shadows of the bed. My mother moaned, not unpleasantly. I sat back, toying with the idea of going back to bed. It wasn't the first time she had brought someone home, and I was sure it wouldn't be the last. Maybe I had been wrong. Maybe what I had heard in her voice hadn't been unease at all. Though something did seem different.

If I had *gone* back to bed, I suppose it wouldn't have made any difference. Nothing would have changed. Except that I wouldn't have been a witness then, and maybe it would have been easier to put it all away without the nightmares.

But I didn't go back to bed.

I stayed and watched and eventually saw the outline of my mother in the Picasso of shadows and light. She was lying on her back, a soft glow of outside light falling across her breasts. I had seen her naked once before, when I was five or six and had walked in while she was bathing. To be honest, I didn't remember the occasion. But my mother liked to tease me about it when she got together with her sisters. "He started to unbutton his shirt," she would say. "And I asked him what he was doing, and he said, 'You look lonely, mommy.' He was all set to climb right in with me." She had always thought that was hilarious, though I had never been able to find the humor in it myself.

Now, she was lying perfectly still, her eyes closed, her mouth slightly open.

The stranger, who was lying on top of her, gazed darkly into her eyes as if he were trying to catch a glimpse of her soul. "What makes you happy?" he asked suddenly. His voice was low and smooth, and I thought how easy it would be to believe in the words spoken by a voice like his.

"You do," my mother said disingenuously. "You make me happy."

"No. The truth."

"Honest," she whispered, running her hand across his chest.

"No, you don't understand, Eve. I'm not looking for a compliment. I'm looking for the truth. I want you to tell me what makes you happy. Truly happy."

My mother's hand fell away from his chest, and though I couldn't read her expression I imagined by the tone of her voice that she had been surprised by his question. "Me?"

"Yes, you."

Empty Vessels

She turned her head away from me, staring thoughtfully out the window. "My boy, Marshall. He makes me happy."

The stranger nodded with apparent satisfaction. Then he took in another deep, uninterrupted breath, as if he thought he could inhale her happiness. "Ah . . . yes," he said, lowering himself again. I could see the glisten of sweat on his bare back, and I heard my mother let out a soft, muffled cry.

There's no pleasure in that *sound*, I remember thinking. I glanced back down the hall at my open bedroom door. I had left the light on. My pillow was rumpled. The sheets on the bed were pulled back. That room seemed a thousand miles away now. I had left it in innocence, but I would go back . . .

There was another cry from my mother.

They had begun to work themselves into an uneasy rhythm now, two strangers trying to get to know one another. Their movements became oddly choreographed, as if they were both mechanically rehearsing a dance they had learned a long time ago and were waiting for it to overtake them.

Another flash of lightning swept into the room. I saw the man run the tip of his tongue across her belly. He licked his lips, savoring the taste, then continued up her body, between her breasts and along her neckline.

"Easy," he said.

A thrust, deeper.

She moaned.

The stranger's face twisted into an ugly grin, and then I witnessed something, something that I still don't fully understand. He opened his mouth as if he were going to yawn, his jaw nearly coming unhinged, and he began to draw the breath from my mother's mouth. It came from her in the form of a long, greenish-gold stream of light that lifted her several inches off the bed. What it was . . . to be honest, I didn't know what it was. Her spirit. Her love. Whatever it is that makes a person real and alive. He took it all in, like a man taking a hit from some fine Jamaican weed, and when he was done, my mother fell emptily back into the mattress.

The stranger shuddered, and caught his breath.

I think I might have shuddered, too. I wasn't sure exactly what it was that I had witnessed. Something horrible, it seemed. Though at eleven, the world was still full of mysteries, and for all I knew, this was just one more of those things that would someday make perfect sense to me. I wanted to believe that, but I think I shuddered anyway.

I don't know what happened in that room after that. I had seen enough. I had seen more than enough. So I left the door slightly ajar and scrambled back to my bedroom, where I turned off the light and buried myself under the covers. When you're eleven, you're supposed to be too old to believe in hiding under the covers. But that didn't matter, and in the end who really knows anyway? Maybe those covers were the only things that kept me alive.

I stayed under them until my muscles ached from not moving. By then, a couple of hours had passed, maybe more. The house had long since fallen quiet. It was still dark out. The rain had stopped. The night temperatures had left the room unseasonably cold. I didn't want to get up, but eventually I was able to scoot out from beneath the covers and cross the floor. I peered down the hallway. At the far end, there was a faint pattern of light forming a misshapen rectangle across the floor.

It was a while longer before I ventured down the hall again. I stopped and listened at my mother's door, heard nothing, then pushed it open until I was certain the stranger was no longer in the room. Unless, of course, he was hiding in the shadows, a possibility I thought unlikely. He was not a man who hid from anything, I imagined. Still, I fumbled quickly for the light switch.

I'm not sure exactly what I expected to find. That the stranger was gone, certainly. That my mother was sleeping peacefully and everything was all right, that was my hope. That she was dead . . . well, as much as I hate to admit it, that was the single worst thought I had allowed myself to consider.

And the stranger *was* gone.

And my mother was not dead. But she looked as if she had come back from the dead. She looked like one of those wax figures you see in museums, pasty and glassy-eyed and not quite right. Her checks, which had lost their fullness, resembled loose skin stretched across a

Empty Vessels

crudely-made drum. There was drool running down her chin, and her adam's apple bobbed horridly as she tried to swallow.

The stranger had left the sheets pulled back. I could see her breathing was shallow, and embarrassed more than I should have been, I used a blanket to cover her breasts.

No, she wasn't dead.

But she wasn't alive, either.

It's been nearly thirty-five years since that night. My mother lives in a convalescent home on the south side. Physically, she functions just fine, though she doesn't get around as easily as she once did and her doctor told me last week that she's developing a cataract in one eye. Nothing out of the ordinary for a woman in her mid-sixties.

But it had never been her physical state that had troubled me.

After her encounter with Mr. Jeffries—that was his name , as I was eventually able to discover: Blaine Jeffries. Sounds a bit aristocratic, doesn't it? A man of royalty, maybe?—anyway, after her encounter, my mother had never been the same. He had left her alive and breathing and with a hole in her heart the size of the Grand Canyon. He had left her an autistic child, emotionally vacant, a woman who could only look past you, never directly at you.

The morning after was a strange timeless dream. I don't know exactly when I became aware of the fact that I was alone with my mother and that things had changed, that in the darkness of the night my world had been turned upside down like an hour glass and presently I was the parent and my mother was the child. Eventually, when I finally did make that realization, I called my aunt.

She called an ambulance.

The doctors at County General kept my mother for a couple of weeks. Her room was on the third floor at the end of the hall, with a window that overlooked the parking lot. I spent a good many hours standing at that window, peering down at the people climbing out of their cars. Even then, I had started looking for him, I guess.

There were a battery of tests, I remember. Mostly neurological and psychological according to my aunt, who tried to explain things to me as they were happening. Neither one of us really understood, though. I'm not sure the doctors understood, either.

"Apoplexy," the doctor said, at the end of a long day of testing. "That's the best we can come up with."

My aunt stared at him, obviously not catching what he was saying.

"A stroke," he tried to clarify. "Apparently a blood vessel in the brain broke. When that happens, there's a sudden paralysis, a loss of consciousness and sometimes a loss of feeling."

"A loss of feeling," my aunt repeated numbly.

"Yes."

I think it was then that she began to understand more than the doctors. It wasn't a loss of feeling my mother had experienced, like when you wake up in the middle of the night and your toes are all tingly and you realize your foot's asleep. It was more like waking up in the middle of the night and realizing that the world was an empty place and you didn't give a damn one way or the other, because you couldn't feel anything.

No love. No hate.

No joy. No sorrow.

Nothing.

That was my mother.

My aunt made the arrangements for the convalescent home. It was a nice place, run by an Italian couple who tried to keep things comfortable and homey. When I went to visit, usually on Sundays, there was always the fragrance of oregano and parmesan in the air. Nothing like the hospital mouth-washy odor I had come to hate so much after her stay at County General. I was grateful for that. I think my mother would have been grateful, too, if she were capable of being grateful.

Things never did return to what you might call normal.

I lived with my aunt, and I guess you could say gradually we worked ourselves into a comfortable routine together. It was a better life for a young boy. Someone always around. No late-night visitors with a few extra bucks and a long list of fantasies.

After I graduated from high school, I moved out and found myself a studio apartment in a neighboring town. I worked at a print shop during the day and attended community college at night, taking one class at a time until I was eventually able to earn an architectural engineering degree through the state university. At the Eleventh Annual Greenhaven Arts & Crafts Faire, I met Elizabeth Banner, a beautiful, joyful young woman who I eventually fell in love with and married. We had two children: Ben, who is now thirteen, bright, and plays a wicked game of tennis; and Julie, who is eleven and loves horses and just about any movie starring Corey Haim.

It's a long, long way from the world where I grew up.

But there isn't a day that goes by when my thoughts aren't drawn back to that dreadful night when Mr. Blaine Jeffries stole my mother's soul.

When I hit my mid-forties, I went through what a pop-psychologist might call a hidden trauma crisis. Over a period of several weeks, I was haunted by a recurring nightmare that took me back to that night outside my mother's bedroom. I was kneeling, trying to catch a glimpse through the crack in the door, when the door suddenly swung wide open. Jeffries, who was startled nearly as much as myself, turned in my direction, his lips curled back, fangs exposed. He growled at me.

"Too late," he said, the words coming from deep in his throat.

I fell back against the wall, the impact sending a sharp pain through my shoulder blades, a pain I hardly noticed at the time.

"There's nothing left for little boys."

He laughed, his voice gruff and irritating, and gradually I became aware of another voice, a soft soprano, joining in. It was my mother.

She sat up, using her stick-like arms as leverage against the bed. Her cheeks were sunken, her eyes distended, and she looked not just malnourished but like a flower, dry and near death. It was almost as if I could see her wilting right before my eyes.

"Nothing left," she said weakly. "Not even for you, Marshall."

And then I would wake up. I'd be drenched from a night sweat, and the dream would still be lingering in the fore of my mind. Sometimes I'd be able to close my eyes and fall back to sleep again, but most of the time I'd end up downstairs at the kitchen table, sipping coffee and trying to forget.

I knew what she meant when she said there was nothing left. She meant she had no love left.

And that, I suppose, had been true enough.

After the nightmares, I hired a private detective. I told him my mother had been raped when I was a young boy, which was certainly closer to the truth than not. I told him that I had witnessed what had happened, which was also as close to the truth as you can come and still not be there. And I told him the time had now come when I felt I had to face the man who had done it.

He was a good detective, maybe because he believed in the case. It took him a little over three months, working part time, with nothing more to go on than a vague description and the stranger's last name, which were all I had to offer. Then one night after Beth and the kids had gone to bed, I got a call to meet him at the local Denny's. He handed me a piece of paper across the table. Printed on one side in blue ink was: BLAINE JEFFRIES. 16289 TICONDEROGA. SARATOGA, CA.

"What are you going to do?" he asked with concern.

"I don't know," I said, just as honestly. I stared at the paper with the name on it, then folded it in fourths and stuck it in my shirt pocket. "Visit him, I suppose."

And eventually that's what I ended up doing.

"Mr. Jeffries? Blaine Jeffries?"

He stood in the doorway, beneath an entry light, and I realized this was the first time I had seen this man out of the shadows. His eyes were dark and weary, the eyes of an old dog that knows its better times are far behind it now. That realization seemed to have settled deeply into many of Mr. Jeffries's features. By his coloring, I gathered he had not been out under the sun in a good long time. His face was lined. His sagging jowls reminded me more of fresh bread dough than the fleshly face of an old man. And beneath it all, there was a sense that here was a man who was near the end of his life.

"I know you," he said, after a good look. "A long time ago, wasn't it? A little boy in a little no-name town on the outskirts of Sacramento."

Empty Vessels

"Greenhaven," I said. "The name of the town was Greenhaven."

He nodded. "I remember." It seemed almost as if he had surprised himself, remembering such a little thing from so long ago. "You hid in the shadows, outside the bedroom door. I . . . don't recall your name, but you were a young man then, a boy, with eyes much wiser than your years. And I see they still are."

"My name's Marshall," I said.

"Yes. And your mother was Eve. Yes, I remember."

I could barely find the restraint to stand there without lashing out at him. Hearing my mother's name spoken through this man's lips . . . it . . . it stirred a rage inside me that I could only assume had been there, waiting, for more than thirty-five years now. It may have settled there, this rage, like sediment to the bottom of a river, but suddenly it was kicking up again, and I was forced to swallow it down, because if I didn't, I was afraid I might very well lose all control.

"She was an exceptional woman," Jeffries said with admiration. He stepped away from the door like a butler inviting in a guest, proper and courteous. "Why don't you come in, Marshall. I'll try to explain the unexplainable; you try to listen and understand."

I hesitated, wondering why I had come here, and what I had expected to find beyond an old man still clinging fondly to his memories. There was a part of me, aside from the rage, that felt surprisingly sympathetic to the man.

"When you stop asking questions," he said. "The answers come naturally."

He raised his eyebrows questioningly. I didn't know if what he said were true or not. I had always asked questions. It was how I got along in the world. Sometimes the questions led to answers. Sometimes not. Maybe I had been asking the same questions for too long now.

I entered.

I think my mother would have described the house as uptown, or out of our league. It had an old European-family flavor. The floor was done in brown British quarry tile, the walls in some sort of imported stone. There was a dank, musty smell inside and I thought how much the house and its master resembled each other.

Jeffries, his feet doing an old man's shuffle across the tile floor, led me through a huge ante-room into an even larger room with a rustic stone fireplace that stood nearly as tall as myself. Near the center of the room was a banquet table hand-crafted from dark wood, perhaps mahogany. He motioned for me to sit, then sat across the table from me. I could feel the heat of the fire against the side of my face.

"You came to me," he said flatly. He steepled his fingers, patiently, apparently aware that he had all the time in the world and that I did not. And it was true: I had come to him, not he to me.

"I want you to explain the unexplainable," I said.

"Ah, my own words used against me." He smiled, with a touch of sadness, and it occurred to me that this was a lonely man sitting across the table. I wondered when he had last held a woman in his arms, when he had last conversed with a neighbor or a friend. It had been a long time, I imagined.

"Where to start?" he said. "Where to start?"

"How about with my mother?"

That smile again. Then he rested his chin atop the bridge of his hands and stared at me as if he could read my entire history with a single glance. His hands were pale and brown-spotted, the fingers thin and delicate. His fingernails were unmanicured and long, and as strange as it was I thought of Howard Hughes and reports of how long his nails had grown near the end of his life.

"She was chosen, you know," Jeffries said calmly. "Your mother was an exceptional woman. Most young ladies in her line of work, they've long since stopped feeling anything. They're dead inside. Maybe it's defensive, I don't know. Or maybe it's a form of self-punishment. Though I rather suspect it's probably a little of both, don't you?"

"I wouldn't know," I said evenly.

Jeffries grinned, a little self-satisfactorily, and I thought it was his hideous side creeping through. His teeth were the color of a dark urine stain against white jockey shorts. I could see something black and fungus-like had begun to form pockets along the line of his gums, and it occurred to me that this man's teeth weren't going to last much longer.

Empty Vessels

"No?" he said. "I would have thought that you were intimately qualified to know such things."

"Then you would have thought wrong," I responded.

"Really?"

"Really."

"I see." He frowned and gazed hypnotically at the fire, and seemed to drift away in his thoughts. Apparently he was fond of where they had taken him, because he seemed suddenly peaceful and at ease with himself.

"I was born in 1887," he said at last. "In a small New England town called Willows Branch. My father was an industrialist, my mother a seamstress. I had two brothers and four sisters, and I was the youngest.

"In those days—much unlike these modern times of ours, I might add—children were expected to contribute to the finances of the family. We worked from a very young age. We did anything and everything just to bring home a few extra pennies."

He sighed, somewhat longingly, his gaze still fixed on the fire.

"And?" I prompted.

"I'm sorry. An old man's thoughts can wonder at times. I'm learning that." He smiled dully, unaffectingly, then sighed again, and if I had taken a deep breath myself I have no doubt I would have inhaled a good deal of this man's loneliness. He was a creature who I suspected had always lived in solitude. And how sad that was.

"I worked for a carriage house," he continued. "As a stable boy. One day, when I was . . . oh, eleven or twelve, a woman came to town. She was a foreigner, with an accent that sounded like a mix of British upper class and Austrian, very different from anything I had ever heard before. I was a good stable boy, and she took a liking to me. And when she was ready to depart after her two week stay, she pulled me aside and asked me what I thought of the idea of immortality."

Jeffries paused and shook his head. "I had never heard the word before. So she had to explain it to me, and it was the kind of dream that sparks a young boy's imagination. The chance to live forever. Incredible. It was absolutely incredible.

"She offered it to me as a gift, though it wasn't a gift at all. Not with the price I had to pay. You see, in exchange for this thing called immortality, she wanted my innocence."

"Is that what you took from my mother?" I asked.

"Your mother had no innocence left," Jeffries said matter-of-factly.

"You killed her, you know."

"I did *not* kill her. I emptied her."

Emptied her. Now there was a polite way of putting it. Though it was true, she wasn't dead. She was sitting in a convalescent home, breathing and eating and getting around with a little help when she needed it, but she wasn't dead. *Emptied her.* I hated the way that sounded.

"Let me show you," Jeffries said, with tired resignation. He climbed, with some effort, out of his seat, and when I didn't follow immediately, he looked down at me. "You coming or not?"

He took me down a flight of stairs to the cellar.

At the bottom, there was a short tunnel leading off to the left. One side was a rubble and brickwork wall, damp and cool to the touch. The other side was a floor-to-ceiling wine rack. There must have been a thousand bottles doing their time here. Blaine lightly tapped one and said, "1910 Chateau d' Yquem." He beamed, like a little boy showing off his prized marble.

The end of the tunnel was blocked by a wood panel that drew back and opened into a small, dimly-lighted room lined with shelves on both sides. It smelled musty here. I took a breath and felt as if I might cough myself silly. Somewhere in the distance I could hear the *plop-plop-plop* of dripping water.

Jeffries stepped into the shadows at the far end.

I stopped at the doorway.

"This is where I keep them," he said cryptically. Except I understood what he meant, the way a husband understands a half-finished thought from his wife. He meant that this was where he kept his collection of whatever it was that he had stolen from my mother and undoubtedly from others as well.

He flipped a light switch.

The room brightened.

Empty Vessels

And I knew immediately this was why I had come here. The shelves on both sides were lined with specimen jars: thick glass, maybe four liters in capacity. Each fell under the soft glow of an individual spotlight. Each was labeled with a brass plate, engraved in black.

I read the one nearest me on the right. It said, simply enough: JOY. Inside was a brightness nearly indescribable. I would suppose—not having experienced such a thing myself—it was something like the light at the end of the tunnel that people who have had a near-death experience often talk about. It was peaceful and serene and most of all it was what it was labeled to be: joyous.

Beneath that, one shelf down, was a jar labeled: ENVY. It was true, apparently, that old saying about turning green with envy. I didn't know where the saying had come from, but the stuff in the container—which resembled a thick, lumpy goo—was the grayish-green color of weathered copper. Green with envy.

"They're all here," Jeffries said.

"All?"

"The emotions. They're all here."

"These are what you took from my mother?" I asked. I was standing over a container labeled ANGER now. Inside was a roiling blackish cloud that seemed to be pressing against the inside of the glass. *It's going to break out someday,* I thought, and I stepped back a pace.

"No," Jeffries said. "Not these. Not specifically. Your mother's emotions . . . I used those up a long, long time ago."

He said it so matter-of-factly that he caught me completely off guard. And for the first time I realized that something was terribly wrong here, something inside Jeffries was not only bankrupt, it was barren. No, this was not a well man. Not physically, and not emotionally. Where was the man's fear? And if he felt he had nothing to fear from me, then where was his joy or his anger or his—

In the glass jars, I thought. They're all in the glass jars.

"You on a diet, Jeffries?" I asked.

"Pardon?"

I nodded to the nearest container. "You aren't partaking, are you?"

He smiled again, and now I could see it clearly. It was a practiced smile, a smile without anything behind it at all. "No," he said solemnly. "Immortality is not all it's cracked up to be, as you might well have guessed already. It's a lonely life, my friend."

"A long, lonely life."

"And what happens if you don't . . ."

"Draw a breath every once in a while?" he said euphemistically. "I guess you could say my immortality would be shortened considerably."

"You'll die?"

"I'll die."

"And that's what you want?"

He inhaled deeply, exhaled slowly, thoughtfully. "It's not so much that I want to die," he said. "It's that I don't wish to be immortal any longer. I hope you can find the distinction there, because there is a difference. It is, perhaps, the difference between the time it takes to say yes and the time it takes to say no, but it is a difference."

I thought I understood what he was trying to say, at least as well as any mortal man can understand such a thing. "So, you're dying?"

"I am . . . aging. I haven't made the decision to die yet. I may not make that decision at all, and by not making the decision, I may die. Or perhaps the decision will be made for me. We shall see what we shall see."

He stared fondly at a nearby container, then ran his hand along the rim of it, like a hungry man staring at a pastrami sandwich that belongs to someone else. It was everything he could do not to empty it, I thought.

"We're all born that way," he said suddenly, as if he could read my thoughts. "Empty, you know. And when our mothers pick us up and hold us and lovingly coo at us, we breathe it all in. One breath after another. And when our fathers jingle the plastic keys in front of us and read us bedtime stories and playfully toss a ball in our direction, we breathe all that in as well. We breathe it in and it becomes part of us, part of who we are and how we see the world and what makes us laugh and what makes us yearn. We're all born empty. All of us."

"It's a little like an addiction, isn't it?" I asked.

"A little."

"And you're the addict?"

"We're all addicts."

And maybe we were. I didn't know for certain, of course, though I knew that it was an addiction that had brought me here, an addiction that I had carried with me since the age of eleven. And I couldn't have said if I'd ever get over my addiction, regardless of what I was about to do. Maybe some addictions are never satisfied.

"It's got to stop somewhere," I said. "Don't you think?"

"Does it?" he asked. He said it in such a way that it wasn't a question as much as a prompt. It was what a father might say to his son, who has come home crying after being picked on by the local bully. The words didn't matter. What mattered was what lay beneath the words, and that part went like this: *So, what are you going to do about it?*

I hadn't come with anything specific in mind. I had come to see what this man looked like, to discover what this man was beneath his mask, but I had not come with the intent to do what I did. I looked at his face, and something erupted inside me, and without thought, I found myself crossing a line that I never thought I was capable of crossing.

"Yes," I said. "It's got to stop."

And I smashed the glass jar nearest me. It was the one labeled ENVY, and the glass shattered much easier than I ever would have imagined. I hit it with the knuckles of my right hand, and when I pulled my hand out, it was covered in grayish-green slime. It felt cold. I snapped my wrist in an attempt to throw off as much of the substance as I could.

Jeffries didn't move an inch, didn't flinch, didn't smirk, didn't react at all. "Feel better?" he asked.

"No." I reached for the next container, this one label ANGER— and oh, how appropriate that was. No fist this time. I simply scooped it off the shelf and let it crash against the concrete floor. It shattered instantly. Glass shards exploded in every direction. For a moment, it looked like a miniature nuclear explosion, a little mushroom cloud expanding upward, black and malevolent.

I gasped and stepped back, and I'll admit without argument that it frightened me at first. But then I felt something inside me like I had never felt before. It was the most unambiguous, most primal passion I had ever experienced. I wanted this man dead. I wanted him dead so bad I could taste it, and I had never been so frightened of myself before.

Jeffries had backed away a step as well, maybe two, and he was pressed against the back wall, holding both hands over his mouth. It didn't occur to me at the time what he was doing—except cringing in a fear of his own—but later it became oh so obvious: Jeffries was making certain he didn't inhale any of the anger. What had he said? *Or perhaps the decision will be made for me.*

I slammed another container to the floor. I can't remember now which one it was. It doesn't matter, I suppose, because they all went, one after another, until the shelves were empty and a small portion of my anger had dissipated.

I leaned back against the doorjamb, bent over, nearly out of breath. Jeffries hadn't moved. "Now I feel better, I said triumphantly. Only it didn't feel triumphant at all. It felt a little sad, I suppose, a little like winning a race because you took a shortcut. Not a victory at all, but a hollow sick feeling because you know that you haven't accomplished much of anything.

"Done?" Jeffries said finally. For all my anger, he was completely unruffled.

I nodded, and straightened again, feeling my breath coming back. "You can rot here, for all I care, I said angrily. "My mother deserved better."

Then I headed back down the tunnel and up the stairs.

And I never looked back.

It was several weeks later, when I was reading the paper, that I came across an article with a slug that read simply enough: MAN FOUND DEAD IN CELLAR. It was about Jeffries. When the mail had begun to pile up in his box, his delivery man notified the authorities. They ended up breaking into the house, and after a thorough search upstairs, they made their way downstairs to the cellar.

Jeffries was found lying at the back of a small room, the floor covered with shards of broken glass. They were still trying to determine

Empty Vessels

his age and how long it had been since someone had last seen him, because the man they found at the back of that room looked as if he might have died of malnutrition. There was plenty of food in the cupboards in the kitchen, and authorities were speculating that he had somehow gotten himself downstairs and was unable to get back up again. After all, the article mentioned, he appeared to be well over one hundred years old.

I took the article with me the next time I went to visit my mother. She was fighting a cold that day, and she was still in bed, so I pulled a chair up and read her the entire piece. At the end, I told her that this Mr. Jeffries was the same man who had emptied her.

How much of what I told her, she actually absorbed, I guess I'll never know. But when she didn't react, not even with a blink or an attempt to raise a hand, I found myself leaning over her, screaming with a rage that seemed as if it had been boiling at the bottom of a volcano for centuries.

A nurse came rushing in before I could do anything crazy. She pulled me away, and scolded me as if I were a little boy who had gotten into a scuffle out on the playground during recess. As she hovered over my mother, making sure I hadn't hurt her, I backed into the wall and suddenly became aware of what I had nearly done.

I had nearly struck her. I had wanted to strike her. I had wanted to knock her on the side of the head until she understood that Jeffries was dead and that I had helped make that decision for him.

I had wanted to hurt her.

Oh, my God.

It was the anger.

I didn't know why I would have walked out of Jeffries cellar with his anger and only the anger. Maybe I hadn't been as susceptible to the other emotions. Maybe the anger was far more potent. Or maybe this was as much my anger as it was his.

I just didn't know.

All I knew was that it was my anger now, and I could feel whatever was left of it still churning inside me.

The Hollow

That day, that mystical day when the warm winds of fantasy first whispered secrets in Michael Carpenter's ears, had been long overdue. It was a summer day, parched and windless and climbing toward the low one hundreds. The kind of day a rabid dog might feel just right about. The kind of day twelve-year-old Michael had spent a lifetime waiting for.

Using a stick of driftwood he had snatched up from the dry, rocky bed of Moss Creek, Michael macheted his way through a field of knee-high grass, looking to kick-up a pheasant or a coyote pup or some such thing. Anything to change the dull routine that shadowed the town of Appleton every January 1st like a dark thundercloud and stayed uninvited all-year round, reminding, always reminding the townspeople that their lives were insipid little lives. He marched helter-skelter through the grass with no particular destination in mind, stopping on occasion and looking back at the serpentine path he had left in his wake, a path that led back home, back to where Cheryl-the-babysitter sat entranced by All My Children or General Hospital or whatever other strip of celluloid nonsense occupied the airwaves at the moment, then he would swallow his loneliness down and turn away again. Off to the wonders of the world, even though in all his summer days of searching he had yet to stumble across anything he could possibly call a wonder.

But this was a different summer day, a new summer day.

In his wandering, his searching for marvels, he came upon a lonely oak which guarded a field of grass as a scarecrow might guard acres of corn. As tall as old Mister Potter's barn, the oak reached skyward on the strength of four arms. The frayed end of a thick cord rope dangled from one arm and Michael knew a swing had once swayed from the mighty branch, swayed with the laughter of summer children and autumn winds. Through the mesh of tiny leaves, the sun slithered and seeped until it fell across his face in a web of spider-lines. And he decided the little bit of shade wasn't all that bad an idea about then.

He slid down the lumpy trunk of the great oak until his butt rested comfortably in the soft, dusty dirt.

If cousin Brian were there, they would tell jokes about school and Buddy Markham and maybe even Cheryl-the-babysitter. And they would laugh out loud before their eyes would meet and suddenly, like two dogs face-to-face in a stand-off, they would each grow perfectly still until one of them couldn't hold it any longer and he would snicker and instantly a wrestling match would break out. Clouds of dirt would fly then, drifting back to earth, back to their squeals of laughter. And it wouldn't seem so hot.

And it wouldn't seem so lonely.

If Brian were there.

Michael sighed.

Then, as he watched a black ant scurrying madly about, herky-jerky here and there, something long and thin and alive soft-slithered out of the hollow of the great oak, floated over the loose dirt and in a blink, sucked the frantic ant from the face of the earth.

Michael Carpenter's eyes nearly exploded from their sockets.

The long, slender *something*—it was surely alive—slithered back into the hidden safety of the old oak hollow.

And Michael listened as the world suddenly held its breath,

The Hollow

hushed by the wonder of what it had seen, waiting expectantly for what would happen next.

"God, did you see that?" he shouted. "Did you see that?"

He was on his feet, staring at the dark hollow of the tree, keeping a safe distance in case the adventurous tentacle—*it was a tentacle, wasn't it? like the wiggly arm of an octopus?*—might dare to snake out into the sunlight again.

"Did you see that?"

It was something incredible, something so wondrous that the town of Appleton would just have to come alive again. Appleton would just have to stir awake from its Rip Van Winkle slumber now. And all because of him. All because Michael Carpenter was in the right place at the right time and had witnessed the weedy arm gobbling up a no-good black ant.

He held tight to the stick of driftwood as he stepped within an arm's length of the hollow. It was dark inside, and quiet.

"I know you're in there," he said, giving the trunk a whack with his stick. "I saw you gobble that ant."

Yes, I'm here.

He heard the words in his head. The *something* was talking to him, talking right inside his head like his very own thoughts did. Like it was right there inside his head with him, filling up the weird furrowed canals of his brain.

"Come out," he said. "I want to see what you look like."

But his head was quiet.

"I won't tell anyone, I promise." As if it made a difference, as if a promise made to a *something*, would otherwise have to be kept, he crossed his fingers behind his back. "Please?"

The raw tip of a tentacle reached cautiously from the darkness. Pink and moist and looking as if a finger-touch would sink deep into its flesh, the tentacle arched skyward, allowing a line of squirming feelers to sniff the air.

Michael moved back a step.

"Come on," he said. "I won't hurt you."

Then another tentacle ventured forth.

And another.

And another.

Until there were six in all, six long slender arms that reached and probed from a strangely-formed body with two dark eyes and a mouth lined with rows of teeth, like the shark-mouth he had seen on television once.

"Wow!" he shouted, feeling his heart pounding against his chest. And he took another retreating step.

The *thing*—now that he had seen all of it, it wasn't any longer a *something*, it was a *thing*—seemed bothered by the sunlight. Translucent inner lids, like crocodile eyes, opened and closed with a slow, purposeful motion. And it stared with a wonder of its own at the young boy before finally extending a single tentacle in Michael's direction.

The pink flesh wrapped itself harmlessly around his finger, feeling like the soft belly of a snake.

"That tickles," he said with a smile.

Then, as if hurt by the comment, the probing tentacle unwound itself from his tiny index finger, and raised a cloud of dust as it fell back to the ground and slithered away.

"I'm sorry."

Huge eyes blinked as if they didn't understand.

"I didn't mean to scare you."

It's hot, the *thing* said in his head. And it waddled back into the shade of the hollow, back so far in the darkness that nothing was left to be seen. As if there had never been a *thing* at all.

"Go on, take a look," Michael told her. "It's there, honest it is."

Cheryl-the-babysitter was kneeling before the hollow of the oak. She had fussed about coming all the way out to the great tree, complaining that she would miss the end of General Hospital. But he had insisted. Even after she had accused him of being a liar, of having an overactive imagination, he had insisted that she come, and he had taken her by the hand and dragged her away from the RCA. After all, she was the babysitter, she was being paid to look after him, wasn't she?

"I don't see anything," she insisted, whisking a fallen strand of

The Hollow

hair back behind her ear. "If you're lying to me, Michael Carpenter, I'll lock you in your bedroom for a week. I swear I will."

"It's there." This wasn't one of his made-up stories. Not like the tale about a man with a mask and long knife that he had seen slipping through the back bedroom window. No, this wasn't anything like that. This was real. "It had six arms with little feelers on the bottom that wiggled and squirmed like white baby worms."

"That's sick," she said, and she started to rise. But before she could, a soft, pink tentacle slithered out from the dark hollow and wrapped itself around her ankle.

"I told you," Michael shouted. "I told you!"

Then a second tentacle wrapped itself around her other ankle. And while Michael was feeling so happy about the sudden appearance, so happy that he wouldn't be thought a liar, the other tentacles were suddenly all there, wrapping around Cheryl-the-babysitter, choking off gurgling screams before they even had a chance to leave her throat.

"No!" Michael screamed. "You're not supposed to do that!" He tried.

He tried to keep the from pulling Cheryl-the-babysitter into the hollow, into the dark of the hollow where no one would ever hear from her again. But the *thing* was stronger than him. And it had six arms instead of only two. And . . . and it was hungry.

That's what it told him. *Hungry*, it said in his head.

Michael fell to his knees and watched in silence until the dust had settled again. *Hungry* kept sounding in his head. *Just hungry*. His eyes followed the tiny drops of moisture leading a path back to the hollow, a thin crust of dirt floating innocently atop the moist redness.

"No!" he screamed, but the scream was trapped somewhere inside his head, trapped with his understanding of what had happened. "You weren't supposed to do that."

Then everything was suddenly too quiet.

Michael wiped away the tears that had stained his face. He looked over his shoulder, back at the path that led home, wondering if he should follow it, wondering if Cheryl-the-babysitter would still be there watching the last of General Hospital, wondering if there was the slightest chance it had all been a nightmare.

111

But he knew better.

Appleton was still asleep back there, minus Cheryl-the-babysitter, but still yawning at its own apathy just the same, as if nothing had ever happened. Nothing at all.

But something had happened.

Things had changed.

Everything had changed.

And Michael had to tell someone. He couldn't simply keep it a secret. Even though he had discovered the even though he had practically fed Cheryl-the-babysitter to it, he couldn't keep what had happened a secret. No, that wouldn't do at all.

Not at all.

He had to tell someone.

Oh God, he had to tell someone.

"In there," he said, pointing an uncertain finger. "Back where it's dark like the bottom of Spinner's Pond. Back inside where your eyes can't see nothing."

"You sure?" Brian asked. He knelt in the dirt, trying to see into the darkness without venturing too near the hollow. He wanted to believe, Michael could see that he wanted to believe. Even though he was a year older than Michael, he was hoping that there really was a hiding in the old oak, still munching on Cheryl-the-babysitter. "Don't look like there's enough room in there for a whole body. You really sure?"

"Room enough," Michael said.

Then, in a soft-whisper, a slender pink arm of the *thing* was there, wrapping itself around cousin Brian like they were long-lost friends, and dragging him screaming back into the hollow.

Michael's muscles locked when he tried to move. He wanted to cup his hands over his ears, wanted to shut-out the high-pitched screams that were calling his name, screaming for him to do something about the hungry But what could he do? It had so many arms, was so much stronger than his twelve-year-old body.

And then he remembered the stick of driftwood he had snatched from the bed of Moss Creek.

The Hollow

And the stick was suddenly in his hand.

And with all his strength, he let the stick fall against the soft pink flesh of the

... again

... and again

... and again

until the had disappeared into the darkness of the hollow, disappeared with cousin Brian under arm, back into the world of the old oak where no one would ever know what it had done.

No one but Michael.

Then the stick slipped from his fingers, falling lifeless to the ground, lifeless like cousin Brian must be, lifeless like Cheryl-the-babysitter must be.

All because the *thing* was hungry.

And he cried.

He studied the trail left by the dragging, and the bright red moisture which spotted the ground, and the redness which coated the end of the stick. And he cried because they were both dead now, because what had begun as such a special day had ended so terribly wrong.

It wasn't supposed to be hungry.

It was supposed to be friendly, just friendly.

That's all.

She stood behind him, his mother did, holding him by the shoulders as he stared through seemingly lifeless eyes at the flashing blue and red lights.

It was dusk now, the sun was sinking beyond the line of distant oak trees which lined Spinner's Pond. The evening air was quickly cooling down the town of Appleton.

Cousin Brian and Cheryl-the-babysitter had been taken away in black, zippered bags. Michael's mother had held her hands over his eyes when the bodies had spilled out from the hollow, but he'd already known what they would look like.

"Just playing," he had answered when someone asked how he had found the bodies. He didn't tell them about the *thing*. They wouldn't have believed him anyway. It was the sort of thing adults wouldn't

believe if it came from the mouth of a young boy. And he was only twelve, old enough now that he shouldn't be making up stories. Even when they showed him the murder weapon, a big old stick of driftwood all wrapped in plastic, he didn't tell them about the Though he thought the stick looked familiar, thought he could almost feel it in his hands as it came crashing down against the soft pink flesh of . . .
    (cousin Brian's skull?)
    (Cheryl-the-babysitter's chubby face?) . . . the *thing*.
    But there was nothing to say, nothing he could add. Enough rumors were already spreading through the town about the drifter that had been seen sleeping under the great oak the night before, the drifter that maybe stopped just long enough to stuff cousin Brian and Cheryl-the-babysitter into the hollow before moving along again.
    There was nothing he could add to that.
    Nothing he wanted to add.
    There was only one thing that really mattered now. Something wondrous had finally happened to the sleepy-eyed town of Appleton. Something the townsfolk would be talking about for years to come. And if Michael Carpenter could only tell the truth, it might keep the good folks of Appleton talking forever more. But it was their secret, just between the two of them—Michael and the *thing*. Because they had both known that morning that Appleton needed a little excitement if it was ever to shake loose from its Rip Van Winkle slumber.
    And now sleepy-eyed Appleton was as wide awake as ever.

Nothing As It Seems

1

Will Cassidy doesn't talk about it anymore. Neither does his daughter, Chantal, who was eleven when it happened and is almost twenty-eight today. In fact, no one in Kingston Mills talks about it. But that doesn't make it any less their history.

2

For six weeks after Will Cassidy's eleven-year-old daughter Chantal had turned up missing, life had been a walk-through, a dreamlike, timeless state of drinking coffee to stay awake, of adrenaline pumping every time the phone rang, of trying to find an answer to the one question everyone was asking: How could this be happening in Kingston Mills?

Chantal's disappearance wasn't the first, though she was the second youngest, right after Bobby Cutler, who was only nine when he vanished. The very first person to disappear was Elmo Stanton, 67, who lived in a small one-bedroom apartment that sat over the Mills Hardware store on Main Street. Elmo had owned and operated the store for a good many years, as had his father before him and his grandfather before that. The Stantons had been one of the first settlers in Kingston Mills.

He had lost his wife to congestive heart failure three years before his disappearance, and though you could still find him at the Community Center on Bingo Night or at the hardware store during working hours, you didn't see as much of him around town as you once did. That was why it wasn't until midday on a Monday, when the store still hadn't opened, that someone finally became worried and a search was begun.

The second person to disappear was Emily Sanders, the town librarian. She had moved to Kingston Mills in 1972, having gone back to school and received a degree from San Jose State after her children had grown and left home. She was forty-two, married to a trucker who spent most of his time on the road, and her favorite activities outside of the library were karate (which caused her to make the long drive into Redding twice a week, usually after nightfall) and mountain climbing (the reason she and her husband had moved to Kingston Mills in the first place).

Emily disappeared on a Wednesday, two days after Elmo.

Robert Underwood had walked her out of the library that night, a little after it had closed at nine o'clock. It was overcast, he remembered, because she had been disappointed in the absence of the stars. They were her reminder of her place in the world, she had told him. Like the stars, even though she was just a single flicker among billions, she had her own shine—we each had our own shine—and there was no telling how far out into space it traveled.

She was in good spirits that night, he said. Looking forward to spending some time with her husband, who was supposed to return the next weekend after a cross country haul to New Jersey. Robert dropped Emily off at the front door of her house a little before nine-thirty, he

Nothing As It Seems

guessed it was. He watched her go in, watched the lights inside go on, and then went about his way.

It was the last time anyone saw Emily again.

The third disappearance came in broad daylight less than eighteen hours later. It was by far the most puzzling of them all, though there were at least half-a-dozen witnesses who swore they saw exactly what happened.

Two of those witnesses, Judy Landers and her husband Tom, were out running errands during Judy's lunch break from the Five and Dime, where she worked as a bookkeeper. They had stopped to pick up a pie from Sandy's Coffee Shop on Main Street, only four doors down from the Mills Hardware, where Elmo had disappeared. Out front, they had bumped into Lily Hanover. Lily, who had just celebrated her fifty-fifth birthday the week before by jumping out of an airplane at 10,000 feet for her first ever sky dive, was excited about her second dive, which was planned for the upcoming weekend.

"You couldn't get *me* up there," Judy said. "Not if my life depended on it."

"Oh, God, you have to try it, Judy. Just once."

"I'd pee my pants."

Tom, who was holding the door open and only listening with half-an-ear, impatiently nudged Judy with his elbow. "Don't forget we still have to get over to the market before you go back to work."

"I know," Judy said. Later, she would confess that she had seen a glow in Lily that she had never seen before, and that in the back of her mind, she was actually wondering if maybe she should try a dive of her own, just for the boldness of it. But Tom was at her elbow and they were in a hurry and . . .

. . . and then Lily seemed to lose her feet all of a sudden. She stumbled backwards toward the door to the coffee shop, the door that Tom was holding open, her arms whirling in the air like an acrobat trying to keep her balance, and in the blink of an eye, she was gone.

Judy remembered a moment of complete dumbfoundedness, when she looked at Tom to verify what she had seen and he looked back at her with an astonished, unbelieving expression on his face. They were both stunned beyond imagination. It wasn't until Martha Haberstein came running across the street, squealing with excitement that they finally snapped out of it.

"Did you see that? Did you? She was right there one second and the next thing—*poof!*—she was gone. Like it was magic. Like one of those silly little coin tricks you can buy for a quarter over at the Five and Dime. Now you see it, now you don't. Absolutely incredible! My heart's pounding a thousand beats a second."

Martha had seen it.

Judy and Tom had seen it.

Two kids from over at the high school, playing hooky for the day, had seen it.

And there were others.

Lily Hanover had disappeared right in front of all of them.

And she wasn't the last. Three more people disappeared before Will's daughter joined the exclusive club. There was Adam Walker, 28, the postal carrier for Kingston Mills; and Teresa Saunders, who was raising two boys after their father had been killed while working for a logging outfit somewhere in Northern Oregon (her boys were staying with their Grandmother, a little closer to town these days); and then there was David Winters, who had sat on the same stool at the end of the counter at the Stop Over Bar just outside of town for nearly everyday of his adult life.

They had all disappeared.

And then one day Chantal had joined them. She had taken the bus home from school, gotten off at her usual stop, and had been walking along the gravel road that ran perpendicular to Bakker Street at the northern edge of town. She was with her best friend, Amy, talking about what they were going to do for Easter vacation, which was only two weeks away.

Exactly what happened, Amy couldn't say. She remembered feeling a chill pass through them as if a sudden gust of wind had kicked up, only it was more like walking into an air conditioned room in mid-August. It was almost as if they had passed through a wall of cold air, she said. Chantal zipped her jacket up and said something about how creepy it felt. And then she was gone.

Just like that.

One moment there, the next moment gone.

Will Cassidy heard about what had happened from his wife, Rachel, who had been home at the time and had heard it directly from Amy only a few minutes after the fact.

It might as well have been hours.

Chantal had joined the missing.

3

For the next six weeks,, almost nothing in Will's life seemed focused. There was a soft, blurry edge to all the questions, to the day-by-day routines that had to be done, like it or not, to everything except Rachel. She had become the only clarity in the foggy haze, the only person who seemed to be able to navigate her way through what had happened and set about trying to do something to get Chantal back.

There wasn't much she could do. There wasn't much anyone could do. Because what had happened to Chantal, like what had happened to all the others before her, was a complete mystery.

Still, Rachel didn't let that get in her way. She had posters made up with Chantal's most recent photograph—as well as photos of all the others who had disappeared—and used volunteers to distribute the posters throughout Kingston Mills, the neighboring town of Round Mountain, and most of the outlying areas of Shasta County. When she wasn't dealing with posters, she was on the phone talking to radio stations or newspaper reporters, to anyone who would listen, to anyone who might help to get the word out.

Will had not been as strong as Rachel. The night of Chantal's disappearance, he had returned from a trip to Chico, where he had spent the day at the Chico State Library researching a feature piece he was doing for the San Francisco Chronicle. Rachel had met him at the door with the news.

She had cried openly that night, freely, telling him more often than he cared to be reminded that she didn't think she would know how to go on if anything ever happened to Chantal.

Will didn't know, either.

And he didn't want to think about it.
He had never felt so helpless before in his life.

4

Several weeks passed, and then Bobby Cutler turned up missing.

Bobby, 9, who walked out of the Five and Dime after buying a pack of baseball cards, had disappeared less than a block away. Once again there were witnesses. And they all told a similar story, the same kind of story that Judy and Tom Landers had told about Lily Hanover's disappearance. Bobby had simply walked into a nothingness and out of existence.

Whoosh.
That fast.
That mysteriously.

And though no one mentioned it, everyone was thinking the same thing: Bobby would not be coming home again. None of them would be coming home again.

5

Will had begun to spend his evenings at the Stop Over at the edge of town. It was a little after eleven as he sat at the bar, nursing a scotch that was the second of two shots he would down all night. He had never been much of a drinker. Chantal's disappearance hadn't changed that much, though it had changed it some. Two shots of scotch were more than he used to drink in a week.

He finished his drink and the bartender, a man by the name of Buddy Wiser—who endured to no end the lame-brain jokes about his name—brought the bottle over and set it on the counter next to him. "Another?"

Will covered his glass.

"It's on the house."

"Thanks, but I'll pass." He got up, feeling a little lighthearted, though probably not so much by the scotch as by the fact that he hadn't moved from the bar for nearly three hours. "Think it's time I better get home."

One of the reasons he found himself at the Stop Over every night was because he didn't want to find himself at home. The house had grown into a mausoleum, a huge, vacuous space, void of everything beautiful and loving that had made up his life.

Rachel was back with her parents. Not permanently, she had tried to assure him. Just until Chantal came back. Without Chantal, the house was simply too much to bear.

It was too much to bear for Will as well.

But he didn't have anywhere else to go.

He tucked in the tail of his shirt where it had pulled free, then zipped up his jacket and looked from the door to the bartender, wondering—like most of the people of Kingston Mills wondered these days—if he was going to make it all the way home tonight without becoming one of the missing.

"See you tomorrow," he said on his way out.

"I'll be here," Buddy answered.

Outside, Will stood on the sidewalk and gazed down the line of old mercury vapor lamps that cast a soft, ghostly glow over the empty street. There was a cool breeze out tonight. He could hear the rustle through the few remaining leaves on the maple trees in the park across the way. That was the only sound he could hear. The people of Kingston Mills did not stay out at night anymore. *No sense tempting the fates* as Robert Underwood had put it.

No, no sense at all.

What happened next would never be completely clear in his mind. All he remembered clearly was this: the night sky was all stars, the air was crisp, and he could see his own breath fog up in front of him as he stepped off the curb to cross the street. A cold front had swept down from Oregon the night before, dropping the temperature to an unseasonably twenty-six degrees. The thermometer had battled back to thirty-eight during the day, but when the sun had gone down, the temperature had plummeted again. The street was littered with patches of ice, many as black as the asphalt itself. Will remembered stepping around more than one. And he remembered seeing a car come around the corner in the distance, its headlights on high beam, nearly blinding him.

That's all he remembered, until he woke up in the hospital.

Rachel was standing over him, holding his hand. There were tears in her eyes, though she had managed to keep them from spilling over the rim. "Welcome back."

"Thanks," Will said through the fog. "Where have I been?"

"The Twilight Zone, I suspect."

He closed his eyes again. There was an incredible throbbing ache pounding away at the back of his head. It felt as if someone had cracked a baseball bat over his skull. "And where am I?"

"The hospital."

"How did I—?" He made a feeble attempt at sitting up, then fell back again.

"Take it easy, honey. You need to rest. The doctor said you gave the back of your head quite a whack."

"What happened?"

"Apparently, you slipped on a patch of black ice." Rachel tried a smile, but behind the smile was the unmistakable presence of worry. "Oh, Will, I don't know what I would have done if I had lost you, too."

He squeezed her hand. "Hey, I'm still here, aren't I?"

"Yeah."

"So quit worrying, you're giving me a headache."

Her smile broadened. "Bet it hurts."

"Dreadfully. You can't imagine."

"The doctor says there's no fracture. So at least that's something. I think he was a little surprised by the x-rays. Especially after the way you looked when they brought you in."

"I guess it pays to have a hard head after all."

Rachel squeezed his hand this time, then sniffled and wiped away the rim of tears that still hadn't overflowed. She had always been a beautiful woman, from the very moment he had first bumped into her going into the old Cascade Theater in Redding. But she had never been quite as beautiful as she was at this moment, he thought.

"Things will be all right," he said.

"I know."

"It's been a nightmare lately..." He had intended to say something about what a screw-up he'd been the last six weeks, about how he was going to knock off the evening visits to the Stop Over, and about how—from this point on—he was going to do whatever it took to get Chantal back again. But something had caught his eye. Will sat up. "Do you see that?"

"What?"

He pointed to a place on the wall, below the clock, adjacent to the door. He wasn't positive, but he thought there had been some sort of chart hanging there a minute ago. The chart was gone now. In its place was a strange, watery opening, rectangular in shape, nearly as big as the doorway. As he stared at it, Will could see ripples forming across the black surface, like white caps, popping up, then disappearing again. "That!"

Rachel glanced at the wall, unimpressed. "The chart?"

"No, where the chart used to be."

She could have looked at him as if he were crazy and needed a little patronizing. *That* would have driven him crazy. But she didn't do that. She looked at the wall and then again at him. "The chart's right there, Will."

"You don't see that?"

"See what?"

"The opening in the wall? It's right there for God's sake!"

She checked again, bless her heart. But by the time she turned back to him, the opening had already begun to disintegrate. He watched the black, watery hole evaporate one droplet at a time as if it had been some sort of temporary aberration in the structure of the hospital. Only he thought it was more likely a temporary aberration somewhere inside his head.

A small patch of the wall appeared, peeking through the blackness in a splash of beige paint, first here, then there, until gradually he could see the chart that had been hanging below the clock. It was a life-size chart of the body's circulatory system. Near the heart, the last of the black, watery aberration glimmered, then vanished.

Will fell back against the pillow, meeting with a horrible shot of pain. He groaned.

"You hit your head pretty hard on the road base," Rachel said, moving up to the edge of being patronizing now. He might have even called her on it, but he had hit his head. And though she hadn't accused him yet, he wasn't so certain that he wasn't seeing things. "The doctor said it was a miracle you didn't crack your skull open."

"Yeah," he said lightly, "But you should have seen the pavement."

She smiled uneasily, and they shared a moment of silence that seemed as awkward as the first time he had worked up the nerve to kiss her. He had always believed that she had been embarrassed for him at that moment, and he believed now that she was embarrassed for him again. He had seen something that wasn't there.

Will looked past her at the chart on the wall. No black, watery hole. No opening to who knew where. No hint that anything else had ever hung there.

It hadn't really been there, had it?

That black, watery hole?

It had all been a figment of his imagination, a side effect of the concussion he must have endured when his head had struck the pavement.

Will wanted to believe that.

He wanted to believe it more than anything in the world.

Then why was it so hard?

6

It was so hard because it hadn't been a figment of his imagination at all. Will Cassidy came to understand this explicitly over the next several weeks.

He was released from the hospital after a little more than thirty-six hours of bed rest and observation. There were still the occasional headaches, though they came less often now and they carried a far more tolerable bang. Besides, he could learn to handle the headaches. It was the black, watery holes that were giving him trouble.

He had detected two more of the aberrations. The first . . . in the hospital cafeteria while eating lunch. The hole appeared in the side of

Nothing As It Seems

the serving counter and ran horizontal beneath the glass sneeze guard. Unlike the first one, this opening—all the while undulating—remained solid for nearly ten minutes as he sat there eating a salad and watching in utter fascination.

The second aberration was a beast of a different nature. He had been walking back to his room after a short tour of duty on the balcony, where for the first time in several days, he was able to breathe some fresh air and feel the warmth of the afternoon sun against his face. The hole appeared beneath a gurney sitting idly in the hallway outside one of the rooms. It was that same black, water-like opening.

He had reasoned endlessly with himself about the holes, arguing on the one hand that they couldn't possibly exist or he wouldn't be the only person who could see them. On the other hand, since he was the only person who could see them, did that mean there was something wrong with him? That he might want to take a closer look at his personal mental hygiene, as he had heard it expressed on the radio once?

But this hole had been even stranger.

Something had poked its hand through the opening.

It was a moment of overwhelming, holy terror. The fear grabbed Will by the heart and shoved him up against the wall and held him there. He watched the fingers flex open, then writhe in the air as if they were trying to gauge the temperature. They were not normal fingers, normal in the sense of being flesh-toned. Instead, they had an eerie metallic, almost chrome-like coloring. Four fingers and a thumb. Everything was there. But it wasn't human.

The hand extended out of the blackness, halfway up the forearm and wrapped its fingers around the edge of the gurney as if it were trying to pull itself free. It seemed to struggle there momentarily. And then another hand, fleshed in the same metallic coloring, emerged from the blackness only inches away. It was this second hand that seemed to sense the hole was going to close. It pulled back almost immediately, vanishing down into the nothingness.

Seconds later, the disintegration began. Millions of black particles began to break away from the hole and vanish, one after the other. It brought to mind a picture of raindrops rising back into the clouds to regroup again in some other place, at some other time.

The hand released its clamp on the metal frame and disappeared into the blackness.

The last of the hole vanished.

The aluminum legs of the gurney came back into view, the beige wall followed.

Will released a breath that felt as if it had been burning a hole in his lungs. He slumped back against the wall, his hands on his knees, trying to calm himself. A cold sweat had broken out across his forehead. He wiped away the perspiration, still working at getting his breathing under control.

He had seen what he had seen, and now he knew—it was real.

Oh, God, it was real.

7

He considered it, but in the end, Will decided not to say anything to Rachel. It was too easy to recall the look on her face in the hospital. She might not have felt sorry for him, but she had felt concerned. He had seen it in her face.

For a day or two after he returned home, she hovered over him, mothering him like she had when they had first started going together. It would have been better appreciated, he supposed, if he had been able to keep his mind off what had happened. But by the second day, he was growing more and more irritable, and Rachel began to pull back.

"What's gotten into you?" she asked him after he had snapped at her about leaving the dishes in the sink to soak. "Are you sure you're all right?"

"I'm fine. I'm just tired of seeing the dishes stack up."

"Then maybe you should think about washing them," she said, standing at the kitchen doorway. "I thought we agreed that Chantal came first over everything. That you and I were going to put all our efforts in getting her back . . . careers and housework be damned."

"We did."

"Then what the hell's this all about?"

It was about little black, watery holes that unfolded here and there and wherever in the fabric of space and time. It was about not being sure that when he closed the door if there was really a door there at all. It was about being . . . terrified.

"I don't know," Will said apologetically. "I guess I haven't been feeling quite right since the accident."

"You want me to call the doctor?"

The doctor had asked him to make a follow-up appointment in two weeks, just to make sure all the synapses inside his skull were still firing the way they were supposed to. Will, though, had no intentions of ever returning to that hospital again. Not if he had any say in the matter.

"No, I'll be all right."

8

Maybe eventually he might have been all right . . . if that had been the end of it. But the next day, while sitting in the den, he became aware of what appeared to be a hot spot forming in the book case across the room. It started out a soft, glowing red, the color of charcoal briquettes when they've finally started to produce some heat. The glow turned bright, then seemed to burn itself out, leaving in its wake the one thing Will was hoping he would never have to see again . . . another black, watery hole.

The opening grew to a span that ran from floor to ceiling, maybe three or four feet wide. A doorway of some sort, he speculated. Or a general fault in the operating system of reality. He wanted to laugh at that analogy, but couldn't bring himself to smile. Jesus, it was happening again. And this time, it was happening in his own house.

He didn't know how long the aberration—if he could still refer to it as such—held him there, frozen. But eventually he was able to stand up and push the chair away. He crossed the room, only distantly aware of the stiffness in his legs, and pulled a book down from the shelves. *Bartlett's Familiar Quotations*, a volume he sometimes used in his writings.

The blessing, he supposed, at least at this point, was that nothing had come clawing its way through. After that little episode with the hands at the hospital, he had spent endless hours wondering what lay on the other side. He had also wondered, though it had been brief and mostly ignored, if the holes were somehow related to all the recent disappearances.

He stood to one side, trying to peer into the glossy, black vent, and found it impossible to see beneath the watery surface. Exactly what the book was going to prove was anyone's guess; but as he stood there, he could feel a draft, slightly on the cool side, flowing silently through the opening. In his mind that proved one thing at the very least . . . a minimum of three dimensions were involved. The book was not going to bounce back.

Not unless someone—or some*thing*—threw it back.

It was a heavy volume, a hardback, five or six pounds if he had to guess. He stared down at it, then said a silent prayer. The worst scenario to scamper through his thoughts—his synapses were working quite well, the doctor would be pleased to hear—was this: just before the book arrived at its destination, a hand would reach out from the other side and catch it. That was not what happened, thank God.

He let the book sail and it was swallowed in one huge gulp.

Gone.

Just like that.

Not even a noticeable disturbance in the watery surface.

It was true then—this vent, or whatever you wanted to call it, was some sort of doorway between the here and now and . . .

And what? he wondered.

And whatever was on the other side.

Will leaned back against the window sill, his stomach clenched in a knot. He had been saving a place in his mind for a chance that the book might simply pass through the vent, bounce off the case behind it, and the aberration would vanish into a cartoonish puff of smoke. No such luck, though. This was the real thing.

What was *on the other side?* he wondered.

He had a caught a glimpse of it, he supposed. Those metallic-like hands that had reached out of the blackness from beneath the gurney at the hospital, *they* were on the other side. And whatever they were attached to. But what else?

Nothing As It Seems

Just go ahead and do it before it's too late.
"Why not," Will whispered.
It didn't matter how close he stood, it was impossible to see past the black, watery surface. It was almost as if the liquid-like veil were there to form a seal of some sort. He touched it with the index finger of his right hand, immediately pulling the finger back. Not because he had encountered heat or cold—though it *was* slightly on the cool side—or even pain for that matter, but simply to make certain that if he was in danger of hurting himself it would be kept to a minimum.

The black, watery vent had swallowed the finger to the first knuckle, and the aberration had felt exactly the way it looked . . . as if it were formed of liquid. The interesting difference, however, was that it had left no residue on his skin. The finger had come back perfectly dry.

Will tried again. This time, he allowed not only his finger, but all of his right hand to dip into the liquid veneer. It felt as if he were dipping into a tub of thick shampoo, the viscous liquid closing in around his pores, sealing them from the surrounding air. He stretched his fingers, then closed them into a fist, taking a certain pleasure in the strange sensation.

It couldn't all be like this, could it?
There has to be something besides this damn liquid, doesn't there?
These thoughts crossed his mind almost simultaneously and were quickly followed by the realization that the vent was beginning to break up. Will pulled his hand free and fell back. The aberration's outer edges dissipated into the air, a thousand tiny dots at a time, like the dismantling of a giant jigsaw puzzle.

The cool draft fell still.
The last of the vent vanished.
Will, his back pushed up against the desk, stared at the bookcase with a mix of excitement and dread. There was a chance, he thought, his heart might actually explode from his chest cavity, it was pounding so savagely.

He raised his hand to the light.
Four fingers and a thumb.

Nothing out of the usual.
Thank God.

9

That wasn't the last of it.
Less than a day later, it happened again.
He had gone into town to see the printer, who had been volunteering both his time and resources to printing posters of the missing Kingston Mills citizens. First, though, Will had needed to stop off to get a haircut, something he had overlooked for nearly six weeks now. He was only a block away from the Four Comers Barber Shop when a new vent opened in the display window of Mary Anne's Department Store across the street.

As Will had learned to do when he first spotted a vent, he stopped and checked the surroundings to see if anyone else had become aware of what was happening. Mrs. Schuster, who sometimes worked as a waitress at the Lakehead Inn, was crossing the middle of the street half-a-block up. Behind her, Terry Bryne and his five-year-old son, Andy, had stopped to window shop at the Book Mark. And there was a car Will didn't recognize, waiting at the stop light at Main and Pine. None of them appeared to be aware of what was going on.

Will stepped to the edge of the sidewalk, his hand wrapped absently around the pole of a street sign which limited parking to no longer than twenty minutes. Only distantly did he become aware of Mrs. Schuster as she reached the other side of the street and started up the sidewalk.

A hay devil—something you rarely saw this time of year in Kingston Mills—swept up several scraps of paper and carried them, swirling into the air in front of the woman. Mrs. Schuster swatted at a candy wrapper near her face, and then . . .

(just like that)

. . . it happened.

It happened so fast that at first Will found himself frozen in place, not sure he could even believe what his eyes had seen. What he had seen was this: as Mrs. Schuster went strolling past the vent, something

Nothing As It Seems

had come out of the blackness and snatched her. Will wanted to believe that it was a man he had seen, but it was like no man he had ever seen before. He was maybe five feet tall, thin, wearing a lightweight jacket over a tee-shirt, both the same color, which was not really a color at all. It was something metallic-like, almost chrome-like, and even more surprising . . . it matched the man's pigmentation perfectly. There was one more thing. He was wearing goggles, slightly too big for his face, the frames and lenses shaded in that same metallic hue.

Mrs. Schuster's purse, which had slid off her arm, dropped to the ground with a thud and the surroundings immediately fell silent. Will glanced up the street at Terry Bryne and his son, who were still transfixed by whatever it was on display at the Book Mark. The car at the stop light had turned right and disappeared. No one else had seen what had happened.

Only Will.

He was the only one who could see the vents, the only one who could see what had just come out of the vents, the only one who knew what was happening to all the missing people.

The black, watery surface of the vent had rippled slightly as Mrs. Schuster had been pulled into it, but it was calm now as Will made his way across the street. He stepped onto the sidewalk, without having put what he was about to do into words yet. It was nothing more than a picture in his head, taken from somewhere far behind him.

He brushed his left shoulder against the light pole, took a few quick steps for momentum, and went sailing into the vent, hands out front, eyes closed, anybody's guess where he was going to end up. He did it all in a single movement, without a moment's hesitation, thinking only of Chantal. If he had thought of anything else, he wouldn't have been able to do it.

On the other side, he landed hard against a concrete walkway, rolled twice, and jammed his shoulder into a bench that kept him from rolling into the street. The impact emptied his lungs in one, huge eruption of air. He grabbed for his midsection, fighting to get the breath back, his mouth working the air like a fish out of water. When it finally came, it burned a path down his windpipe and into his lungs. He gasped and sat back, grateful to be alive.

David B. Silva

It was another thirty-seconds before he was able to take in his surroundings with any measure of discern. The black, watery surface of the vent where he had come through had settled again. Will made note of that before anything else, with a footnote to himself that at least temporarily he still had a way to get back. The strange thing was that he wasn't sure how far he had actually come.

He was lying on the sidewalk in front of Mary Anne's Department Store, almost as if he had bounced off the vent and had fallen to the ground. But he had gone through the vent; he was certain of that. And this wasn't Mary Anne's Department Store. At least it wasn't the one where Chantal had bought her first party dress for last year's Sadie Hawkins dance. It was close, the design, the items in the window, the name, its location on the street. Close. But the store was like everything else here: it had no color. Like the sidewalk beneath him, the bench he had rolled into, the streets, the other buildings, like all of it . . . it was a blinding, crippling monochrome.

Same as the man, Will thought.

Out of the corner of his eye, he caught a movement and tried to pull his feet, which were splayed across the sidewalk, back into his body. It was a boy he had seen, maybe a year or two younger than Chantal. In his hands, he held a comic book, the lettering and illustrations all done in a strange sort of three-dimensional embossing.

That's how they work around the monochrome, Will thought distantly.

He had pulled his feet back, but he had not pulled them back far enough to prevent the boy from tripping over them. It wasn't a bad stumble, just a missed step or two before the boy caught his feet again. Then there was a moment when the boy looked down at Will with annoyance, and Will realized it was the kind of annoyance you shoot at a high spot in the sidewalk. As if the boy had not actually seen him there at all, but had looked right through him.

"Sorry," Will said, startled by the sound of the word as it came out of his mouth. It had sounded amplified somehow, and drawn out, almost guttural. This place was not only different by its lack of color, he realized, but also by the distortion of its sounds.

The boy disappeared down the street.

Nothing As It Seems

Heading for The Collector's Corner, Will thought as he climbed to his feet. He brushed the monochrome dust off his jacket sleeves and the front of his pants, then looked up the street, past the Five and Dime at the bookstore (which was called the Book Cover on this side). Beyond the bookstore, he could see the sign for the barbershop, and beyond that, in the distance, just a glimpse of Hattie's Antiques.

Where to start?

The Abductor (as Will had already come to think of him) had taken Mrs. Schuster somewhere nearby. It couldn't have been far, because Will had come through the vent only seconds later. How far could they have gotten in a matter of seconds?

Only two places came to mind. The first was an old warehouse that had been split into a machine shop on one side and a wrecking yard on the other. That place was right around the corner, less than two blocks from here. The other place was the old abandoned railroad station, up the street and to the left. The kids liked to play there. At least they did on the Kingston Mills side. Then there was a third possibility, now that he thought about it—the Haberstock Mill, which had been closed down in the late Sixties. It sat near the edge of town, though, a fairly decent hike from here.

It was the warehouse, then.

That's where he would start.

10

It was surprising how disorienting the monochromed landscape could be. As he moved down the street, he found it next to impossible to simply put one foot in front of the other without weaving unsteadily. Everything felt slightly off center.

He managed to stay on his feet, though, at least long enough to make it to the old warehouse. The machine shop, a place called Anderson's Tool and Die, was closed on Sundays, according to a sign posted in the window next to the door. Will leaned against the glass, his hands cupped around his eyes, and tried to get a peek inside, but it was too dark to see anything.

Next door, there was a man out front dismantling what looked like an old Ford Pinto. He had just ignited a cutting torch and had flipped the visor to his helmet when Will walked past him.

Otto's Auto Wrecking was the name of the place. It was not a far cry from the junk yard that sat in the same spot on the pigmented side of Kingston Mills. The same corrugated tin panels (only monochromed, of course). The same caustic mix of oil and gasoline in the air. And while Will had only been there once or twice, he had learned that the only way to find what you were looking for was to start scavenging through the piles one by one. This time, though, he was scavenging for something a little different.

He checked the office first, then a small machine shop in the back, another room that appeared to be used for warehousing small parts, and finally a bathroom where the monochromed dirt, several shades darker, was visibly noticeable. Chantal was nowhere to be found. Neither were any of the other missing Mills residents.

On his way out, it occurred to him that if no one could see him, then he must be to this world what the Abductor was to the colorized version of the Mills . . . some sort of invisible predator. He didn't know how he felt about that, but he couldn't imagine feeling good.

At the curb, he stopped to get his bearings and was surprised to discover that a new vent had opened across the street. It consisted of that same black, watery surface, about the size of a doorway, this one overlying the front of a brick building. It had not been there when he had entered the wrecking yard.

He stepped forward, curious. There were the usual questions that came to mind about how long it might remain open. But the question that was most unsettling was this: Did this mean the other vent had closed and he wouldn't be able to get back again?

Before he could give it much thought one way or the other, the vent began to disintegrate. In a matter of seconds, it had splintered into millions of minute particles, each particle evaporating almost as quickly as it had been formed.

The vent disappeared.

Will sank back against a light pole.

Somewhere inside him it felt as if a hole had opened and it was slowly devouring any hope he might have of ever finding Chantal again. He felt that and he felt something else. He felt a strange weariness working its way into his bones like a strain of super flu. It hadn't hit him yet, not fully at least, but it was—

Half-a-block up, the Abductor came running around the corner. He was wearing his goggles—the monochromed version of sunglasses, Will imagined—and carrying a small rectangular box in his hands. No sooner was he around the corner, than he glanced down at the box and suddenly dropped out of his sprint. He walked a few steps further, then came to a standstill, visibly disappointed.

Too late, Will thought. *The vent's already closed. That's what that little box of yours just told you, isn't it?*

The Abductor turned around, his shoulders slumped, and headed back the way he had come.

Will took after him.

11

They ended up not at the old railroad station or the Haberstock Mill as Will had originally thought they might, but at a private residence one block over from the city park. On the colorized side of Kingston Mills, this was a house that used to be occupied by Henry Bascom and his wife, Edith. They had packed up and moved south to the Bay Area after the mill had shut down. To the best of Will's knowledge no one had occupied the place since. That was on the colorized side.

On this side, things were apparently a little different.

The Abductor climbed the front steps of the old Victorian and entered the house, stopping only a moment to check the box in his hands one last time. Will went through a side gate to the back of the house. In the far back corner, at the end of the gravel driveway, sat an old, detached garage. He peered through the window at the darkened interior, looking past the car (which resembled a Plymouth Duster), and finding nothing much else of interest.

The house, assuming the layout didn't stray far from the Bascom house, was a beautiful two-story Victorian with three bedrooms and a bath upstairs; the living room, a parlor, a kitchen and a huge walk-in pantry downstairs. There was also an attic and a basement.

Will leaned against the corner of the garage, feeling slightly short of breath and wondering what was wrong with him. Through the back porch windows, he watched the Abductor fiddle around in the kitchen, then disappear back into the depths of the house. A moment later, the light in the basement went on.

That's where you've got 'em, isn't it, you crazy bastard?

Two short casement windows had been mounted just above ground level on either side of the back porch. Will got down on his knees, then his stomach and peered into the basement. He would never admit to being surprised, because surprise was only the tip of the ice berg. They were all there. Elmo Stanton. Chantal. Mrs. Schuster. All of them. The Abductor had them sealed off in a corner of the room, caged liked animals. But at least they were there and they were alive.

The casement windows were locked. He looked around for something he could use to break them open, and when he found nothing, he took a more direct approach. He sat back and landed a solid right shoe to the centerpiece of the sash. The frame collapsed into the room, followed almost immediately by both panes of glass.

Will went through, driven more by adrenaline than thought.

The Abductor, who had been toying with the rectangular box at his work bench, turned, the startle unmistakable. The box slipped out of his hands and landed on the concrete floor, somehow remaining intact. One hand shot up to cover his eyes, while the other grabbed for the goggles which were hanging around his neck. He worked them into place, then seemed to gain control of himself again. He smiled sardonically.

"Out of your element?" he asked. His speech was marked by that same drone-like, low-pitched slur that seemed to mark all the sounds in this place.

"You're the one wearing the goggles."

"Minor inconvenience. Temporary. Until I adapt." He was a nervous little man, full of high energy, rocking from foot to foot. It was hard to imagine him ever relaxing, ever closing his eyes and sleeping.

"Adapt?" Will asked.

"To your side. Yes."

"Then the vents that keeping popping up everywhere, they're . . . yours?"

"Apertures. Yes. Mine." He smiled, almost to himself. "There's here . . . and then there. All bright sights and clear sounds. You don't appreciate it. Yes. Can't appreciate it. No."

Behind him, someone stirred. Will didn't turn to see who it was because he didn't want to take his eyes off the Abductor. Not for a second. But when he heard the voice, even in that low-pitched slur, he knew immediately that it was Chantal.

"Daddy, you're here. How did you get here?"

"Are you all right?"

"I'm just a little tired, that's all."

The Abductor grinned at him. "Tired? You, too? Yes?"

He was feeling tired. Not sleepy tired, but worn-out tired. And it was something he preferred to keep to himself. "Tell me . . . why all the people?"

"Think of your bodies, then of mine. Think of physiology. Yes?"

It made perfect sense once he thought about it. Chantal and the others . . . they were test subjects, guinea pigs, a means of understanding how the body handles all the sounds and colors. The stimulus was like a narcotic to him. There was the pleasurable experience, and then there was the overload. He was trying to master the overload.

"This is all on your own, isn't it?" Will asked quietly.

"Of course. Who else?"

"No one else even knows what you're doing here."

"No one."

Will glanced back at Chantal, who was standing now, with her hands wrapped around the monochromed bars. Her face was drawn, deep lines that didn't belong there etched into her cheeks, shadows beneath her eyes. He didn't want to stretch this out any longer than necessary.

"It's time to let them go," he said calmly. "They have families and—"

"No. They stay."

Then someone from behind him said, "He keeps the key in the drawer there, under the work bench."

Will made the mistake of turning to see who was talking—it was Elmo Stanton. In that instant, the Abductor closed the distance between them and struck Will hard across the side of the face with something that felt like a baseball bat. Will fell back against the door to the cage, hitting his head against the metal bars, and thinking distantly to himself that he knew better than to take his eyes off this guy. How could he have been so stupid?

Somewhere far away, he heard Chantal scream, "Daddy!"

The Abductor closed again, and Will could see this time that it wasn't a baseball bat he was holding in his hands. It was a gardening hoe. He swung it again and it landed near the crown of Will's head, leaving behind a strange numbness that seemed less painful than disorienting. Will backed into the bars and curled up.

It shouldn't hurt this bad, he thought from faraway.

"Not so big on this side. Not so strong," the Abductor said.

"Stop it!" Chantal screamed. "You're hurting him!"

The Abductor reached back for another swing, and this time Will was able to get his arm up to block it. The handle of the hoe landed flush across his forearm. It hurt, there was no mistaking the hurt, but he was still able to grab on.

"Let go! Let go!"

He didn't have the strength to wrestle the hoe away, but he managed to hook his arm over the handle and lock the blade behind him. With a violent tug, the Abductor dragged Will across the concrete floor, away from the cage, as if he were nothing more than a house dog with his teeth clenched around one end of an old rag.

"Not strong here. Just a tired old man. Yes."

It was true. Will hated to admit it to himself, but it was true. For whatever the reason, every movement he made seemed to drain his strength a little more. This little, five-foot troll was going to overpower him, and there wasn't much he was going to be able do about it.

The Abductor dragged him another couple of feet across the floor, Will holding on for dear life, and then he stopped and bent over in another attempt to wrestle the hoe from Will's grasp. Instinctively, Will fumbled for something to grab onto—a hand, an arm, a fistful of hair, anything. What he came up with were the goggles.

The Abductor let out an immediate scream that sounded like pure agony. He dropped the hoe and fell back, shading his eyes with his hands. For a moment, as he was stooped over and trying to rub the pain out of his eyes, he resembled the Hunchback of Notre Dame—a sad, almost sympathetic, little man.

Will climbed to his feet, sucking air and feeling like a man twice his age. It was all he could do just to toss the hoe aside and pick up the goggles.

"The keys!" someone yelled from behind him.

He found them in the drawer, where Elmo had said they would be, and tossed them to Chantal, who unlocked the cell. "Why don't you take everyone upstairs," he said. "And wait for me out front. All right?"

"What are you going to do?"

"Just say good-bye, that's all."

The Abductor, who had huddled into the far corner with his hands still covering his eyes, peeked through the thin splay of fingers like a child checking to see if the monster was still there. "Can't go," he said. "No."

Will crossed the room and picked up the rectangular box that had earlier been dropped. It was what he had expected—some sort of electronic grid, all done in monochrome and three dimensions, similar to a relief map. He ran his fingers over the surface, trying to decipher the landmarks, and suddenly the box began to put out a low-pitched vibration. A moment later, a small square, enclosing an X, rose up out of the grid in what could only be construed as some sort of electronic marker.

"I do believe you've got another vent opening up," he said. He thought their current location was landmarked by a circle within a circle, which meant the vent wasn't more than a block or two away. "Guess it's time for me to be getting back home. I appreciate the map."

"No. Leave the map." The Abductor made a feeble attempt to reach out and grab him with one hand.

Will pushed him away with almost no effort, which was a good thing, because he didn't have much effort left. The fatigue wasn't getting any worse, but it wasn't getting any better, either. "Sorry. No can do."

"Please! "

"Maybe next time." On his way out, Will stopped at the top of the stairs and looked back. The Abductor had crossed the room and was standing at the bottom, looking up through splayed fingers, still cringing from the blinding colors.

He isn't going to give up, Will thought. *This is all he has, all he is.*

Out front, he met up with the group again. Lily Hanover was leaning against a four-by-four porch support, looking as tired as he had ever seen her. "Don't you hate it?" she said.

"What?"

"Everything painted this silvery metallic color. No blues or yellows or reds. No rainbows. No flat white. No glossy black. It's enough to drive a person insane, don't you think?"

Will nodded and looked down at the map in his hands. He didn't think the new vent could be far from here, and when he glanced up to gain his bearings, it was a pleasant surprise to find it across the street, only two houses down.

Chantal came up beside him and put her arm around his waist. "How do we get out of here?"

"Right there," he said, pointing at the vent. Only she wouldn't be able to see it; he had forgotten that little fact. If he hadn't fallen and struck his head, he wouldn't have been able to see it, either. "Come on, I'll show you."

They crossed the street as a group, moved down the sidewalk, and came to a stop in front of a rundown Victorian that Charlie Weaver had inherited from his father two years ago. He hadn't got around to renovating the house yet, but it was something he said he had always wanted to do. The vent was at the foot of the front porch steps, shimmering black, open for now, but for how long no one knew.

Will stepped up next to it. "Elmo, why don't you come on up here. You were the first one to have to endure this nightmare. Let's see if we can't get you home again."

"What the hell you talking about, Will Cassidy?"

"Just trust me, all right?"

Elmo stepped forward. Will took him by the arm and guided him

up the first step and through the vent. He crossed over one piece at a time, with his right leg
disappearing first, followed shortly by his left arm. In less than a breath, the black, watery vent had closed in around him and he was gone.

Bobby Cutler came up and stood next to Will. "Where'd he go?"

"Home. He went home, Bobby."

"Can I go next?"

"Sure." He ushered the boy up to the steps, his hand resting in the small of Bobby's back. "All you have to do is climb the steps."

"That's it?"

"That's it."

"Will I see you on the other side?"

"In a few minutes. Now, go on."

After Bobby, Lily Hanover went next, and then Teresa Saunders and Mrs. Schuster, until one-by-one they had all stepped through the vent—Chantal being the last—and Will was the only one left behind. He glanced down the street, then down at the grid map in his hand. The emblem for the vent—the square with the X in its center—had begun to vibrate again. That could only mean one thing. The vent was getting ready to close.

Chantal called out from the other side. "Daddy?"

"I'm coming, baby." He took the first step up, then the second, and suddenly found himself straddling the two worlds, caught half-here and half-there. Something had caught him from behind. When he turned and stuck his head back through the vent, he discovered that the Abductor had taken hold of the tail of his jacket. The little man was tugging for all he was worth.

Chantal, who was standing at the foot of the steps in front of him, reached out for his hand. "What's wrong?"

"He's got hold of my jacket," Will said, acutely aware that the outer edges of the vent had begun to break into thousands of tiny, swarming specs. In a matter of seconds, they were going to start flying off, tens of thousands at a time, and he didn't want to know what that would do to him. "You've gotta help me through!"

"Someone help!" Chantal screamed. "He's caught!"

Adam Walker, a man Will had never met before today, came running up the walkway from the street, as did David Winters and Emily Sanders. Chantal motioned to Walker, the closest body. "Grab his hand!"

He grabbed Will around the wrist, using both hands, and together with Chantal, neither of them actually able to see the vent, they managed to pull him free. Or at least free of the vent. The Abductor was still holding on, half-in, half-out of the opening, his eyes clamped shut to the sudden brightness.

"No! You stay!" he was screaming.

It was too late to shed the jacket.

Too late to pry his hands loose.

The vent completed its disintegration in a matter of milliseconds.

Whoosh! It was gone.

The Abductor let out an agonizing scream.

His upper torso, from just above the shirt line, separated from the rest of him and fell to the ground in a lifeless heap. What remained behind was anyone's guess. It had either disintegrated with the vent, or it was lying on the ground in a similar heap on the other side. Either way, what was left here was a horrific mess.

For a long while, Will found himself holding Chantal against his chest, trying to spare her the gruesome sight. It was only later that he realized she couldn't have seen it anyway.

12

Will doesn't talk about it anymore, but he worries sometimes.

The vents have never stopped opening and closing. They still pop up out of nowhere every once in awhile, and Will is still the only person who can see them.

And while no one else besides the Abductor has ever come through, he dreads the thought that someday that might change.

Ice Songs

Record Searchlight
August 28, 1961
Mysterious Chunk of Ice Falls From The Sky
Cottonwood, California
Local experts in astronomical and meteorological phenomena were questioning a report yesterday that a large piece of ice fell out of the sky and landed in the back yard of the Hollerman family.

Michael Hollerman, 11, said the ice block was larger than twelve inches square when it first hit. The strange chunk of ice crashed to earth only a few feet from where the boy was playing baseball with a neighborhood friend, Leonard Perry, also of Cottonwood.

According to the National Weather Service, the skies over Northern California were clear yesterday, temperatures ranging in the high nineties, low one hundreds.

The two boys were the only witnesses.

Dallas T. Morgan, the regional director of the U.S. Meteor Society said the ice could have come from a comet. In somewhat similar

David B. Silva

circumstances, a 50-pound piece of ice fell in French Gulch in 1954. Another chunk of ice reportedly fell out of the sky over Shingletown as recently as 1958.

"A lot of people who consider themselves intelligent, like to say it just can't happen," he said.

William Bickert, a professor of astronomy at Shasta Community College, discounted the comet theory.

"It certainly wasn't from a comet. It would have melted. Ice particles are vaporized by the heat of the sun," he said.

Bickert believes it was more likely that the chunk of ice was either picked up from somewhere else and carried on the turbulence of a small thunderstorm, or came from a jet engine high in the atmosphere.

I keep that newspaper article in my wallet, behind my California Driver's License, face-to-face with my last four-year extension. It's yellow now, and ragged at the seam of the fold. But I've carried it around with me all these years, every now and then reading through it one more time, because the story never seemed to have an honest ending. Not if you were there. Not if you were Michael Hollerman or Lenny Perry. I don't think the story's ever ended for either of us.

It was a young boy's day, that long ago hot August afternoon when Michael and I were playing catch out in the pasture behind his house. There was the sharp tang of turkey mullein in the air, the distant soft whisper of the creek at our ears. The sky was a forever blue, an empty palette waiting for the stroke of a brush to give it a cloud or a moon or some other such stroke of imagination.

Michael's parents had taken the old Chevy pickup into Redding, hoping to talk Sam Johnson down at Tire Surplus into letting them have some retreads on credit. So Michael and I, we were tossing an old hardball back and forth. He was trying to get his wrist to snap out a curve, but the stitching had gone soft in late July and the ball wasn't having any of it.

"Just throw it straight," I was telling him.

"I'm trying," he said. He began a new wind-up, but it never fully materialized.

"What's the matter now?"

Ice Songs

"Listen, Lenny. Can't you hear it?"

"Hear what?"

"Listen," he said, shading his eyes and looking toward the sky. "Don't you ever listen?"

I heard the whistle of the wind, and I found myself remembering another time when my Grandfather had whittled a small chunk of wood for me—smooth and conical. He wrapped a piece of shoe-box string around the thick end, turned it upside down and pulled. A whirligig, he called it as it spun its way across the tabletop. I laughed because the spinning was such a surprise, and the sound it made—a gentle windsong like the flap of hummingbird wings—was like someone whispering in my ear, tickling me. That was almost the same sound I heard falling out of the sky that hot August day with Michael.

Then Michael pointed. "There!" he said. "There it is!"

Across the field, next to the road, there was an old oak tree. That's where the chunk of ice crash landed. It snapped off a couple of branches, tore away the old tire swing Michael's dad had put up a summer or two before, and hit the ground with a thud. Dust kicked up, then softly drifted away.

"Christ! Did you see it?" Michael screamed.

I can still see the shimmering heat reflecting back a strange dream-like image of him running through the pasture, like an endless line of mirrored similitudes, all shirtless and wearing frayed cut-offs, all holding on tight to a San Francisco Giants cap with one hand, waving me to follow with the other.

"Lenny, you'll miss everything!"

It seemed odd, that moment. The way a minute will sometimes go cold on you, and everything slows down, dream-like and crystal clear. I could hear his voice, a long squeal of excitement, carrying on the breeze as if it had wings. *Did you see it? Did you? Did you?* All that exuberance kicking up behind him, and all I could feel was fear.

The chunk of ice was partially buried in the ground, but I saw as much as I wanted to see from where I finally came to a safe standstill. It was the size of a gunny sack, like the ones we used to stuff with hay and use for bases when we played baseball down at the school. It was giving off a chilly vapor; its color—almost glowing through the vapor's tendrils—was gray and cloudy, the way ice cubes left too long in the freezer sometimes cloud up.

Michael knelt next to it, brushed away some strands of hay with his fingers, and smiled. "What do you suppose—"

"You shouldn't touch it."

"Don't be dumb. What's not to touch? It's just ice, that's all." He reached out, his index finger long and thin and trembling just enough to be noticeable, and when he touched the glistening mass and nothing happened, he grinned. "See? Just ice," he said, wiping his finger across his bare chest.

"Right out of the sky like that? Everything as hot as hell today—the grasshoppers are hunting for shade, for crissakes—and a chunk of ice falls right out of the sky? It doesn't make sense, Michael. Not a lick of sense."

"Sure it makes sense, Lenny. A chunk of ice doesn't just fall out of the sky without some sort of sense to it."

"Leave it be, Michael."

He glanced up at me, his expression a question. "Aren't you itching to know where this thing came from? What it is? Don't you want to know everything there is to know about it?"

"Wait till your dad gets back. Let him take a poke at it."

"Then it wouldn't be ours, would it?"

Michael's eyes were all lit up, and I knew he was dreaming dreams that I couldn't even imagine. That was the difference between the two of us. Michael, he could see the lines of history etched across the flesh-red colors of broken granite, great movements of the Earth recorded there, Neanderthal scratchings, wall paintings, arrow tips. He could see anything and everything, because there wasn't anything unimaginable when he closed his eyes. It was never like that for me. Close my eyes, I'd see black. Open them again, I'd see white.

"Whatever it is you're thinking," I told him, "forget it."

He smiled, and I couldn't tell if he was smiling at me or if one of his *dreams* had just passed through his mind and delighted him. It was a half-smile, a self-possessed smile.

I sat in the grass a few feet away, watched him lift the ice into his lap as if it were a soft pillow.

Ice Songs

"It's cold," he said with a shiver.

"What did you expect?"

He shrugged. "I don't know." Then he painted his initials in the frost of the smooth surface. MJH. Michael James Hollerman. As if it were the dusty tailgate of his dad's pickup. "Maybe nothing," he said quietly. He seemed taken by something he was seeing inside that cloudy block of ice, as if he were catching eyes with something that was staring back. "Maybe everything."

"What are you seeing in there, Michael Hollerman?"

"Shhh," he said, a finger over his lips. "Can't you hear it?"

"Hear what?"

"It's singing," he said.

"Can't be."

He started rocking back and forth then. *Hear it?* The smile on his face had gone cold, almost there but not quite, just a faint curl at the corners of his mouth. *Can't you hear it?*

I couldn't hear it then.

I'm not even sure I wanted to hear it.

But I know what that sound was like, it was a soft humming sing-song, the mournful cry of tiny voices, a little like the continuous hum-song of the mercury vapor lamp my father had bolted above the loft of our barn the summer before. A little like that, but not quite the same.

"Hear it?" Michael asked. "Singing like the Christ Our Savior Choir on Sunday mornings, a thousand voices all happening at once? Enough to send a chill right through you. Hear it, Lenny? Tell me you hear it. Someone else's ears should be hearing this, not just mine."

I lied to him, told him I heard.

Then his smile unfolded. "Our secret, right? Just you and me, brothers of the blood and the moon? No one else knows, right?"

"No one else."

"Not a single soft whisper to another breathing soul?"

"Just you and me, Michael. That's all, just you and me."

He seemed happier then. "Have you ever heard of such a thing? Have you ever read about the sky raining ice on a hot summer day? Ever? Anywhere? In Egypt or New Zealand, even Iceland? Ever?" He shivered, then wiped his palm across the cold block, gazing again at its fogginess. "What do you think it is, Lenny?"

"Something unnatural," I almost told him, but I knew he wouldn't be listening. Michael was like that. Always an open ear for things that seemed like magic, but throw a warning his way and it was like pouring hot wax in his ears, 'cause he wasn't going to hear you. He just didn't believe anything could be evil. "I don't know," I told him.

"But it's ours. Isn't it, Lenny?"

"Not ours, *yours*. It's all *yours*, Michael. You heard it first, you were the first one here. It's yours to keep, Michael. All yours."

He whispered a soft *thanks* that drifted away in the breeze.

"So what are you going to do with it?"

"I'm not sure," he started to say, then he tenderly traced a fingertip along the top edge of the ice, as if he were wiping away a tear. It was an eerie gesture, deliberate and purposeful, and for a strange moment, I had the uneasy impression that I had just witnessed some sort of an exchange between ice and flesh. Cold to warm. Warm to cold. A communion between animate and inanimate.

"You okay, Michael?"

"You know what it is, Lenny? What it's doing?"

"Singing, that's what you said. Singing its song."

"I was wrong."

"Then what?"

"It's dying." He held his finger in the air—the same finger he had used to trace the outline of the block—and we both watched as a lonely drop of moisture trailed down the finger, leaving a glistening path across his palm and down his forearm before dropping off into the grass. There were tears in his eyes, shining soulfully in my direction, and I knew he was asking me to prove him wrong. "That's what it's doing, Lenny. Isn't it? I know enough to know it's dying, don't I?"

"You can't be sure," I told him.

"But I know enough . . ."

(I shivered, because suddenly everything rational was slipping away from me, and it frightened me that I was almost *believing*)

". . . don't I?"

"It's just a block of ice, Michael. Frozen water, that's all.

Ice Songs

Something that's already dead can't go and die on you. You breathe in that icy cold vapor long enough, Michael, it plays tricks on you. And pretty soon you're thinking things that just don't make any sense."

"But the song?"

"The sound of melting ice, the sound of popping air bubbles. Not a song at all. It's a chunk of ice, Michael. Out of the sky on a hot summer day or cold winter night, it's still just a chunk of ice."

His eyes, dark brown and endless like polished black agates, had glazed over—suddenly looking as cold as the sheen of the ice held in his lap—and I knew he wasn't listening. Maybe it was the song he was hearing, maybe it was something else, something inside himself. But that was the first moment I really understood the difference between the two of us. Like Nightshade and Galloway, we were. Michael all ready to follow his heart, me all ready to follow my brain

In the distance, a cloud of dust came rolling up the road behind the Hollerman's old Chevy pickup. It was late afternoon, the sun still hours above sunset, and the pickup was shimmering behind a curtain of heat waves. I shaded my eyes, thinking, *Let your father hold it, Michael. Let him hold the icy thing in his lap and let's see what he has to say about it.*

"Your folks are back," I started to say, but Michael was already off to a gallop in the other direction, his summer-blond hair flapping in the wind, his baseball cap left on the ground where he'd been sitting under the white oak. There was a small damp spot in the dirt where the ice had been melting.

. . . ice tears . . .

"What are you doing?" I yelled after him.

"Saving its life!" he yelled over his shoulder.

By the time I caught up with Michael, he was already inside the garage, bent over, hands on knees, sucking in as much breath as he could hold onto. His face had gone pale, almost as icy white as that vaporous block. He was standing next to a wall of shelving on one side—lined with a hundred jars of canned goods Mrs. Hollerman had put up the last several months—and an old Philco freezer on the other side.

"It was melting," he said between breaths.

"You're going to keep it?"

"I have to."

"But . . ."

"Promise you won't tell, Lenny. Brothers of the blood and the moon, just you and me, promise. Please?"

I could see the Hollerman's pickup breaking through the curtain of heat waves, coming up the drive, into clear focus.

Please, Lenny?

"I hate this."

Please?

"There's something not right about that piece of ice, Michael. You know that, don't you? It's not just me, feeling colder than I should on a hot summer afternoon. It's more than that. You know that, don't you?"

. . . brothers, Lenny, of the blood and the moon . . .

He didn't have to say another word. Michael had a way about him that made you trust him. Maybe even more than you knew you ought to at times.

"All right," I told him. "Our secret."

"Thanks." His face came alive again, and a half-smile came out long enough to make me feel as if maybe I hadn't made such a godawful promise after all.

But I had.

Next morning, the *Record Searchlight* carried the story I still keep in my wallet behind my driver's license.

Brothers of the blood and the moon, just you and me, he'd said.

But Michael was Michael. He just wasn't the type to sit still with a secret tucked away in his back pocket, all buttoned up tight where no one could see it. Sooner or later, he had to open up that pocket and take another look. And I guess when that wasn't quite satisfying enough, he decided to invite the rest of the world to get a good a peek of its own.

Ice Songs

"I saw the paper this morning," I told him when I'd finally caught up with him. It was on the noon side of 10:30. Mr. Hollerman was off to Eureka to pick-up something or other. Mrs. Hollerman was in the house, putting up apricots. I found Michael in the garage, of course, standing back in one corner, with one hand reaching out of the shadows and resting on top of that old Philco freezer as if to make sure it didn't wander away from him.

He coughed, from deep within his chest.

"You forgot to tell them about the freezer," I said.

"I didn't forget."

"Maybe tomorrow you'll tell 'em, huh? Or the next day? Or the day after that? Because they'll have to know sooner or later, Michael. We gotta tell someone sooner or later."

He coughed again, and I thought his insides were going to come up. "Do we? Do we *have* to tell? The two of us knowing, maybe that's more than enough, don't you think, Lenny?"

"Just you and me?"

"Who else?" he said, but it wasn't Michael's voice I was hearing. And the hand that was resting on top of that old Philco freezer, when I looked again, it was a pale, wax-like thing. Not Michael's hand at all. "Don't you see?" he asked. "Nobody can take it from us, Lenny. It's ours. We found it, and it's all ours."

"Your ears heard it, Michael."

"There's never been another single soul who's come across such a thing, Lenny. Not one. Not in all of time. We're the first."

"Your hands touched it."

"And *your* hands clapped, didn't they?"

"They trembled, Michael."

"From what? From fear? Is that what's got hold of you, Leonard Perry? The hand of fear? Your ears so full of wax you didn't hear the magic in that ice song? Is that it? I hear magic, you hear danger? Because if that's what's bothering you, Lenny, then you can forget about it."

Michael stepped out of the shadows then. Pale as a ghost, but smiling just the same. His eyes were ice-like crystals, pupil-less blue-white orbs all clouded over so you couldn't see into them today the way you could the day before. I wanted to be able to see into those eyes. I wanted to be able to see what was behind them, because it couldn't have been Michael.

"It's not evil," he said, his cold breath fogging that warm August air as if he were standing outside on a mid-winter's day. "Honest, Lenny. It's not like that at all."

He reached a hand—all powdery white and icy cold—out to me.

I took a step back.

"It's more like a sleepless dream." He coughed again, spewed out a cold white cloud that nearly bent him in half. When he straightened up, his face was like a mask, sculptured crystal, hollow and ghost-like. "Remember the full-mooned night the Miller cow gave birth to the two-headed calf? Remember in the back of the barn that night, under the eyes of that full moon, how we each drew blood and pressed our palms together because we knew, we just *knew* there was something magical about that night? Remember that, Lenny? Because that's the way it is in here."

(*in here?*)

His hand reached out again, further this time, and I knew if I took hold of that brittle icy skeleton it would break off in my hand.

I took another step back.

"Please, Lenny. We can share it. Just you and me."

"I can't," I said.

"But there's no one else, Lenny."

"I can't."

"Please?"

I backed into one of the garage door springs, felt the jagged edge of metal rip open the back of my shirt, then I stumbled a few steps before turning and breaking into a run.

"Lenny!"

All the way down the drive (dust kicking up with my heels) I kept glancing over my shoulder, expecting to see him there, floating right alongside me, sweating the same way that vaporous block of ice had sweat the day before. But he never moved from that dark corner of the garage, as if he knew he couldn't wander far from that Philco freezer.

"Brothers of the blood and the moon!" he yelled, but I never

Ice Songs

answered, because I couldn't be sure if it was Michael's voice calling after me or if it was one of those ice songs singing temptations to my heart instead of good sense to my brain.
Brothers of the blood and the moon, Lenny!

Michael died shortly after that.

I went by the Hollerman place the morning after Labor Day to visit, because I couldn't stay away. But it was too late by then.

Mrs. Hollerman answered the door. I guess she had done most of her crying by then. She didn't shed any tears while I was standing there on her porch, and I didn't notice the redness that comes from crying too much. But just the same, they were empty, those eyes of hers. Hollow and cavernous.

"Pneumonia," is the way she explained it at the time. I guess I could have asked for more. We both knew more than we were letting on.

I stopped by that old Philco freezer on my way back home, thinking if nothing else, maybe I could put an end to whatever in hell that block of ice was all about. The door was ajar, held open with the help of a short length of two-by-four. But the plug hadn't been pulled, there were chilly tendrils rising from the crack. When I looked inside, it was nearly empty. No sign of the vegetables Mrs. Hollerman liked to put up for the winter, or the meat Mr. Hollerman sometimes brought home from his hunting trips. Just a block of melting ice.

And suddenly I couldn't let it die.

It was a number of years later, when I returned to Cottonwood for a family reunion, that I met again with Mrs. Hollerman and she finally told me the truth about Michael's death.

"He came in late that night, after sundown," she said, her eyes faraway with the memory. We were sitting on her back porch, her in an old rocker, me on a nearby bench. Mr. Hollerman had died the year before, after a long bout with lung cancer.

"It wasn't like him," she was saying. "Coming home late, not saying a word, then hiding himself in his room. You knew him, Lenny. He was all full of fun and life, that boy."

Always running one step ahead, I thought.
"There was this music coming from his room . . ."
Ice songs, Mrs. Hollerman. You were hearing the ice songs.
"And it kind of pulled us along, Michael's father and me, up the stairs until we were standing right outside the boy's bedroom." Mrs. Hollerman stopped her rocker then, and she sat forward, elbows on knees, eyes still faraway. "The door opened by itself, Lenny. And there was Michael, standing in the middle of his room, glowing like one of those fluorescent necklaces they sell at the County Fair, and looking like something cut from a block of ice. All pale, he was. And his arms, they were outstretched the way Jesus always has His arms open to welcome in the lost.

"And Michael, his eyes all alight, said, 'I was the first, mom. I found it, I heard its icy song before the notes touched another human ear. Can you imagine it? Can you?'"

"There was this music playing somewhere, his *icy song* I suppose, and it was filling up the room with its noise. 'I love you!' he screamed. 'Don't ever forget that, mom. I love you!'

Mrs. Hollerman shuddered, her voice caught, and she sat back in her rocker again. "It wasn't pneumonia that took him, Lenny. It wasn't anything as natural as that.

"When Michael reached a hand out to me, I guess I couldn't resist taking hold. So bad was my wanting to pull him out of that room, away from that music, and into my bosom. But when our hands touched . . .

"He was so cold, so brittle and cold . . .

"He simply . . . *shattered* . . . like a dropped mirror, cracks running up his arm and down his body, head-to-toe, until he suddenly shattered into a thousand jumbled pieces with no sense at all to them.

"And I tried to piece them back together again.

"I tried."

Mrs. Hollerman buried her face in her hands then, and when she cried I thought they were the tears she had kept cooped-up inside her ever since that chilly summer night when Michael—as withered and brittle as a marrowless bone—had shattered with her embrace.

I cried with her.

Ice Songs

That was more than ten years ago, and I never told Mrs. Hollerman that Michael still came to visit me. On hot August nights, he comes. Still icy-cold. Still looking eleven years old, coughing out a white vapory mist. And he always asks the same question, "Hear it, Lenny? Can you hear it? Singing like the Christ Our Savior Choir on Sunday mornings, a thousand voices all happening at once! Enough to send a chill right through you!" Then he smiles a smile that says, *It's not too late, Lenny*, and he reaches out a wax-like hand, and I hear him say, *brothers of the blood and moon, Lenny*, because that's what we were supposed to be, Michael and me, and I catch myself wondering if the ice song is a death song or a life song or a song from some other "side", some *inside*, and what it would be like to be *inside* there with him, and I fight against that part of me that's curious enough to want to know, the same as I fought against it twenty-some years ago.

(*but maybe no longer*)

I want to hear angels instead of air bubbles, I want to know what it's like to feel excitement burning in my veins like hot cinnamon blood, like Michael always felt—(*still feels*)—because even a death song is better than no song at all, Michael knows that, no one could know better, and he's the only one who knows if the ice song I heard yesterday, pouring out of that chunk of ice I saved from a melting death on Labor Day 1961 is the same cold song that sung to him with a voice like the Christ Our Savior Choir . . . it's the song I imagined, the same song I've heard in my head a thousand times since, and if I *really* heard it yesterday . . . then maybe it means it's my turn . . . and maybe when Michael reaches out for me tomorrow night, saying, *Can you hear it, Lenny?* saying, *brothers of the blood and moon, Lenny?* maybe if I take hold of that wax-like hand of his, maybe then the laughter will come back to me, like when we were eleven, and we used to play baseball in the pasture out behind the Hollerman house.

Because the laughter died after that day.

Because I Could

1

I turned fourteen in 1970. My parents separated that year, in late August, and after a bout with emphysema and a stroke, Grandpa Myles died in bed. I remember that year for both of those reasons, though one more than the other, because it's the one that won't let me forget.

We lived in the north state where the biggest event of the year was the annual County Fair Demolition Derby at Three Gates Park on the other side of the river. My grandfather took me there once, when I was eight or nine years old. I got sick on cotton candy and threw up on an elderly woman who was sitting next to me in the grandstands. That was the last time we ever went to the Derby together. Grandpa Myles never took me back.

Doesn't matter, I guess.
That was a long, long time ago.
I just wish it would let me be.

2

My earliest memory of Grandpa Myles was at a dime store called The Depot which sat at the edge of town, just before you hit pasture. Kids liked to hang out there after school, maybe read the newest Superman, maybe toss around a Frisbee in the parking lot. Most of the time, they just liked to hang out.

Grandpa Myles stopped there to pick up some groceries on the way out to Aunt Trudy's place for Sunday supper. I was with him because Mom and Dad had gone down the state to attend a wedding. I was eight years old, and it was the first time I had ever been alone with my grandfather. It was also the first of two trips to my Aunt's house that I'll never forget. The reason for that being this: it was the day I realized I wasn't alone in what I could do.

"You stay put," he said as he climbed out of the Corvair. He slammed the door, then leaned in through the open window to say something else. He had just started wearing glasses with gold, wire-rim frames that appeared to trim an inch or two off the width of his face. He hadn't shaved that morning, or the morning or two before, and the stubble that had shown up was silvery-gray and white and patchy in places. "I'll be right back, so don't go tootin' the horn or playing with the brake, you hear?"

"I won't."

When he returned, he pulled an Eskimo Pie out of the bag of groceries, handed it to me, then thought better of it. "No, you better let me fix that for you."

I let him take it back. He tore off the wrapper, fashioned it into a paper cone, then pushed the ice cream stick through the bottom. Before he handed it back to me, he stole a bite out of one corner.

"There you go," he said with a grin.

His voice had changed recently. Mom and Dad had both commented on it after hanging up the phone the last time they had talked to him. The sounds he made came from somewhere deep in his throat, peppered and incredibly low. I didn't know it at the time—I don't think he did either—but eventually the doctors would tell him the huskiness in his voice was an early symptom of the emphysema.

Because I could

"What do you say?"

"Thank you."

"You're welcome, Lee. You're mighty welcome."

Aunt Trudy's place was a thirty mile drive. You could make it in twenty-five minutes if you took Deschutes and missed the after school rush at the middle school in Palo Cedro. After that, it was pasture north and south, then foothills and scrub oak, and finally—in some magnificent whim of Mother Nature—you were traveling through miles and miles of pines and cedars and giant white oaks.

I don't remember how long it took us to get there, but it didn't seem long at all. Not like the usual trip, with Dad driving and Mom sitting next to him in the front seat, staring out the window, occasionally engaging in short snippets of conversation when it seemed unavoidable.

Grandpa Myles wasn't much of a talker either, I decided. After we had left The Depot, he had grown quiet, staring off into the horizon, driving on automatic, like he had something on his mind that he wanted to share but just didn't quite know how to go about it.

Over the years, he had learned to keep his secrets.

I understand that now.

I tried to sneak a borrow—the only word I knew at the time that seemed to say what it was I did . . . sort of like borrowing his thoughts for a moment—but all I came away with was a lonely feeling, like the way I sometimes felt when it was raining outside and I had to stay in the house.

(Later, near dusk, when we were sitting on the back porch of Aunt Trudy's, just the two of us, he said, "Some things aren't for sharing, Lee. You understand that? Everyone has his secrets. You hold yours close to you, and you stay away from those that belong to someone else." He looked at me. "Is that something an eight-year-old boy can understand?" I nodded, understanding only a little, but thinking back to how I had tried borrowing from him, and feeling ashamed.)

I finished my Eskimo Pie, did the stick up tight and proper in the wrapper, and placed it in the ashtray. We were approaching the foothills now, near the slight incline where brown grass gradually gave way to sparse patches of green foliage.

David B. Silva

Coming the other way, I watched a logging truck accelerate out of the bend at the bottom of the foothills. A blue International. He was hauling a full load of Monterey pine, a familiar sight this time of year. The truck blew past us. A gust of warm summer air whistled through the windows.

I closed my eyes, feeling the warm, peaceful breath against my face, and suddenly the borrow I had tried to pull out of my grandfather just a few miles back was playing inside my head:

It's night, the sky crisp and clear, stars shimmering across a long stretch of railroad track. Grandpa Myles is up ahead, standing at the side of the track, a dimly-lit lantern on the ground next to him. In the shallow sphere of the light, I can see the dim outline of another man. He's kneeling, in the middle of the tracks, struggling to get his pants leg loose from a tie.

"Myles, you can't leave me here like this."

"That's the thing, you see, I can."

"But why?"

"Because . . . it's a good time, a good place."

In the distance, a rumbling sound rises out of the still night,

"Time to be on my way, Larry."

"Jesus, Myles, please . . ."

The whistling wind died away. I opened my eyes. Across the seat from me, Grandpa Myles had both hands wrapped tightly around the steering wheel, as if he were trying to hold onto something—anything—that was solid and real. I stared at him, overwhelmed, realizing he had shared something with me that I only partially understood, and knowing without a doubt I would never be able to forget the face of the man I had seen struggling on the tracks. It had been the face of someone who knew he was about to die.

I gazed at my grandfather for a long time, then asked the only question I could think to ask, "Why?"

"You and me, we have a gift," he said softly, a slight tremor in his voice. He still hadn't managed to unlock his hands from the steering wheel; the knuckles had turned nearly white. "You see things, don't you? You close your eyes sometimes, and . . . and you just see things."

I nodded uneasily.

"What's that word you like to use?"

"Borrow."

"Yeah," he said, as if it was a good word for him too. "You close your eyes, and you borrow a look, don't you, Lee? Right inside a person's head."

I didn't say anything.

"But that's not the all of it, I bet. 'Cause if you're anything like me—and I'm betting my life you are—sometimes you can even make things . . . happen. Can't you, my boy? Like moving the cereal box across the table when you don't feel like reaching for it."

"The man on the tracks?" I asked.

"His name was Johnson, Larry Johnson. He worked as a photographer for the Office of War Information . . . it doesn't matter. It was a long time ago, and some things . . . well, they're over the heads of little boys. He wasn't a bad man, but he wasn't a good man either. That's all little boys need to know. Even special boys like you."

"Did he die?"

"Yes."

I fell silent, distantly aware of what it meant when you died. It was something bad, and it lasted forever. That was as much as I needed to know.

"I'm not proud of it," Grandpa Myles said. He looked at me, his eyes dark, his shoulders slumped, as if the weight of what he had done had grown heavier over the years. "It happened during the war, when I was working as a brakeman for the Southern Pacific. We were hauling oil, came up on a broken rail late one night, and this guy Johnson, who was supposed to be snapping off PR photographs . . . him and I . . . we'd had a little too much to drink. I don't even remember what the argument was about. All's I remember is walking along the tracks with him, thinking how much I'd like to tie him down till the next train came along . . ."

My grandfather went into a short coughing jag then, finally tearing one hand away from the steering wheel long enough to cover his mouth. When he was done, his eyes were watery, and his voice had a new huskiness about it.

"That night, I guess I thought about it a little too much," he said solemnly. "It never should have happened. I lost control and a man died."

He looked at me again, his eyes not quite as dark as they had appeared before. "Am I scaring you with this?"

I was scared. Scared and fascinated and curious, all wound together like a tightly-coiled spring. I told him no, though. Sometimes it's just too hard to tell the truth.

"The only reason I'm telling you this, Lee, is because you and me . . . we're two of a kind, you know. Sometimes it gets lonely, knowing you got a secret you can't tell anyone. It's like having a million dollars buried in the backyard, but you can't spend it 'cause you had to rob a bank to get it. You might live a whole lifetime without ever getting a chance to share that kind of a secret with someone. You understand?"

I nodded.

"There aren't many folks in the world who can . . . borrow the way you and me can, Lee. I don't want to scare you. But at the same time, I want you to know you aren't the only one."

We drove in silence for a long time after that, Grandpa Myles with his eyes on the road, me staring out the window. Finally, he said, "There's something else you should know. That night, when Johnson died ..."

I looked at him.

"Something happened to me that night. I guess some might call it guilt, but it was more than that. It was like . . . you ever see black smoke shooting out the stack of a steam engine? Like that. A black cloud that started growing inside me. It's been growing inside me ever since, Lee." He looked across the seat at me, his face emotionless except for his eyes, which were as frightened as any eyes I had ever seen. "I think it's killing me," he said.

There are a lot of things you don't understand when you're eight years old. But one thing you've already learned by then is that it's better to say nothing when you're in over your head. I turned my attention back to the scenery, watching the landscape slide by, wondering what he had meant about the black cloud growing inside him. I'd had a headache once that felt like that.

When we drove down the gravel road to Aunt Trudy's place, he looked across the seat at me again, studying me. "Our secret?"

"Yeah," I said, knowing it was a secret I had already been keeping. Only now the secret was a little larger. And he had been right: there weren't that many people in the world who could borrow the way him and I could.

I've never met another one.

3

I always thought I'd remember Grandpa Myles as the old brakeman who took me down to the railyards on warm summer afternoons to watch the trains roll in from the south. On those rare occasions when a steam locomotive came through, he almost always slipped into some sort of foggy recollection of years gone by. "That's an Alco," he'd say. "Manufactured by the American Locomotive Company. One of the best ever made. You don't see those anymore. Not since the diesels came along."

He would sigh then, his eyes dull, looking like someone who was happiest when reliving old memories. Those favored years had passed him a long time ago. But for Grandpa Myles, his best friends would always be the railroad, the war, and the steam engines.

Some six years later, in early 1970, my grandfather suffered a stroke that forced him to move in with Aunt Trudy. ("Where I can keep an eye on the old coot," she'd say in good humor.) The stroke left him partially paralyzed on the left side of his body, with almost no feeling in his arm and leg. It took months before he finally regained movement in his hand and the left side of his face. In the end, though, after all the improvement had run its course, his left arm continued to dangle uselessly at his side, and the only way he was able to get around was by dragging his leg behind him.

He refused a cane or a walker. Instead, he would lean his weight against the wall, or the back of a chair, or whatever happened to be handy that might support him. I guess I couldn't blame him for that (though Aunt Trudy certainly found it a nuisance having to walk every step with him just in case he tipped a little too far to one side). It was a difficult time for everyone in the family. This was a man who used to work on the railroad, who used to travel across the south on mighty steam engines hauling oil for the war effort, who used to drink until dawn in little out of the way bars in out of the way towns. Back then, he had been a free man. Now, suddenly, he had become a burden.

4

My last visit with Grandpa Myles came near the end of 1970. It was a Sunday afternoon, in the middle of the school year. Mom had decided to take what had become a rare trip up to Aunt Trudy's for a visit. It was the second trip to my Aunt's house that would forever stand out in my mind.

Some things . . . you don't deserve to forget.

My parents had officially separated during the latter part of the summer. Unofficially, I suppose they had been separated for the better part of my life. It had been sorely overdue—their parting of the ways. I ended up living with my mother because she insisted while my father remained silent. Then in early October my father had headed south to the Bay Area to live. "To escape the line of fire" was the way he put it before he said goodbye for the last time.

It surprised me when I realized how much I missed him.

And seeing Grandpa Myles again . . . that was a surprise of a different nature, I suppose. Though it felt much the same.

I'm not sure what I had expected to find. On the way to Aunt Trudy's my mother made a somewhat clumsy attempt at preparing me. "Sometimes," she said, her eyes straight ahead, keeping a safe distance, "when you're old like your Grandfather is . . . well, time catches up with you." Then she told me how his health had been failing the past few weeks. He had never fully recovered from the stroke, of course. And I had witnessed what I had thought was his emphysema over the years, stealing a little of his strength here, a little more of his breath there. But when I had last seen him, he had been a different man.

I remember standing in the doorway of his bedroom, staring. Someone had propped him up in bed—using three or four pillows to do it—and he looked almost . . . breakable. He had lost weight, at least forty or fifty pounds. Pounds he could hardly afford to lose. There was the sour smell of urine in the air. The lower half of his face was hidden behind an oxygen mask, but his cheeks were pasty and damp, almost surreal, the cheeks of an aged mannequin.

"Lee."

"Hi, Grandpa."

He motioned me further into the room, his frail fingers making an effort out of the motion. The nails of his left hand had all turned black.

I took two or three steps, then stopped and leaned against the wall. This was as close as I wanted to get, because I already had a pretty good idea of what was happening just across the room from me. "You're dying, aren't you?"

He nodded, taking a long swallow of oxygen—the mask over his face seemed to make the effort more troublesome for him. Then he spoke again, the words leaking out of him, breathy and asthmatic. "I've run . . . out of . . . steam," he said, almost smiling.

"Does it hurt?"

"Feels . . . heavy."

Next to the bed, someone had strapped the oxygen tank to a handcart; a plastic tube ran from the tank to his mask. Above that, an IV had been hung from a metal stand; another tube ran from there to somewhere beneath the blankets. A plastic bag had been mounted on the side of the bed, fed by yet another tube, this one from a hidden catheter.

It looked horrible.

And I realized then that I had gone to Aunt Trudy's with the faint hope of finding the man who had—all those years ago—let me borrow from him, who had told me stories about steam engines and the war, who had later let me follow him down to the railyard. I needed that

David B. Silva

man. He was the last anchor on a drifting ship. But as I stood there, leaning against the wall, afraid to move any closer, I felt betrayed. It had suddenly occurred to me that Grandpa Myles wasn't much different than my father. They were both men trying to "escape the line of fire." They had simply gone about it in different ways.

Grandpa Myles was going away, and he was never coming back.

I don't know how long I stood there in silence before my mother came through the door behind me. She glanced without warmth or concern at Grandpa Myles, smiled without emotion, and said a weak hello. Then she turned to me. "Your Aunt and I are going into town to pick up some groceries. Someone needs to stay here with your Grandfather. You mind?"

I looked at him, seeing a man who reminded me of that other man, Johnson, who had been so completely aware that he was going to die soon.

"Lee?"

"I'll stay with him."

Grandpa Myles closed his eyes, and I listened as my mother and Aunt Trudy gathered up their coats and purses. His breathing had become shallow, almost peaceful. I wondered if he was aware of what was going on around him.

"We're leaving now."

"Have a good time," I said.

Faraway, the front door closed.

Grandpa Myles opened his eyes again. Over the rim of the oxygen mask, he looked at me, tired yet focused. A dull ache rose up inside my head. I saw a splash of black, a sprinkle of white, then felt him make an effort to borrow from me. Only he was sending, not borrowing.

"What are you doing?"

I want you to understand, he whispered in my head. *I want you to understand what it's like.*

"To be dying?"

Yes.

"Tell me."

He closed his eyes again, peacefully this time, as if he might never open them again. And in my head, he said, *I'm not . . . afraid,*

Because I could

Lee. Not of death. I want you to know that. It's the blackness that scares me. He swallowed up another deep breath and surprised me as much by what he didn't say as what he did. I had expected him to tell me how godawful it was to be attached to the network of tubes that fed him and pissed for him and breathed for him. Instead, through both bitterness and fear, he said, *It's been at it a long time, Lee. Since that night on the railroad tracks. Growing inside me like a black cancer. It's not emphysema, Lee. And it wasn't a stroke. I guess you could say it's the price you pay.*

When he looked up, his eyes were shining with tears.

I took a deep breath. He didn't need to say anything more, I knew what he wanted.

I suppose if I had had to do it by hand, if I had had to pinch off his oxygen tube with my own fingers, I couldn't have done it. But I was lucky—if you could call it that—because I had a touch of a different sort. I only wish I had understood what he had tried to tell me.

It was, in fact, easier than I care to admit, easier than I ever would have imagined. That was the part that scared me the most that afternoon. How easy I made it seem.

I focused on the plastic tube running from the tank to his mask, and in a matter of a few seconds, it collapsed in the middle.

The air stopped flowing.

I guess I thought it would be peaceful. And at first, it was. Grandpa Myles nodded to me, gratefully it seemed, then closed his eyes once more.

There was a moment when it seemed as if it was all over.

Then his body went into a sudden, violent throe. He grabbed for the oxygen mask with his right hand, struggling to pull in another breath, the effort both courageous and strangely ineffective.

Lee?

Please, Lee, I was wrong.

"No you weren't," I whispered. "You were right."

Please, he said inside my head.

Something aloof and emotionless had settled over me like a fugue. I couldn't stop. I didn't care.

He opened his mouth wide, and I heard a faint, faraway gasp as he struggled for another breath. The sound slowly trailed away. His mouth went slack. And he closed his eyes one last time.

The voice inside my head grew faint, then disappeared altogether.

5

Everyone has his secrets, my grandfather had told me. You hold yours close to you, and you stay away from those that belong to someone else.

This was my big secret.

I stood there, leaning against the wall, staring at him, for I don't know how long. I remember crying. It had been so unreal, I had half-expected him to open his eyes again, to look at me and smile and start talking about the old Alcos. Instead, the room turned bitterly cold, and I cried.

I didn't kill him to save him from suffering. I killed him because I could, and because he was going to leave me anyway, and because at that moment I lost control and didn't think it would make any difference.

But it did.

That afternoon, something thick and black was given birth inside me. My grandfather had described it as being like black smoke shooting out of the stack of a steam engine. I hadn't understood him then. I'm not sure I fully understand even now. Only that it's not like black smoke from a steam engine. It's more like a hole that starts out the size of a pinhead and slowly, methodically devours everything healthy and decent in a person.

They did an autopsy on Grandpa Myles. Eventually, without my assistance, he would have died his own death. His organs had all turned black, had all begun to harden. The medical examiner said he had never seen anything like it. Even the man's arteries had taken on a grayish-black discoloration.

Call it guilt, if you want. Call it justice. I guess you could call it the price you pay. It doesn't really matter.

There aren't many people in the world like my grandfather and me.

Maybe that's a good thing.

Alone of His Kind

All of them strangers.
For some reason, Foss hadn't prepared himself with the idea of meeting strangers. Now that he was standing inside the doorway, though, he realized that was exactly what had brought him to the soup kitchen. Not just a chance to get out of the apartment again, but a chance to re-introduce himself back into the company of other people. After Ellie had died, because he didn't think he could stand being in bed without her next to him, he had slept on the living room couch for nearly six months. Now, he was trying to find out if he could stand being back in public without her.

A woman, with a baby in one arm and a dirty-faced six year old boy hanging on the tail of her sweater, opened the door behind him. Foss moved to one side, pulling the collar of his coat tighter around his neck. An angry gust of cold January wind ushered her through. For the briefest of moments, he shared a glance with her, two lost souls, neither able to conceal the desperation that brought a person to a place like this. It was a straight-in-the-eye moment. Her pupils were pure black marbles, no peaceful dreams behind them, no promising tomorrows. But neither were there any visible regrets. She tried to smile, though it looked painful on her face, then she hoisted the baby higher in her arms and started toward the serving counter at other end of the room.

Foss closed the door. Without another thought—he was here now, there wasn't much sense in turning around and leaving—he fell in line behind the woman and her two kids. The dining hall was a long, narrow room, lined on both sides with row after row of empty cafeteria-style tables. The walls were papered with an endless gallery of flyers and posters that had been taped and stapled to the plaster, a giant bulletin board of information on government and private services, even the local Bingo night at the Grace Baptist Church on the corner of Fourth and Saint Thomas. Not the kind of place where a person came if he had another choice.

In a corner near the front door—where the fluorescent lighting fell short and it was dim around the edges—Foss managed to find a table to himself. He settled in there, with a plate of hot beef stew, and watched the steady line of new faces come wandering through the door, half-frozen and twisted with hunger, until eventually the faces all started to look alike to him. After awhile, he quit glancing up when he heard the door open. It was easier than admitting he didn't care. Or he couldn't care. Since Ellie's death, it was hard to tell the difference.

"Any papers?"

Foss looked up from his plate, startled, and encountered a man in his late thirties, early forties, about the same age as nearly everyone else who had come through the front door this evening. He was bundled up for the winter weather, wearing an over-sized pea coat with the collar up above the tips of his ears, black gloves, heavy boots, a Giants baseball cap. It wasn't until he quit leaning against the table and stood straight up that Foss noticed one arm was easily six inches shorter than the other.

"Huh?"

"Newspapers? You have any newspapers?"

"No," Foss answered. "I'm sorry."

"No reason to be sorry." The man started away, dragging his right foot behind him; and it was at the same instant that Foss realized one leg was shorter than the other, that the man stopped and turned around. "You do read, though, don't you?"

"Not the newspaper."

"Too depressing?"

"Sometimes."

"That's why I quit reading them." He motioned to the empty chair across the table from Foss. "Mind if I join you?"

"No. Go ahead."

"Name's Jas." He pulled the chair out, sat down, and reached out with his misshapen limb to shake hands. "First time you've been in here, isn't it?"

Foss froze, staring uneasily at the stranger's hand. The fingers were fat and stubby, little dwarf fingers, about the size of Vienna sausages. He was frightened by the thought of shaking that hand, afraid that he might somehow make it worse than it already was. "Herb Foss," he said finally. The handshake was quick and frail.

"First time, right?"

"Right."

"Thought so. The food any good?"

Foss shrugged. "It's a little like eating at a school cafeteria."

Jas smiled. "I never take a meal here. The stuff can kill you."

Foss glanced down at his plate. There was a layer of coagulating fat already beginning to take shape across the top of the beef stew. *When the man speaks the truth . . .* He pushed the food discreetly aside. "If you aren't here for the food, then what are you doing here?"

"Papers. I'm collecting papers."

"Thought you didn't read?"

"They aren't for reading."

The woman who had come in right after Foss, went by on her way out. The baby in her arms was on the verge of falling asleep, but the little boy was slapping each table he passed with the palm of his hand, full of renewed energy now that his stomach was full. She seemed mechanical in the way she moved, completely unaware of the world around her. When she opened the door, another gust of wind blew in. Then she was gone.

"What about you?" Jas asked.

"Huh?"

"What are you doing here? It can't be the food."

"No, it's not the food." Foss stared at the door a moment longer, wondering briefly if the woman had a husband, where she stayed at night, what kinds of childhood memories her children would have when they were grown. Loneliness was scary no matter what form it came wrapped in, no matter how you chose to wear it. "Just feeling sorry for myself, I guess."

"Nothing wrong with that."

Briefly, his mind wandered off to Ellie. It was nearly impossible to remember her before the cancer had hollowed out her body. When he closed his eyes, he saw sunken cheeks and pencil-thin fingers and eyes nearly submerged in their sockets. Thank God she had never stopped smiling. That was one feature the cancer had failed to wipe from his memory.

"... lost someone close to you, didn't you?"

"I'm sorry. What?"

"I said, I bet you recently lost someone close to you."

Something deep inside Foss let out a long-held sigh of relief, and he tried a smile that didn't feel right. "It shows?"

"Enough."

"My wife," he said quietly. "I lost my wife." Then he buried his face in his hands, because it was all right there again, right on the surface, as brutal as the day she had died. It took a deep breath to bring him back under control. Then a heavy silence slowly floated down around the two men. The surrounding pandemonium faded further and further into the background, like a scene from a movie. When it was done, they were the only two people left in a world where everyone else was too busy.

Foss used his dinner napkin to wipe his face.

He took another deep breath. "God, I miss her."

"I lost a daughter," Jas said quietly. His voice had the sound of a far-away echo. For a moment, his gaze had drifted off to the other end of the room, then he stared down at the Styrofoam cup Foss was holding in his hands, as if the words were safer spoken to something inanimate. "In an automobile accident when she was eight. Her name was Purdy."

"We never had kids," Foss said.

Alone of His Kind

Jas smiled, mostly to himself. "You missed something special," he said softly. "Kids have a way of reminding you what it's like to be alive. It's too easy to forget, otherwise."

An old man, carrying a battered suitcase, came through the front door. He stood there a moment, soaking up the warmth, before finally moving to the serving counter at the far end of the room.

Jas watched him walk by, then turned to Foss again. "It still hurts. It'll be four years, Christmas Eve, and it hurts like it was yesterday. I wish I could tell you something different."

"I wouldn't believe you if you did."

"Maybe not. But you'd want to."

One of the volunteers finally had to ask them to leave. They had talked—on and off between periods of quiet reverie—for nearly two hours. It was 7:30 now. The evening temperature had dropped ten to fifteen degrees since Foss had first arrived. It was cold enough for the first snow of the season now.

Foss took a deep breath. Behind him, the fluorescent lights inside the dining hall went off. The entire city block seemed suddenly darker. "Getting late," he said, blowing warm air into his cupped hands. "Maybe I should be going."

"Which way you heading?"

"Seventh Street."

"I'm heading that way, if you don't mind?"

"Not at all."

The street, cast beneath a veil of grayish-black shadows, was shouldered by a series of abandoned store fronts, their plate-glass windows boarded over, their walls spray-painted red and orange and black with graffiti. A month's worth of garbage had collected in the gutters, some of it rotting and infested. Two blocks up, the northwest corner of a neglected tenement building had begun to crumble, dusting the sidewalk with the thin, grayish-red color of brick and mortar. Not many vehicles found their way down here, not this deep into the underbelly of the city.

They crossed the street, toward a broken street light, Jas limping more noticeably now.

"You never told me," Foss finally said.

"What?"

"About your leg."

"Oh." Jas glanced down, giving his limb a quick, cursory look. "I was born this way. Part of the Thalidomide generation."

"Sorry."

"Hey, it's not a tragedy," Jas said blithely. "You don't miss what you've never had. I was born this way. I learned how to make do from early on."

"Must have been hard when you were a kid."

"Because of the other kids?"

"Yeah."

"It didn't matter once they got to know me."

They had finally arrived at a well-lit corner, Seventh Street still several blocks ahead. Jas stopped next to a Community Savings Bank that had gone out of business a couple of years earlier. He leaned against the red-brick building, staring quietly off into the darkness of the side street, as if he were saddened by a moment that had arrived too soon. "'Fraid this is where we part company, my friend."

"As far as you go?"

"'Fraid so." He nodded over his shoulder toward the side street, where the black of night had thickly gathered. "I'm about half a block from here."

"Oh . . . well then . . ."

Jas grinned. "I've got a bottle, if you'd like to share a nip."

"I don't drink."

"Probably better for you."

"I just never acquired a taste. Neither did Ellie."

"A cup of coffee?"

Foss stared down the street, feeling cold for the first time, and remembering how cold and empty the apartment had felt since his wife had died. "Hell, I ain't got anywhere to go but home."

"Good."

Half-a-block down, they stopped outside a tenement building that still had the scars of a recent fire. Half-inch sheets of plywood had been nailed across the front entrance and the only two windows on the first floor. Someone from the city's Public Safety Department had tied a bright yellow banner across the face of the doorway, the word CONDEMNED repeated in inch-high black letters from one end to the next, just in case some poor near-sighted soul might stumble by.

"This is it."

"You're kidding."

"I knew you'd like it." He waved his Thalidomide arm in the air. "You can't get in through the front, we have to go around back."

Foss couldn't bring himself to move. "The building's condemned, for Christ's sake."

"No noisy neighbors that way."

They passed through a narrow alleyway along the right side of the building, and ended up climbing in a basement window that opened horizontally after Jas gave it a little shove with the palm of his hand. Jas crawled through the window first, into the dusky underworld.

"Careful," he said.

Foss followed, stepping down atop a crate of some sort, then down again until he was standing on a cement slab floor. There was the strong odor of smoke in the air. From somewhere outside, a diffused cast of light cut a rectangular swath across the basement floor, though it was difficult to define the shape and orientation of the room. Now that he was inside, it felt a little like trying to find your way to the bathroom in a strange house at two in the morning.

"This way." Jas nudged him in the direction of a stairwell. As they began to climb, their footsteps echoed back a hollow, lonely sound that seemed to come from half-a-landing above, sounding as if someone else might be crazy enough to be inside this burnt-out shell of a building. That wasn't true, though. There were only two crazy men here, and Foss caught himself wondering if this wasn't the dumbest thing he'd ever done.

"You really live here?"

"Nearly four months now."

"What about your wife?"

"Jean? We split up after Purdy died. She said every time she looked at me, she saw Purdy, and the pain started all over again. It took a heavy toll on both of us, I guess. Jean finally moved to the Midwest somewhere. I heard she remarried." Three steps ahead, Jas suddenly stopped and turned around, his face cast in shadows too dark to see. "I missed her, but I learned to live without her. Purdy was a different story, though. I've never stopped hoping that somehow she would come back again."

Another landing popped up.

"Fifth floor," Jas said flatly. "It's right down the hallway here."

They stopped at the third door on the right. The frame had been blackened by fire, but the door appeared solid and in one piece. A taut, rusty bicycle chain had been wrapped around the knob and padlocked to a solid steel bar wedged between the wall and the floorboards. Jas fished around in his pocket, pulled out a key.

"You're kidding. You really keep a lock on this place? In this building? You worried someone might break in and steal something?"

"Everything I own is in here."

The door swung half-open and struck something. There was a nearly-pure absence of light on the other side, but Foss thought he could make out the faint outline of a row of boxes stacked floor-to-ceiling.

"Just a minute." Jas disappeared inside, then suddenly a light kicked on. "I broke the seal on the meter box. It'll be months before the power company figures it out. No one pays much attention to a building once it's been condemned. Come on in."

At first glance, the room appeared no larger than a narrow entryway. There were boxes rising from floor to ceiling on either side of the doorway. But on second glance, after his eyes had had a chance to adjust to the sudden brightness, Foss realized they weren't boxes at all. They were tall stacks of newspapers.

"There's nothing to be afraid of."

"I know. I'm not afraid."

"Then come in. The living room's through here."

He led Foss under an archway of magazines and paperback books, newspapers and packing materials. The apartment was a labyrinth of man-made tunnels—seemingly mindless tunnels—and Foss slowly realized this wasn't the kind of place where you found your way out again. Once here, if you wanted to visit the outside world again, someone was going to have to point you in the right direction, someone was going to have to offer you a way out. Otherwise . . .

"Do a lot of reading?" he asked, to free his mind.

Jas smiled as they rounded a stack of Look magazines. "I'm not a reader; I'm a collector."

They passed beneath another archway—this one made from old *TV Guides*—rounded a corner, and at last they were standing in the living room. On one side, a niche had been carved out of the stacks to make space for a well-worn sofa, the stuffing showing through small rips in both armrests. On the opposite side, the room was lined with Georgian sash windows that looked out on the street below.

Jas motioned for him to have a seat, then leaned back against a waist-high pile of newspapers that were double-strapped with twine. Behind him, a dim light filtered through the windows, mingling with the stir of dust.

"Why did you invite me here, Jas?"

"Because you were hurting. Because we're two of a kind." He glanced out one of the windows, staring safely up the street. "Because I wanted to show you something."

"What?"

"Purdy," he whispered, off somewhere faraway. "I wanted to show you Purdy."

"I thought you said she was dead."

Outside, a car rolled slowly down the street, its engine the only sound in the air.

"When I told you there wasn't anything special about being a Thalidomide baby, I lied. The loneliest thing in the world when you're a kid is being different."

"We're all different."

He held his arm in the air, as if it were the work of the Devil. "Not like this, we aren't. This is the first thing people see. It's like a flashing neon sign: *freak!*"

"You're not a freak, Jas."

Momentarily, he seemed stunned, as if he might cry. Then he closed his eyes, took a breath, and stared up the street again, following the sound of the car as it faded off into the distance. "As far back as I can remember, the only time in my life when I wasn't lonely was when I was with Purdy."

Foss's mind turned to Ellie.

"That's the way it was with you, too, wasn't it? Your wife was the only person in the world who could make you feel like you were alive."

He stared at him, unable to say anything.

"Wasn't it?"

"I suppose."

"And if you could have her back?"

"I can't."

"But if you could?"

"I don't know."

"Yes, you do. You'd take her back in a second." Jas stood up, his body a gray-white silhouette against the window, and it wasn't the shrunken arm or the short leg which Foss immediately noticed; it was the way the man stood, as if he had suddenly *overcome*. "I want to show you something," he said, the sound of excitement creeping in his voice.

"It's getting late, Jas. I really should be on my way."

The man waved a hand at him and started across the room toward the far corner, still dragging his right leg heavily behind him, almost—but not quite—like a caricature of a man dragging a ball and chain. "The empty apartment can wait a while longer, can't it?" He stopped somewhere just beyond the outer edge of the light, his upper body disappearing out of sight as he bent over another stack of old newspapers and brought something out from the darkened corner. He tossed the object across the room at Foss, who caught it with both hands.

Foss sat forward on the edge of the sofa. "A papier-mâché arm?" he said, turning it over in his hands. It was made from newsprint, the paper soft and pliable, the core hollow. "So what's your point?"

"Look again."

"I've seen it. So what?"

"Take another look."

Foss stared sharply at the man, thinking: *I'm crazy for being here, crazy for staying this long.*

Jas returned the stare with his own brand of firmness. "If I had to offer an explanation, I'd say it has something to do with emotion. At least that has a measure of possibility. A kid with Thalidomide limbs, he knows he'll always be different, and he knows there's nothing he can do about it. But every morning of his life he wakes up hungering to be like the rest of the kids; and a hundred thousand times he breathes that hunger in and out of his system until finally, years later . . . in some mysterious, inexplicable way . . ."

"It happens?"

"Look again."

When Foss arrived home that night, he closed the door behind him, locked it, then leaned heavily against the wood frame. The apartment was cast in black, a single line of yellow-orange light seeping in through a crack in the living room drapes. The blood was still pounding behind his temples.

Maybe it had moved, maybe it hadn't.

The mind can play tricks on you if you aren't careful.

Foss thought he saw it move. He thought he saw each finger—one right after the other—slowly curl into a fist, then unfold again. A reasonable man, though, after a few hours of reflection, might argue that he had simply been caught up in the moment. Jas had spent several hours with him, planting possibilities in his head, and he had—quite innocently—let himself believe. Yet, reasonable man or not, it was fresh in his mind, the crystal clear picture of that papier-mâché hand closing into a fist.

He flipped on the light switch next to the door, and a lamp in the corner of the living room came silently on, casting a soft-white glow across the room. On the end table, next to the couch, there was a studio photograph of Ellie and him, taken three years ago after she had nagged at him for nearly a month to have it taken. *It won't hurt you to dress up for a couple of hours.* He had finally given in, donning his only suit, a brown tweed that made him look fifteen pounds heavier. Ellie wore a crepe dress with a lace bodice overlay. She was absolutely stunning.

I miss you, El.

His mind drifted back to the papier-mâché hand.

It was a long time before he was able to pull his thoughts out of that scorched tenement living room again, away from the stacks of newspapers and old magazines, back to his own apartment. He hung his coat in the entryway closet. On his way to the kitchen, he stopped and placed Ellie's photograph face down on the end table. Then he fixed himself a can of Vegetable Vegetarian soup, took a shower, and headed off to bed.

Jas was in his dreams, waving an arm in the air as if it were an American flag on the Fourth of July. *A kid with Thalidomide limbs, he knows he'll always be different, and he knows there's nothing he can do about it. But every morning of his life he wakes up hungering to be like the rest of the kids: and a hundred thousand times he breathes that hunger in and out of his system until finally. years later . . . in some mysterious. inexplicable way . . .* "Pay attention, Fossy." His shirt sleeve was rolled up above the elbow, exposing an underpinning of elastic straps which held the arm and hand in place. He unfastened a single strap, letting it dangle from his arm as if it were an eviscerated artery. Then another strap. And another. Until, suspended at an impossible angle, the limb had taken on the almost-surreal appearance of a broken arm. With a twist, he snapped it off altogether and held it in the air over his head. The fingers, like nightcrawlers exposed to sunlight, were squirming for their lives. "Need a helping hand?" He tossed the limb across the room. Foss caught it somehow, the fingers still struggling to grip the air, as if they were trying to play an invisible piano, and he screamed . . .

He managed to sleep through the dream, though he woke up exhausted the next morning, and while getting dressed—as he slipped his right hand through his shirt sleeve—it came back to him like the aftershock of an earthquake, more vivid than the original dream.

For three days, he never left the apartment.

Three weeks later, nearly a foot of snow had fallen.

It had begun to snow again the evening Foss returned to the burntout tenement building. He stood across the street, leaning against a wrought-iron spiked fence, watching the fifth-floor windows for some sign of life. The picture of the papier-mâché hand was still remarkably fresh in his mind, those stiff, glove-like fingers curling into a fist as if they were trying to squeeze every last ounce of energy out of the ink and newsprint. And that's why he had come back. Because three weeks ago, something too fantastic to even imagine had happened inside this building.

He didn't have a long wait, maybe ten minutes, before a light went on upstairs on the fifth floor, the northeast corner window. Night had come early to this part of the city. The street and alleyways were already clothed in endless black shadows. Against nightfall, the fifth-floor light radiated a soft, ghost-like glow, the only sign of life in the neighborhood.

Foss leaned forward, pulling his overcoat tight around him. The catch to all this—to standing out in the snow, watching a man he barely knew—was that he still wasn't sure what it was he wanted. No, that wasn't true. The truth was that he wasn't sure if what he wanted was even possible.

And if it was—

There was movement at the window, a dark shapeless cloud that slowly came into focus, the silhouette of a man. It was a silhouette that was dream familiar now: a nearly middle-aged man wearing a baseball cap and a pea coat, dragging one leg behind him as if it carried the weight of all his burdens.

Jas. Picture perfect. Only the Thalidomide arm in nonattendance.

It's there.

You just have to peel back yesterday's Sporting Green.

Foss started across the street, keeping a watch on the window, both anticipating and fearing what he might see through that pane of glass. Whatever was about to happen, he was here because he had to be. It had taken him a few weeks, but he'd come back. He realized now this wasn't about burnt-out buildings and papier-mâché arms. It was about making things whole again, about taking back what never should have been lost in the first place. That's what Jas had been trying to tell him. He had started sleeping on the couch again, the same night he met Jas. Though *sleep* was probably a poor choice of word. His eyes had drifted shut a few times, but his mind never stopped replaying the movement of those paper fingers. Over and over again. Until it had slowly sunk in, the reason why Jas collected his newspapers, the reason why it still haunted him to this very moment.

The blend of anticipation and fear had turned to adrenalin but he was standing outside the fifth-floor apartment now. The padlock was open, hanging from the steel bar anchor, and somehow the idea of protecting this place made more sense the second time around. *Everything, I own is inside here.* Everything in the world that mattered.

He knocked.

Inside the apartment, there was the sound of lagging movement, the sound of a Thalidomide leg being dragged across a floor cluttered with newspapers. It stopped near the other side of the door. Then complete, unnerving silence.

"Jas?" His throat went suddenly dry, suddenly swollen with unspoken words. "I came to see her, Jas."

The door swung open, the light nearly blinding after he had journeyed through the darkness of the stairway. Jas stood to the left, slightly hunched over, dwarfed by an immeasurable background of printed material. He appeared not at all surprised, nor terribly pleased. Though it was difficult to read his expression; from the chin down, his face was hidden behind a black winter-scarf. "There are no straight lines," he said with a tired voice. "All things circle back to where they started."

"I want to see her, Jas."

"Purdy?"

"Yes." Foss pushed by him, into the labyrinth of newspaper stacks. "It's the Thalidomide, isn't it? That's how you do it. The damn drug didn't just screw up your genes, it screwed up something inside you, something inside your psyche. That's what you were trying to tell me. That's what you meant when you said you wanted me to meet Purdy. Somehow, you've managed to bring her back, haven't you? After practicing with newspapers, modeling them and reworking them, you finally learned how to bring her back, and—"

"And if I could do it for Purdy, then I could do it for your wife?"

"Yes! Yes, exactly!"

Jas stared at him, his expression unreadable, his hand still on the doorknob, his body stiff and steadfast. "It was a mistake, Fossy. Go home and forget about it."

"Go home? I can't go home. I don't have a home. Not without Ellie."

"It's not what you think."

"You brought her back, didn't you?"

"You think it's that easy?"

Yes. Oh God, Yes. It has to be.

"I want it to be."

So do I. Jas seemed as if he were going to say. The actual words were never spoken, though, but something in his expression quietly changed. He softened his stance, and stared off into a distant corner of the room. "You really want to meet Purdy, then I'll introduce you."

"Thanks," Foss whispered.

"Don't thank me. Not yet." He shook his head, then started to move. "Over here, on the left. You'll have to wedge between the Chronicles and whatever the hell that other stack is."

They shouldered their way along a narrow aisle carved out of stack after stack of old magazines and newspapers. Jas went first, stopping every so often to flip a light switch. Apparently, he had torn a wall out between the adjoining apartments, that was the only way Foss could imagine the seemingly endless layout. Straight ahead, at the entry to an unlit room, they finally came to a standstill.

"You're sure?" he asked.

"Yes."

He flipped on the light, and there she was—though not quite as Foss had expected to find her.

In his mind, he had pictured a beautiful eight-year-old girl with dirty-blonde hair and piercing-blue eyes, with a child's smile and canyon-wide dimples. He had expected, as crazy as it now sounded, that she might even say a sweet, "Hello." But that's not what happened. She was sitting on the floor, her back against the wall, her hands folded stiffly in her lap; and from where he was standing, a good eight feet away, he could see where over time her skin had mummified. She wore a smile, sure enough, but it didn't belong to a happy child. No helloes from this little girl, her voice had turned to dust a long time ago.

He turned to Jas. "She's ..."

"Dead."

"But I thought you could bring her back?"

"I never said that."

"But the hand, the papier-mâché hand?"

Jas turned the light off, leaving both of them standing in a grayish-yellow glow not much different from the color of Purdy's skin. "I tried to tell you—"

"Jesus, Jas, I thought . . ."

You weren't listening. It wasn't the Thalidomide. It was emotion, pure emotion."

"But you didn't bring her back."

"No." He shook his head, a sense of unease showing through now. "I didn't bring her back. Not the way you were hoping I would. Not like that."

Foss felt something cold flow through his veins. "Like what, then?"

"More like a doll, I guess. A paper doll."

"Like the hand?"

"Yes."

"One that looks like Purdy? That moves like her?"

"What I'm telling you is that it isn't Purdy." He started to shuffle back down the aisle of newspapers toward the front room, as if that were going to be the end of the conversation. But it wasn't. "I don't know you as well as I should, Fossy. I don't know what kind of a man you are, what's important to you, what you're willing to sacrifice. I don't know how much you and I are alike, if we're alike at all."

"That didn't seem to bother you last time I was here."

"Things were different then."

"What's changed? I'm still the same man."

He stopped and turned slowly about, as if he wanted to make sure that what he was going to say would hit home. He looked older than a man in his thirties. Foss thought maybe it was the lighting in the room. "But I'm not the same man," he said in a hoarse whisper. "You give a little; it takes a little."

"I don't understand."

"I know you don't." He started walking again. "That's the point."

They stayed to the left, following a corridor that cut through a room of what—at a glance—appeared to be romance novels with their covers torn off. In the end, they turned up in the living room. On the other side of the Georgian sash windows, it was still snowing, the flakes looking like white butterfly wings fluttering in the air. For an instant, Foss was as peaceful as he had been since Ellie's death. But that was lost the moment he caught a small movement out of the corner of his eye.

She was sitting on the couch, a life-size paper replica of an eight-year-old girl. Mechanically, her head turned toward him—making the dry, crinkling sound of paper being crumpled—and she smiled. It was a child's smile, with canyon-wide dimples.

"Jesus, it's actually alive."

"She can't talk," Jas said, sitting on a nearby stack of newspapers. "Does it matter?"

"No. Not to me. I just thought you should know."

Foss knelt before the paper girl, mesmerized, and touched the back of his hand to her cheek. Every part of her was perfection — the eyes, the ears, the lips, the hair, a paper sculpture that seemed more alive than some of the people he had known during his life. Her cheek felt cool and soft, and dusted with something that felt like paper fuzz. Before he drew his hand away, she reached out to him, wrapping her tiny paper fingers around the soft flesh of his arm. As if she needed his touch as much as he needed hers.

It was all he could do to keep from crying. "Oh dear God," he said softly. "She feels, doesn't she? Like a living, breathing human being, she feels."

"Yes."

Foss glanced over his shoulder, his eyes watery. "And Ellie? Can you bring her back, too? Like this? Can you make her this alive?"

Jas nodded, though something grim swept across his face. "But not me. You. You have to do it. And there's something else you should know."

What?

"It started a few days after we met at the soup kitchen."

It doesn't matter.
Whatever it is, it's not enough to make me change my mind.
"You need to understand what you're getting into," Jas said ruefully, as he unwound the black winter-scarf from around his neck. With great care, he removed the last layer, as if it protected an open wound. Underneath, in the soft glow of the 75-watt bulb, it appeared as if he had pasted a column from last week's food section across his neck. Dry, dirty-white newsprint. Red and black ink. Fused into his flesh, like a scab over an abrasion.

This is, Foss thought dimly, a man who loves his daughter.

"It's a trade-off, you see. A little of me for a little of her."

"Can't you stop it?"

"I'm not sure I want to."

"For God's sake, why not?"

"Because I'm not alone anymore."

That's not enough.

Foss felt his legs weaken. He sat flat on the floor, staring at Jas and realizing—more clearly than he wanted—this man was his reflection; and worse: maybe it was enough. Isn't that what he'd come for? To put an end to the loneliness once and for all? He glanced from Jas to Purdy, noticing for the first time the patch of pink skin fused into her paper neck.

"You want your wife back?"

The way I remember her? That perfect? Or something just close enough to take away the ache inside, to fill the emptiness she left behind?

"I don't know."

"Tell the truth, Fossy."

The truth? Christ, could there still be such a thing? If there was any shred of it left in him, it had to be something that went like this: With Ellie, even a paper Ellie, at least a little piece of him would go on living. Without her, everything inside was eventually going to shrivel up and die.

That was the truth.

The cold, painful truth.

All the truth Foss had ever needed.

The Night In Fog

1

I'm going to tell you this story and you might believe it, and you might not. It doesn't matter to me one way or the other. I've been carrying this around for nearly twenty years now and even though it's Rick's story and not mine, if I don't let it out it's going to eat a hole in me. So I'll tell you as much as I can . . . you believe as much as you want . . . and maybe that will be the end of it.

2

This was how it all came up again:
"I need to see you," Rick said.
It was the first time I had talked to my brother in nearly five years.

I'm ashamed to admit that. Family ought to stand for something. But life has a way of taking you where it will. It had taken Rick and me down strikingly different roads.

"Can you come?"

I glanced at the calendar pressed against the side of the refrigerator and held there with a Hersey's magnet. It was Friday, October 30th. Tomorrow would be Halloween and I had promised Traci I would take the kids on their rounds. Then on Sunday there was dinner with her parents. I flipped the page and glanced at the following weekend. "When?"

"Tonight."

"Christ, Rick."

"It's important, man."

"I've got a full weekend already. Can't it wait?"

"She's back."

It had been such a long time since he had talked about her that it nearly went right past me, unnoticed. My first thought was . . . *she*? Then it registered, the tone that had been in his voice as he had said that singular, difficult word . . . *she* . . . and a sick, dreadful ache stirred inside me. Not again, I thought. Please, not again.

"We've been over this," I said. "A thousand times."

"It's different this time. It's happening to someone else."

3

This was how it all came up in the first place:

Rick, who was twelve and still doing time at Buckeye Junior High where I had done my own stint two years earlier, said, "You won't believe what happened today." We didn't have much in common. Never had. Rick was one of those kids who for the life of them couldn't seem to fit in. He was the square peg: bad jokes, glasses, kind of a geeky-looking kid who spent most of his time alone.

"Probably won't, so don't bother me."

"I ate lunch with a girl."

"So?"

He said her name was Jude Fairclough. She had transferred in only two weeks earlier from some school down in the Bay Area, and she sat in front of Rick, two rows over in English. Her hair was reddish-brown, he said. Her eyes light blue, her face sprinkled with freckles. He never said it out loud, but it was easy to tell he had a crush on her.

I guess I thought that was okay.

At least until I began to wonder if Jude Fairclough even existed.

4

"Just this one last time," Rick said over the phone. "I'll never bother you again, Bryan. I promise."

I knew that wasn't true. There would always be one more time. It was never going to end. Not in Rick's mind. And I hadn't missed the significance of the date, either, though he probably thought I had. October 31st was tomorrow. Halloween. That was the first time the real monster in Rick had come out.

"Where are you?"

"I'm renting a place in Weed."

"Uh-huh," I said, digging around in a drawer for a pen and a piece of paper. I didn't know what I was going to say to Traci, but when she heard it was Rick, she would probably be okay with it. She had always been concerned about my relationship with my brother. I found a pencil instead, and an old envelope from Pacific Gas and Electric. "What's the address?"

Softly, he said, "Thanks, Bryan."

"It's okay."

After that Halloween night, Rick had spent the next nine years behind bars. I had visited him only twice. Both times shortly after he had been sent to the Youth Authority. Both times in the company of my parents. My mother died two years later from a heart attack, no doubt largely due—at least in my mind—to the living hell Rick had put her through. I never went for another visit after that. Dad went alone, struggling hard to hold onto what little family he had left, even in the face of what Rick had done.

5

From my brother's letters over the years:

Jude Fairclough . . . she was a truly beautiful girl, Bryan. You've got to remember, when you're twelve, you scare easy. The dark scares you. Being alone at night scares you. But most of all, pretty girls scare you. I wouldn't admit it then, but she really stirred up something in the pit of my stomach, something I'd never felt before. It wasn't a feeling I liked much, Bryan. Not then, and not now. But it was a feeling I didn't want to lose, either. Kinda like riding the roller coaster even when you know it makes you sick.

That first day, like I told you before, I caught up with Jude in the cafeteria, maybe twenty minutes into the lunch hour. She was sitting alone at a table in the back. There was a banner on the wall behind her with huge red-and-black letters announcing the Halloween dance, which was only a week away. I remember that as clear as can be. She looked tiny and lost sitting there beneath it, and I remember thinking how hard it must be transferring into a new school already a couple of months into the year.

"Hi."

She looked up from her plate, where she was still working through her peas and carrots. Her smile was like sunshine, warm and bright. "Hi."

I sat down across from her. "So what is it you want to show me?"

"It's right here."

I watched her rummage around in an old canvas tote bag that looked something like the reusable shopping bags old ladies take to the grocery stores these days. It was the size of a small painting, with wide straps that she curled back as she peered down inside. I thought of a magician, you know, reaching into his top hat and pulling out a rabbit, that old routine? And like she had read my mind, she came out with . . . not a rabbit, but an old cigar box.

The Night In Fog

She placed it on the table between us.

There was a moment of truth, Bryan, when I thought she was seriously giving thought to whether she should share it with me or not. Looking back on it now, you've gotta know that I wish it had never happened. I wish to God she would have thought long and hard, then shaken her head and said, "No. This isn't right."

Maybe that would have been the end of it.

Right then and there.

Maybe none of the rest would have ever happened.

But we both know it didn't go like that.

I looked at that box, Bryan, and it reminded me of Grandad. He used to love to smoke cigars. You remember that? The same brand. Dutch Masters Palmas. I used to keep a collection of his cigar boxes at home at the back of my bedroom closet, on the floor. Used them for baseball cards and marbles and stuff. There wasn't anything fancy about them. Dutch Masters was printed in red across the front edge, and in black, bold letters across the top. Next to the label was a portrait of four men wearing those wide-brimmed Pilgrim hats they were always wearing in our early U.S. History books.

I looked at her. "Yeah, so?"

"What's your favorite season?"

"I don't know."

"Spring? When the flowers are in bloom? Or maybe Fall, when it's still warm, but the sky's gray?"

"Winter," I said, thinking of snow. It never snowed much in the valley, but remember the snow on Lassen and Shasta? What was it? Maybe an hour's drive, maybe a little more, to either place? I doubt I ever told you, Bryan, but I always liked the snow. There was something about the crisp air and the pure whiteness everywhere. It always made me feel alive.

She nodded, then motioned to the box. "Go on. Open it."

It was too late not to open the box by then. I mean, it had probably been too late the moment I had found Jude sitting in the corner by herself. But this is the God's honest truth, Bryan: some roads in life don't allow you to turn back.

I raised the lid, which was hinged with nothing more than a thin

sheet of cardboard, and up out of the box came a huge breath of cold arctic air. It felt as if I had opened the freezer door at the Holiday Market. I know this sounds incredible, but it was actually snowing.
White, crystal flakes swirling around the edges of the box.
Frost in the corners.
Cold enough to make you shiver.
Snowing! It was *snowing*!
It was like nothing I had ever seen before, and I stared at it, couldn't move a damn muscle, for a good long time before I looked up at Jude.
"Like it?"
I nodded.
"Thought you would."
"How did you do that?"
"It's the way you imagined it, isn't it? The cold wind . . . the snow . . . like opening your bedroom window in the middle of winter?"
"Yeah, but how did you—?"
"Close the lid. I want to show you something else."
The cigar box had turned cold in my hands. Across the front, a thin film of ice had formed, the white crystals making it nearly impossible to read the words: Dutch Masters. But the moment I dropped the lid, in an instant, I mean no longer than a snap of your fingers, the ice was gone.
"Now, open it again," she said.
I gave it some thought, Bryan. I swear I did. Not much, I admit, because I was curious, just like you would have been curious. But I gave it some thought, then I raised the lid, and I watched a thick, syrupy blackness rise up like a cloud of volcanic ash. Inside the box, it was suddenly as if I was standing on the edge of a cliff looking up at the sky. Far in the distance, I could see a quarter moon, and beyond that . . . the glitter of billions of stars.
I snapped the lid closed.
"Something, isn't it?" Jude said.
It *was* something. I didn't understand it, but it was the most amazing thing I had ever seen.
I opened the box again, and this time I did one of those stupid

things you do on a dare. I reached into it, past the brim, and found myself buried up to my elbow in the darkness. It was as if I had dipped into a pool of water at night when the surface and everything beneath is as black as oil.

"It feels cool," I said, wiggling my fingers. "How deep is it?"

"How deep is the sky?"

"I mean . . . what would happen if I fell in? Where would I be?"

"It's a cigar box. You can't fall in."

"But if I could?"

"Then I guess you'd be . . . *lost*."

But I was already lost. I just didn't know it. I wouldn't know it for another week, and by that time, it would be too late to do anything about it. That was, of course, if I had *wanted* to do anything about it. Everything in life is a choice, Bryan. The choices we make are a reflection of who we are and what we want. But it's the choices we don't make that tell the true story. The moment I opened the cigar box, I never even thought of turning back.

"How do you do it?" I asked.

"It's the box," Jude said. "It's all the box."

But that was a lie.

6

I had gone up to the attic, to the old steamer trunk in the far corner, where Traci kept what she liked to call . . . our memories. On the outside of the trunk, blue ink on white construction paper, she had attached a handwritten sign that read: *Things Not To Be Forgotten*. Inside, the dark corners were filled with things I had spent a good part of my life trying to put behind me. Mostly old newspaper articles about what had happened. But there was also the stack of letters from Rick.

They were sitting on the seat next to me now, as I headed north on I-5. It was a little past two in the morning. The sky was crystal clear, the night air cool and crisp. I had rolled down the passenger window to keep me from drifting off to sleep, but the truth of the matter was I didn't need it. One by one I was revisiting those letters, hearing every word Rick had written, and trying to understand what had gone wrong inside his head.

Weed was still another six hours away.

7

From my brother's letters over the years:

I couldn't get it out of my head, Bryan. After dinner that night I went to bed early, afraid that if I stayed downstairs and watched television with the family eventually Mom would take a good look at me and she would know. She would know what Jude had shown me. And even worse, she would know that I wasn't frightened by it.

I thought about Jude all night. I thought about her maybe as a girlfriend, since I'd never had one. But mostly I thought about the magic in that box of hers and what it would be like if that box belonged to me. I suppose that's a terrible thing to admit, but when you're twelve, you're always looking for shortcuts, and Jude . . . she seemed like my only chance to finally make people take notice of me.

You know it, Bryan. You know I've always been a nobody. A *goof*. This was the first time in my life I ever had a chance to be someone.

At lunch, I found her sitting in what had already become her regular spot at the back of the cafeteria. She looked lost sitting beneath the huge Halloween banner by herself, and believe me, I knew how she felt. I had felt the same way almost all my life.

"Hey."

"I knew you'd be back," she said.

"Yeah?"

"It's the box, right?"

I shrugged. "Maybe."

"You want more, don't you?"

It should have been obvious to me right then, I suppose. She had dropped the first bread crumb and I had picked it up exactly as she had known I would. But shortcuts don't always lead where you think they do, and in all honestly I should have been paying more attention. I missed the obvious, Bryan. And I've paid dearly for it.

"You want to see something really scary?" she asked.

"Like what?"

"That depends. What scares you?"

I remember this so clearly in my head. The first thing I thought was: *You, Jude. You scare me.* It flashed like lightning across the screen behind my eyes, then I saw the image of an old woman cloaked in a black robe, then that creature from the movie *Pumpkinhead*, then suddenly I found myself thinking how immune I had grown to the things that scared me when I was a kid. It wasn't the monsters that scared me now, I thought. It was—

"You're wrong," Jude said.

"What?"

"About the monsters. They *do* scare you."

I swear, Bryan. I never said a word about what I was thinking. Not a single word. She just . . . *knew*.

"Trust me," she said. "They scare everyone."

I watched her dig around in that magical tote bag of hers until she brought out a plain, brown-paper sack. It had been folded in half, then half again, and I sat there, nervous as all get out, as she painstakingly reversed the folds.

"Where's the cigar box?"

"I didn't bring it."

"Why not?"

"Because I brought this instead." She flattened the bag against the table, then slid it across the smooth surface at me. "Go on. Open it."

I took the bag, shook it out, then set it back on the table between us. It was full of air now, standing upright on its own.

"You've never really been scared before, have you, Rick?"

"Nope."

"Bet *I* can scare you."

The bag made a rustling noise.

I stared down at it, not frightened, but surprised.

The brown paper walls expanded, then contracted, then expanded again, as if they were alive and breathing.
Jude grinned. "Go on."
"What?"
"Reach into it."
"No way."
"Scared?"
"No."
"Then do it. I dare you."
It was only a bag, I told myself. A brown paper bag. Nothing more. But it *was* more than that, Bryan.

I raised myself up and stared down at it, all the way to the bottom, where I could see the flaps folded and pressed one over the other in a perfect fit. The bag was empty. I found a tremendous sense of relief in that fact, and sat back again, feeling confident as I finally reached in with one hand.

Now, this is the weird thing, because I can't explain it, but I felt my fingers brush up against something. I don't know how to describe it exactly. It felt thick, I suppose. Stringy. Like a ball of yarn. But in my head, there was another flash of lightning and I caught a glimpse of something so . . . gruesome, so scary . . .

I couldn't pull my hand back fast enough.
"It won't hurt you," Jude said.
"What is it?"
The bag rustled again.

Hot air rose out of its paper walls, the smell reminding me of the stench that sometimes came up from the garbage disposal at home when Mom made us do the dishes.

"Trust me," she said.

And I did. I don't know why, Bryan. I still don't understand that part of it . . . how I could be led so easily to do the things I eventually did . . . but this was one more step in the process, I believe. It seems so unreal now, looking back. Blurry around the edges, like a dream. It was almost as if I wanted to see how far I could take it before I woke up and it was over.

I did it all in one quick move. My hand dropped inside the bag . . . my

The Night In Fog

fingers wrapped around what felt like a clump of long, coarse hair . . . I pulled . . . and up came the head of this . . . this *creature*. It had deep-set, bright-golden eyes. Huge nostrils spewing out hot, sour air. A sloped, Neanderthal forehead covered in a thick mat of brownish-black fur. A mouth that seemed almost too big for its head. Incisors that reached halfway down the creature's chin.

I had never seen anything like it in my life.

I screamed and pulled my hand back, then found myself falling backwards over the bench, head over heels. I landed hard on the floor, my heart pounding like a hammer inside my chest, an ache at the back of my head where my head had struck the linoleum.

Jude laughed. "I told you it wouldn't hurt you."

"What . . . what was that?"

She took back the bag, folded it neatly into fourths, then stuffed it into the canvas tote.

"A daydream."

"What?"

"*Your* daydream to be more specific."

"But what about yesterday?"

"That was yours, too."

"The snow? The stars?"

"All of it. Yours."

"Impossible."

"But true."

"Prove it."

"Close your eyes," she said.

I may be a *goof*, Bryan, but I'm not an idiot. I wasn't going to trust her again. Not that easily.

"Okay, don't close your eyes. Just focus on something in your thoughts."

"Like what?"

"Anything. It doesn't matter. An apple. A poster. Your favorite movie. A Halloween mask. Anything."

It should have been easy, but it wasn't. My head was reeling with the image of that creature. I tried to think about familiar things: my room at home, the desk, the television, the last movie I

197

had watched, the knife I had received from Uncle Chet on my birthday.

And it happened just like that. The knife appeared. It was that tactical knife Uncle Chet called a Generation IV. Remember that one, Bryan? It opened smooth as velvet, nice and easy, like a key locking in place? Remember that? The ported grip? The matte-silver finish?

It was a nice little knife, but it was hovering in the air right in front of my face.

"How do I get rid of it?"

The blade slid out of the handle grip, the tip inches away from my eyes.

"Jude?"

"Think of something else."

"What?"

"Anything. It doesn't matter."

You find yourself staring at a knife and your mind goes into its own little version of panic, Bryan. Let me tell you. I mean, your thoughts really aren't your own anymore. They pour through your head like alphabet soup, some of the letters forming words, most of them forming gibberish. I don't know where I got the image of the feather, but suddenly there it was . . . floating in place of the knife, the color striations as clear and as real as if I had just plucked it out of the tail of a pheasant.

Jude laughed again. "See, that wasn't so hard."

I watched the feather float back and forth on an invisible current until finally it touched down on the table. Then it was gone.

"What happened to it?"

"It lost your attention."

The cafeteria was nearly empty now. There were some fourth grade girls across the room, dressed in Brownie uniforms and huddled around a tray of beads one of them had brought for making necklaces. The last of the food had already been removed from the serving line, the stainless steel counter cleaned up, most of the kids on kitchen duty let go. It was as alone and as quiet as it ever got at school.

"How come I couldn't do this stuff before?"
"Before when?"
"Before you."
"You weren't ready," Jude said.

8

Weed was an odd little town. Just south of the Oregon border. Flat, nestled in a sprawling valley, the elevation somewhere around three or four thousand feet. It looked a little like a forgotten town, a place where people a hundred years from now might stop and visit because over the past century it hadn't changed much.

I got off I-5, off the beaten tract, and found myself driving through old town, past the Cedar Lanes Bowling Alley, the Palace Theater, The Pizza Factory. Rick had given me directions, but in my haste to get them down my handwriting had been so sloppy that I was having trouble reading it now. Though . . . if it turned out that I couldn't find the place that might not be so terrible when all was said and done. I could probably convince myself that I had at least made the effort. More of an effort than he deserved.

I wondered what he looked like now, how much he had changed. I wasn't sure I would even recognize him anymore. It had been nearly twenty-five years. A person changes in twenty-five years. I had changed.

I glanced again at the letters on the seat beside me, then pulled to the curb to see if I could figure out where I was and how I was going to get there from here. It was no longer a matter of hours now. Only a matter of minutes.

9

From my brother's letters over the years:
What scares you, Bryan?
I mean *really* scares you.

Sleep does it for me. That's when I don't have any control over the pictures in my head. I close my eyes, drift off to sleep, and the movies start rolling. I'm just another member of the audience. What happens, happens.

That night I dreamed about Halloween. I think that's what she wanted. I think that was what she had in mind from the very beginning. Halloween. Looking back on it now, it was the perfect time, wasn't it? All Hallow's Eve. The festival of the dead. A time when the devil and the witches are free to roam the earth and cause their havoc.

In the dream, I was at the school Halloween party, though it was outside, at a beach somewhere, with a huge bonfire and flames reaching ten or fifteen feet into the air. Everyone was dressed in costume. From the Mad Hatter to the Wicked Witch of the West. I was the Grim Reaper. It felt weird, but I liked it. Jude was there, too. Dressed as a ghost. Her white, airy gown flowing like wings on the ocean breeze. I don't remember much of what went on during the dance, only that at the end when everyone stood in a circle around the fire and removed their masks, *my* mask wouldn't come off.

It was a cause for amusement at first. The others gathered around, taking some sort of twisted delight in watching the *goof* struggling with his mask. I fell to my knees, prying my fingers under the edges, trying to rip it away from my face, nearly suffocating in the process. But it held on. It wouldn't let go. And gradually, one by one as it dawned on the others that the mask wasn't going to come off, the laughter began to turn to fear.

You know why, Bryan?

Because suddenly I wasn't the *goof* anymore.

Suddenly I was the Grim Reaper!

I woke up with a start.

The bed was soaked; I had been sweating like a damn race horse. I pushed back the covers, sat up, and leaned against the wall, my mouth dry, my breath short. There was a faint hint of sulfur in the air, a thin layer of smoke hovering just above the level of my desk, tendrils of the stuff still rising out of the wastepaper basket.

I didn't even get out of bed to open the window. I pulled the covers up around me, then sat there for what seemed like hours, rewinding the

The Night In Fog

dream over and over again until I couldn't find a way around it any longer. A door had been opened, Bryan. It was as if I was standing in the doorway looking in on an ugly part of myself, a part I had always suspected was there, but had managed somehow to keep hidden.

I slept the rest of the night sitting up, my back against the wall. In the morning, the room was still full of that smoky musk. I opened the window to air it out, then discovered the pile of ashes in the wastepaper basket next to my desk. Left over from the dream, I figured. Because dreams and daydreams were kissing cousins, and if daydreams could get me a feather, it only made sense that the ashes—in all their smoky glory—had made their appearance in the same fashion.

But there was something else, too. I had been only vaguely aware of it last night, but this morning, it seemed remarkably clear in my mind. Someone or some*thing* had been in the room with me.

I asked Jude about it at lunch that day.

"Residue," she said.

"What?"

"Leftovers. From your dreams." She leaned forward and lowered her voice. There was something different about her. I didn't know what it was exactly, only that something wasn't quite right. "You don't get it, do you?"

"Get what?"

"It's all made of the same stuff, Rick. Your dreams. The snow in the cigar box. The feather from yesterday. They all come from you. From inside your head."

In all honesty, Bryan, I don't think I really understood any of it before that moment. Then it came home to me like a light going on and the shadows scurrying back into the recesses of a darkened room with only the stairs illuminated. The magic was in *me*. Not the cigar box. Not the paper bag. Not even Jude. It was *me*.

"Residue," I said, mostly to myself.

"Exactly."

"Wow."

"Yeah. You're starting to get it now, aren't you?"

"I think so," I said, looking into her blue eyes and finally realizing what it was that was different about her. The cafeteria was awash in fluorescent light, casting a false brightness over everything. Everything except Jude, who looked as if she had just stepped out of a slightly overexposed photograph. The color had begun to fade from her face. *That* was what was different.

"Are you okay?"

She looked past me at a group of girls exiting the cafeteria. It was almost as if her eyes were both luminous and transparent at the same time. "I didn't think it would happen so soon."

"What would happen?"

"Nothing important."

The cafeteria was nearly empty. Outside, the sun had shown itself for the first time in nearly two weeks and even the Brownies were soaking up the warmth. I could hear the clatter of dishes coming from the kitchen, a teacher's voice as she scolded some kids for littering, and in the back of my mind I could hear Jude's voice whispering, *It's just the residue, Rick. Residue.*

She didn't just look *different*, I realized. She looked *ill*. She looked like an old tee-shirt with the color washed out. Pale, I suppose you might say. But more than that. If the light had been at her back, I think I might have been able to see right through her.

"No. Something's wrong with you," I said. "You don't look right."

"I'll be fine."

There are different kinds of monsters in the world, Bryan. I know you think I'm the biggest monster of all, but you're wrong about that. And you're wrong about what you think happened that night at the Halloween party. Jude knew what was going to happen long before she ever met me. And she knew it would make her well again.

10

There are different kinds of monsters in the world.

I turned into the parking lot of the Motel Ranchero, and drove slowly around the outer edge, past an old Chevy pickup with a camper shell, past the weeds growing out of the asphalt, past a dimly-lit cubby-hole with a handwritten sign on the door that said *Office*.

Rick hadn't mentioned anything about staying at a motel. I had assumed the number he gave me was an apartment number. But I probably should have known better. I don't think he ever stayed longer than a month or two in any one place.

I pulled into one of a long line of empty spaces, turned off the engine and sat for a moment, staring at the door to room 118. It was morning now. A bank of angry-looking rain clouds was rolling in over the mountains to the west. The temperature had dropped a bit.

I don't know exactly how long I sat there, but eventually, Rick pulled back the curtains and peered out through the motel window at me. He looked like a stranger I guess you could say. His hair was shoulder-length, stringy, gray over the ears. He held a pack of cigarettes in one hand, along with a lighter, and an unlit cigarette in his mouth.

He waved me in.

It was a long walk from the car to that motel door. I hadn't told Traci this, but I had come here because I wanted to put an end to the letters and the calls, and I knew the only way that was ever going to happen was if I looked my brother in the eye and told him in no uncertain terms that our relationship was over. We had been brothers once, but that had been a long time ago. Maybe not in Rick's mind, but in my mind, it was a dead relationship.

He opened the door before I got there. "Oh, man, you came. I knew you would. I knew it."

Rick didn't look any better up close than he had at the window. It had been three or four days since he had shaven, and his beard, unlike the gray in his hair, was as black as ever. He lit the cigarette in his mouth, blew out the match and tossed it at the ash tray on the table next to the window.

"Come in, man. Sit down. I know it ain't the best place in the world, but I cleaned it up for you."

I sat in the nearest chair.

"Let me get a shirt on, okay?"

The first thing I noticed, besides the fact that he had, indeed, cleaned up the room, was how thin Rick had become. He was a couple of years younger than me, almost thirty-eight, and he had always been on the slight side, but he looked haggard, as if he had been living on the streets a good part of the past twenty-or-so years. I also noticed the tattoo. It was on his right arm, up near the shoulder. The Grim Reaper, holding his scythe in one hand and flipping off the world with the other.

"Look," he said, reappearing with a shirt. "I know you think I'm a nut case. And I don't blame you. But what happened that night . . . it's not what you think."

"What *did* happen?"

He had opened the bottom drawer of the dresser and was digging through it, looking for something, when he stopped and gave me a crooked glance. There was the oddest expression on his face. For a moment, I thought he might break down and cry, but he didn't. He nodded slightly instead. "You know, that's the first time you've ever asked me that question."

"Is it?"

He nodded again, more visibly this time, then pulled an old shoe box out of the drawer and sat in a chair across the table from me. He placed the box on the table between us. "You really want to know?"

"That's why I asked."

"It was like a dream, Bryan." He gazed through the window. A middle-aged woman, her husband and two kids, were hauling luggage out to their Datsun. Shadows moved across the parking lot as a cloud blocked the sun and swallowed them up as if they were only shadows themselves. "I mean sometimes I think back to that night and it's like it happened to someone else. It's like a scene out of movie, something I saw as a kid that belongs to me now."

I shifted uncomfortably in my seat.

Rick took a long draw on his cigarette. "Jude was there, you know. At the party? *Go on*, she kept saying. *Do it.*"

"Do *what?*"

"You've got to understand, Bryan. It was Halloween. That was the whole point. I just thought it would be a big laugh. That's all." He took another long draw on his cigarette, then stuffed it out in the ash tray. "But she wouldn't let up. *Go on, have a little fun*, she said. We had talked about it for days, and I won't deny it sounded like fun. Fact is . . . once it got going, for awhile at least, it *was* fun."

The Night In Fog

"Rick," I said.

He looked at me.

"You're stalling."

"Yeah, I guess I am." He pulled a pack of cigarettes out of his shirt pocket, looked at them, then tossed them aside. "They were everywhere that night. It was like snapping your fingers. I didn't even have to close my eyes. An image would come into my head and there it was, alive and kicking, right in front of me. Just like that. I can't remember them all, there were so many. I remember the scarecrow. He had this dirty straw face with these two empty eye sockets, nothing else, and he was carrying this scythe with an old rusty blade that looked like it had been out in the rain for years. I remember that. And I remember this huge griffin or gargoyle or some such thing, I don't know exactly what the hell it was. Its wing span was like . . . just incredible."

Rick stared off into his memories, his voice just above a whisper and fighting through a tremor. "There were others. This guy that was nothing but bones and a little hanging flesh. He had these perfect teeth. All I remember about them is how they kept chattering, like he was trying to say something. God, there were so many others. Snap! Just like that they were everywhere."

I looked at my brother, who seemed a thousand miles away, and felt an odd mix of loathing and sadness. It had been more than twenty years and Rick was still entwined in his own self-denial. I remembered the scarecrow, too. Or at least the story of the scarecrow. The part Rick always seemed to forget, though, was that *he* had been the one who had taken the scythe to the party. I still don't know where he had gotten it from, but for weeks afterward the newspapers reported that he had wrapped it tin foil to make it look like a harmless prop.

"At first it was kind of funny, you know. Watching the kids freak. Half of them were out the door before anything happened. And the other half were heading out right behind them. I didn't think anyone was going to get hurt. I mean, that never even crossed my mind. It was just supposed to be a prank."

Rick glanced at me, as if he were checking to see how much of this I was going to believe, then his dark-eyed stare returned to the window. "I don't know exactly when things started to go wrong. I guess I didn't realize anything *was* wrong until I heard the screaming and saw one of the kids fall. I think it was Manny Bunkin who went down first. The griffin swooped down on him from behind. It just seemed to fly past him, as innocent as that. Then Manny's head kind of fell off to one side of his shoulders and he collapsed. It was crazy after that. I mean you couldn't make any sense out of what was going on."

"Thirteen kids were dying," I said tightly.

My brother fell silent.

"Thirteen of them, Rick."

"Don't you think I know that? Don't you think I haven't had nightmares about it every night since it happened? I was there, man. I saw the blood. I saw the dead bodies."

"You *made* the dead bodies."

"No. It wasn't me. It was never me. I never brought those things to life. It was Jude. From the moment we met she had a chain around my neck like I was a trained animal. It was all to get me to that night."

"*You* killed them, Rick. You used the scythe and *you* killed them."

"I was only twelve, man. You really think I could have done that? It was her. I swear it was. That's why I wanted you to come, because I can prove it to you."

He fumbled to get the top off the shoe box and when it was more of an effort than he had the patience for, he turned the box over and dumped its contents onto the table. It was a pile of newspaper clippings, some old enough that they had begun to yellow around the edges.

"Look at this. It's right here somewhere." He rummaged frantically through the pile, his face twisted into an expression of pure mania, his hands shaking, until he came up with what he had been looking for. "Yeah. Here it is. Look at this. You remember this photo?"

He flattened out the newspaper clipping in front of me. It was from the Record Searchlight. The day after the Halloween tragedy. The caption read: Rick Freeman escorted out of the County Courthouse by police. In the photograph, he was at the top of the steps, wearing handcuffs and a bulletproof vest, his eyes staring out in a lifeless, vacant gaze. I remember my mother looking at that photo and remarking how frightened she thought Rick looked. But I never saw any fear in that expression. I never saw anything in it.

"Look. Look right there," he said, pointing into the crowd of spectators in the background. "See her? That's her. That's Jude."

The police had never been able to verify the existence of a Jude Fairclough. No one was registered under that name at the school. And none of the other kids could recall anyone with that name. In the end, they had concluded that she simply did not exist.

"Now, look at this one." Rick flattened out another clipping in front of me, using both hands like an iron, then pointed to a similar crowd of spectators in another photo. "You see her? Right there? Next to the column?"

The caption read: Sheriff's deputies escort young suspect out of court building. The article was from the Dispatch. It had been written two years after my brother had been arrested. The "young suspect" in the photo was not Rick. It was some kid I had never seen before.

"That's Jude."

It might have been.

And it might not have been.

It was an old grainy clipping, and I couldn't be sure one way or the other.

"And here," Rick said, ironing out another article. "Look at this one. Right here, in front of the fence. There she is again."

This was from the Herald. The photo was of a group of students gathered around a chain link fence where they had apparently built a memorial of flowers and cards in honor of the victims after a high school student had opened up fire in the school parking lot. The girl in front, the one Rick had pointed out, looked slightly older here, maybe sixteen. I glanced at the date. The article was from November 2, 1981, six years after what Rick had done.

"It goes on and on," he said, adding more clippings to the pile. "Every couple of years. Always right around Halloween. Always somewhere new."

I sifted through them randomly, looking at the photos, studying the faces of the girls. "You can't tell anything from these."

"It's her."

"If that's true, then why is she always the same age? You've got stories here spanning twenty years."

"That's the whole point. Don't you see? That's what it's all about. That's why she does it. To stay young."

I stared at him a moment, a little dumbfounded I suppose, though I probably shouldn't have been. I had expected something like this. Rick had never made an effort to own up to what he had done. He had always been long on excuses and short on responsibility. "This is crazy. I don't even know what I'm doing here."

"She's here," Rick said. "In Weed."

"Oh, Christ. You're kidding."

"That's why I wanted you to come up, man. So I could show you in person."

I glanced down at the photos again, not even sure what words would work under these circumstances. I guess there was a part of me, some sense of family left over from when we were children, that wanted to believe in him. It was not the only struggle going on in my mind at that moment, however. I also wanted to prove him wrong, to show him once and for all that there wasn't any Jude Fairclough, that there never had been, and to force him to finally own up to what he had done.

"She's in everyone of them," Rick said as I sifted through the clippings. He had calmed down some, though I had the sense that he was never really at peace, even when he was sleeping.

"What do you have in mind?" I asked.

11

I'll regret those words the rest of my life.

Rick was convinced that Jude was going to make an appearance at the elementary school dance, less than seven hours away. Just as he was convinced that she had been making similar appearances under similar circumstances over the past twenty-odd years. I wasn't going to change his mind.

He sat across the table from me, exhausted from his own agitation, and slowly gathered up the clippings. "I want you to see, that's all. Just

come to the school with me. Let me prove it to you. She'll be there, Bryan. She'll be there and so will those *things* she creates."
"And if you're wrong?"
"You tell me. What do you want?"
"First, you take responsibility for what happened that night."
"You got it."
"Then you get yourself some help."
"I'm not crazy, man."
"That's the deal. Take it or leave it."

12

The next seven hours went like a wait at the dentist's office. We got a bite to eat at McDonald's, then returned to the motel room. Rick brought out a deck of cards and we played cribbage for awhile, the same as we had when were kids. For an hour or so, the gulf between us was put aside. Things seemed to settle into an air of . . . *routine* I guess you might call it.

After the third game Rick came down with a headache. He slept for a few hours. I watched the sun go down and felt the temperature drop. The storm coming over the mountains from this morning finally settled over the valley.

It started to rain.

I stared out the window, watching puddles take form in the parking lot, and thought about Traci and the kids and how nice it was going to be to get back home again.

13

We arrived at the school a few minutes past eight.

Rick had been quiet and withdrawn since his nap, saying something about his headache not getting any better. He didn't look well, and I found myself watching him a little closer. I don't know what I was expecting to see, but his sudden sullenness had me worried.

"It's over this way," he said as we climbed out of the car.

"Hey, are you okay?"

He nodded. "Yeah, fine. Why?"

"You've been awfully quiet."

"I've got a lot on my mind."

The gym was really an all-purpose room that doubled for the cafeteria and served as the gathering area for school assemblies. There was a teacher at the main entrance, a short burly man with a queer little bald spot that made it appear as if he had purposely shaved his head in that area and that area alone. Rick stopped and talked to him long enough to convince him that I was some kid's uncle and we were making sure the kid had shown up like he had said he would be. The man seemed to take it all in stride. No big deal. People come and go all the time. Go on in and make yourselves comfortable.

It was dark inside, the lights kept dim, except for a string of red, blue and green bulbs outlining the stage at the far end. The music was blaring, so loud it took a moment before I recognized *Wonderwall* by Oasis. Rick motioned toward the other side of the room and I followed him around the outer edge. He stopped under a basketball hoop, then scanned the crowd.

"See it?"

"What?"

"Right there." He pointed toward the refreshment table. "In the corner, behind the kids. The thing in the robe. It's still taking form."

I don't know to this day what I was expecting to see. Probably nothing at all. And I can't say for certain one way or the other that anything was there. But I thought I caught a glimpse of something, one of those out-of-the-side-of-your eye things. It stood head-and-shoulders above a group of nearby kids, clothed in a robe, a gaunt, drawn face staring out through two bright-red orbs. The robe was open in front, and I thought I could see ribs and a breastbone.

It was a glimpse, though. Nothing more.

A second. Maybe less.

And then it was gone.

"And over there," Rick said, pointing across the dance floor.

There was a folding table against the far wall. On top of the table,

The Night In Fog

on display, were a number of carved pumpkins, each with the light of a candle flickering through the openings. Next to the table, stood two kids, one dressed in a leather-jacket with his hair combed back, the other wearing the fangs and white face of a vampire. There was something else there, too. I couldn't tell exactly what it was, only that it had a vague shimmer about it, like an aura. And a foreboding sense of doom. I remember feeling the weight of that doom settle heavily on my shoulders for a brief moment. Then it was gone.

"We don't have much time."

"What's that supposed to mean?"

"It won't be long before they take full form."

The music wound down. For an eerie moment a hush fell over the room and everything seemed to grind to a standstill. I caught another vague shimmer of something lurking in the shadows near the trash cans. It looked something like a baboon, with an elongated snout and teeth too large for its face. Then it was gone and the music came up again, this time with Alanis Morisette singing *Isn't It Ironic.*

I turned to Rick to say something, but he had already worked his way down the room ahead of me. I could see him overlooking the crowd, searching the faces, his eyes as wide and as white as I had ever seen them.

Finally, he stopped, looked back at me, then motioned toward a little girl, sitting in a chair near the stage. "It's her," he mouthed. "It's Jude."

She was such a tiny thing. Dressed in white, with papier-mâché wings, and a silver-glitter wand in her lap. She reminded me of my daughter Peg, and I found myself wondering what I was doing here instead of being at home, escorting the kids around the neighborhood with their little pillow cases in tow. There are only so many Halloweens before kids no longer want to be seen with their parents, and I had wasted this one.

I looked to Rick, who had started across the room in the direction of the girl. Those white eyes of his flashed again inside my thoughts, and suddenly, for the first time, I realized what he'd had in mind all along. He hadn't brought me here just to see Jude. He had brought me here to see Jude *die.*

David B. Silva

I can't you tell you how I knew this. Only that it was one of those things that instantly seemed self-evident. Like when you realize a half-second too late that you aren't going to make a yellow light.

Rick started his way through the crowd, in no apparent hurry, never taking his eyes off the girl. I moved with him at a different angle, step for step. It was the only angle I had, and it quickly became evident that it wasn't going to be enough to get me there first. He had the line on me and he had the jump. All I could do was hope to get there before it was too late.

But if that's what I was thinking, then I was fooling myself.

Maybe half-a-second more . . .

Maybe then . . .

Just before he arrived at the girl, Rick pulled a knife from the inside pocket of his jacket. It was the same knife Uncle Chet had given him when Rick had been a boy. The Generation IV. He kept it low, at his side, but the colored lights reflected dully off the matte-silver finish, and I saw it clearly. I saw it and I realized my brother was playing out the same fantasy he had played twenty years ago, or something as near to that fantasy as he could construct in his mind.

He pounced on the girl, knocking over the chair and sending her sliding across the floor on her back.

No one around them seemed to notice at first. It was as if the two of them were ghosts, playing out one final death scene for the benefit of no one but themselves.

Rick leaned over her, pausing momentarily to study her face. Later, he would say that he had stopped to look into her soul, to make certain she was really Jude. Then he raised the knife above his head.

Someone screamed.

I fought through the last hurdle of kids.

The girl, whose name I would later learn was Kimberly Hall, looked past my brother and stared directly at me. Her eyes were light blue, the color nearly drowning in its own white terror. Her mouth opened wide, but the scream inside her never made its escape.

Rick plunged the knife into her chest, nearly all the way up the shank.

The girl took in a depth breath that slowly gurgled out again. A trickle of blood ran out of her mouth, down the side of her chin. She stared toward the ceiling, her eyes instantly glassy, her mouth opening and closing like a fish gasping for air.

I pulled Rick off and looked down at her, thinking of Peg, thinking of everything that had brought me here, to this moment and place, and the thousand things I might have done to prevent it.

She closed her eyes.

"Just watch," Rick said.

"Shut up! You hear me? Just shut your goddamn mouth, Rick!"

"Watch."

There was nothing else I could do but watch. I had never seen a person die before, and in all honesty, I hope I never do again. I watched her eyes close, then I watched a subtle change ripple through her features like a wave. It reminded me of the shimmering I had seen earlier. Only this time I thought I caught a glimpse of something more. I thought I caught a glimpse of a hundred-year-old woman, deep black sockets where her eyes should have been, loose, weathered flesh, a mouth of rotting teeth . . .

It was there.

And then it was gone.

And she was dead.

Kimberly Hall was dead.

14

That was twelve years ago.

Rick was convicted of murder and sentenced to death. He's run his course of appeals. Tomorrow he's scheduled for execution in the electric chair. Which, I suppose, is what stirred this all up again.

He never stopped writing, though I admit I stopped opening his letters years ago. I couldn't endure the pain any longer. They all read alike.

There are nights when I still can't close my eyes without seeing her face staring up at me. I don't know if what I saw at the moment of her death was real or not. I guess I'll never know. Traci tells me it's something I use to protect myself from my guilt, and I suppose that's as good an explanation as any. But I pray she's wrong. I pray it really was Jude Fairclough who died that night. Because, as Rick said in one of his letters: some roads in life don't allow you to turn back.

Metastasis

"It's back," Melanie said.
The bedroom window was open, the curtains drawn back. Midnight had swept through half-an-hour or so earlier. The month was July. Nine days earlier, a high pressure system had locked in over the coast, bringing high temperatures and a sopping humidity. It was rarely comfortable inside the apartment before the sun went down.
"What's back?" I whispered.
"The cancer."
"Jesus, Melanie."
The moon had risen above the apartment complex across the way. Its light poured into our bedroom, grayish-white, and fell across her body like velvet. "I can feel it inside me," she said.
I sat up, and stared numbly out the window. There was nothing I knew to say. Nothing that could express the dryness in my throat, the fear in my stomach. We had both known the cancer might return. It was just that . . . that things had been going so well. I ran my hand across her bare back in wide circles, not saying anything at all.

"I love you, Jimmy."
"Maybe it's something else," I whispered.
"Maybe," she said, not really believing.
I stared through the bedroom window at the peaceful night, wondering when it was all going to end, this cancer stuff. Night became a conscious, faraway dream for me, dark and sulking. The silence between us became a bottomless pit, its mouth open wide, waiting to taste the next spoken word.
There were no more spoken words that night.

We slept in late the next morning, till nearly ten o'clock. It was Saturday and the only item on the calendar was a mailing Melanie had promised to do for a local environmental group called Earth Care. The newsletters (which focused on a recent *Time* article about the greenhouse effect and global warming) had been delivered the day before. They were sitting in stacks on the dining room floor, a little more than a thousand copies altogether.
It was noon by the time we finished breakfast and moved into the dining room. Melanie cut a handful of newsletters off one of the stacks, and sat down at the table. "Get a chance to read the article?"
I nodded. "Last night. Before I came to bed."
"And people think nuclear war is scary."
"It *is* scary."
"I know," she said. "I didn't mean it to sound like that. It's just that no one seems worried about what's going on in our own backyards. The things we eat. The way we acquiesce to every scientist and politician and quote—*professional*—unquote who happens along. Doesn't it make you wonder sometimes if we aren't giving away too much of ourselves?"
I stared at her, trying to look past the words, because they didn't sound like they belonged to her. "Are we still talking about the article, or are we talking about something else?"
"The article," she said.
I didn't believe her, but I left it alone.

We worked on into the afternoon.

Metastasis

It was another wicked day. Mid-nineties. High humidity. The air conditioner had given out its last breath of cool air on the previous Wednesday, and the manager had promised to replace it within the week. For the time being, though, we were forced to keep the windows closed and the drapes drawn during the day. Inside, it felt dark and oppressive and peculiarly isolated.

We worked in silence for another ten or fifteen minutes. The process becoming mostly mechanical, a chance to drift off into your own thoughts. Then Melanie looked up from the newsletter in her hands, and said evenly, "I've decided to make an appointment to see Dr. Perry."

"You already have a checkup scheduled, haven't you?" I looked at her, realizing unmistakably that I had secretly hoped last night had been the end of her cancer talk. It was a bitter realization, followed by an equally bitter taste of guilt.

"That's more than a month away. This won't wait that long."

"You really believe it's the cancer?"

She nodded solemnly.

"Want me to call him for you?"

"No, I'll do it."

Ovarian cancer.

Melanie had been thirty-three years old when the doctors first diagnosed it, almost two years ago. She liked to swim at the Y in the afternoon, and play volleyball at the high school on Wednesday nights. She liked to read mysteries before she fell asleep in bed, and bake berry pies when the berries were in season and she could pick them fresh off the vines. Maybe that was the thing I loved most about her, that indefatigable enthusiasm she had for life.

We had lost our only child, Ruby Ann, to a miscarriage in '86. It was a loss that nearly tore apart our marriage. A year went by when everything had seemed shrouded in a thick, dismal fog. Sometimes I would wake up, the bed next to me cold and empty, and I would find Melanie sitting at the kitchen table, drinking a warm cup of coffee, staring blankly out the kitchen window. I wondered at times like those if I would ever have her back again. In the end, though, she stubbornly

217

pulled herself out of her depression, and for awhile we were able to piece our fragile lives back together.
Until the cancer.
The awful, consuming cancer.

"There's nothing showing up on the scan," Dr. Perry told us a week after Melanie had first brought it up. We were gathered together in a cramped examination room; Dr. Perry on a small stool in front of us; Melanie sitting on the examination table, dressed in a hospital gown, her fingers gripping the rounded edge of the stainless steel table.

"Then you've missed something," she said quietly.

For God's sake, I thought, *listen to the doctor.*

"We didn't miss anything, Mrs. Slayden."

"Yes, you did."

The good doctor sighed. "Your white cell count is normal."

"So was the scan, honey." I took her hand in mine, as if she were a child (later, I'd hate myself for patronizing her like that, for not listening to her). "And so was the doctor's examination."

"We're talking about my body. I know what I'm feeling. I've felt it before. The cancer's back."

I looked to the doctor, who folded his arms and leaned back on his stool. He had seen this reaction before. Maybe many times before. "I know you've been through hell and back . . ."

Melanie's chemotherapy had ravished her body nearly as much as the cancer it was supposed to fight. They had kept her overnight when her temperature hit 104 after her first session. A few days later, she received a blood transfusion for her anemia. Then her hair fell out, and it was at that point the secret was out and the denial had become pointless.

She slept long hours during the six months of chemo. Sometimes I would stand in the bedroom doorway, studying her, thinking how different she looked from the woman I had married. Her face lost its color. Her eyebrows disappeared. By the end of her chemo she had vomited away nearly fifteen pounds.

When her hair finally grew back, it was dark and curly. She didn't

care much for the way it looked. For months afterward, she would stare at herself in the bathroom mirror, fingering her hair or her cheeks—which had become sallow and sunken—turning from one profile to the other, wondering out loud what had happened to her.
She *had* been through hell and back.
And she had survived.
Listen to the doctor, I thought.

Three or four weeks filed by, temperatures consistently hitting the low-to-mid nineties, the humidity hovering right around eighty percent. The air conditioner still hadn't been repaired. At night, we opened the windows to the cool breeze blowing in off the ocean. Mornings, we woke up early—before the temperature had started to climb—closed the windows, drew the curtains, and hoped the night breeze would keep the house cool a few extra hours.
The summer had turned out to be one of the hottest on record.
More than the heat, though, Melanie had been bothered by our last visit with Dr. Perry. On the way out to the car, she had hardly said a word.
"What is it?" I asked during the trip home.
"I want a promise out of you," she said without looking at me.
"What kind of a promise?"
"I want you to promise that whatever happens to me, you won't call a doctor."
"Don't be ridiculous."
"I mean it, Jimmy."
"You're just upset."
"Promise me."
"How can I—"
"*Promise* me."
I shouldn't have—in fact, I remember crossing my fingers, like a child trying to make peace with a little white lie—but I did end up giving her my word. I guess I figured that would be the end of it.

After that, a slowly-widening abyss seemed to grow between us. It was more than just between the two of us, though. It was between

Melanie and the rest of the world. She became withdrawn, silent. Sometimes it felt as if a dark cloud had settled over the apartment. I would look at her from across the room while she was reading or watching television and a foreboding somberness that belonged to her would stir inside me. That was as close as she let me come.

More honestly, that was as close as I wanted to come.

Between Melanie and the doctor, I wanted most to believe the doctor.

Melanie wouldn't let me do that.

In mid-August we sat down to do the next Earth Care mailing. The Cupertino Courier, a local newspaper, had run an article a few weeks earlier about a study in western Ontario where scientists had slowly made Lake 302 more acidic by adding sulfuric and nitric acids to the water. The purpose was to observe and chronicle the chemical and biological damage.

"Did you get a chance to read it?" Melanie asked as we were working.

"Not all of it."

"Nearly all of the species in the lake, in adapting to the higher acidic levels, went through an evolutionary change. The crayfish developed harder shells. The white suckers adopted larger eyes. That kind of thing."

"Over a period of how long?"

"The changes came relatively early, but after seven years there wasn't a species in the lake that could reproduce. Even the white suckers, which had initially thrived, had begun to disappear." She placed the last newsletter on top of a stack, then studied me for a reaction. "Every form of life in Lake 302 died out, Jimmy."

"Isn't that what they expected?"

She stared at me a moment longer, as if she couldn't believe my question, then she turned quietly back to folding newsletters.

"Well, isn't it?"

"I suppose," she said softly.

"Then what's the matter?"

"I don't know. Nothing, I guess." She shrugged. "I was just thinking . . . how sometimes it feels like we're turning the world into a giant science lab. I mean we've got test-tube babies and lakes with experiment numbers and—"

"That's how we solve problems, Melanie."

"Yeah, I know. It's just that . . ." She stopped there. Her gaze, both faraway and thoughtful, drifted toward the open window.

"Hey, are you okay?"

"I don't think so," she whispered.

"What is it?"

"I'm scared, Jimmy."

The apartment became an empty church at midnight, hushed and listening. I moved around the table, put my arm over her shoulders, and she melted warmly into me, one frightened soul into another. Entwined with her, I felt both helpful and helpless. Maybe we both felt that way. "I love you, babe."

"I know."

"What can I do?"

"Nothing."

Late afternoon faded into evening, evening into night.

Before going to bed, I pulled back the curtains and opened most of the windows in the apartment. The cool breeze off the ocean had shifted south. Here, the air was stagnant and hot, the temperature hovering near the 85 degree mark. It reminded me of the time we went down to Texas to visit Melanie's sister. That had been in the middle of a late-summer heat wave as well.

"Jimmy . . ."

"Yeah?" I climbed into bed next to her. It was the first time in weeks we didn't immediately roll away from each other, looking for sleep on the wallpaper patterns of opposite walls.

"Do you believe in God?"

"Only when I need him." I thought she would smile, but she didn't. "Why?"

"I don't know, just wondering."

A familiar silence maneuvered its way between us, and I caught myself thinking back over the past few weeks, wondering what was happening to Melanie, to our relationship, to everything I had always held close to me.

"What's happening to us, Melanie? Why won't you tell me what's bothering you? All this silence, it's driving me . . ." I stopped short of saying it, though I'm not really sure why. It was the truth. I had already inched up to the edge and looked into the abyss that was threatening to swallow us both. The blackness, the quietude, were maddening. "It's the cancer-thing, isn't it? The visit with Dr. Perry."

She didn't answer.

"We can try another doctor, if that's what you want. Someone from a different hospital."

"No," she said firmly. "No more doctors. You promised."

"Then what do you want me to do?"

She paused, and even in the shadowlight I could see her switching emotional gears again. Softly, as if it hurt getting it out, she said, "You can hold me."

We held each other for a long time.

Sometime around midnight, the heat inside the apartment finally broke. Melanie opened her eyes for the first time in nearly an hour. "I love you, Jimmy Slayden."

"You're such a fool," I said lightly. I snuggled up against her, inhaling her wonderfully sweet scent, not wanting to ever lose the memory of that smell. "Just don't lock me out, okay?"

"I won't," she whispered.

But she did.

That night proved to be the last time we made love together.

Shortly after that, Melanie began to change. Perhaps that's what she had been trying to tell me, that she knew she was going to start changing and there was nothing I or anyone else could do about it.

The changes came gradually, over a period of three or four weeks. She grew increasingly fatigued during the day, awake and active during the night, after the outside temperature had cooled down. I guess I'll never know if she was bothered by daylight, but she seemed more comfortable secluded inside the apartment with the curtains closed, the lights off. Often, I would come home after work, only to find her standing in the shadows, a ghost-like form frightened of being seen.

Then one night, after nearly two days without anything to eat, she began vomiting up a brown, watery liquid. I sat next to her on the bed, holding a stainless steel kitchen bowl under her chin because she no longer had the strength to make it to the bathroom.

"I've got to call the doctor," I told her.

Out of the corner of her eyes, she peered up at me. Her face was sallow and sunken, much the same as it had looked after her chemotherapy. She shook her head.

"You're not eating . . . nothing seems to be staying down . . . Jesus, Melanie, you'll dehydrate if this keeps up."

"No doctor."

"At least take some Compozine."

Her stomach lurched again, a dry heave this time.

I wiped her face with a damp washcloth. "You've got a couple bottles left over from the chemo."

"No."

"This is getting crazy, Melanie." I wrapped her hands around the now-warm sides of the bowl, and got up from the bed, wanting to distance myself from what was taking place. "I can't sit and watch you killing yourself like this."

"I don't want anything else in my body," she said. Then she coughed—or it might have been another heave, I'm not sure—and the convulsion bent her almost in two, loosening a soft weeping sound from the back of her throat.

I sat down again, and rubbed the back of her neck. "I feel so helpless."

"I know."

Her skin had lost a great deal of its elasticity. As I rubbed her neck, I realized layers of skin were beginning to crumble and flake. Underneath, I touched something hard and scaled.

A chill rattled through her. "I itch all over," she said, showing me her hands. The fingers were swollen, and the backs of her hands were peeling much the same as the back of her neck. "They put all that crap inside me, Jimmy."

"What?"

"I never should have let them do that." Another chill shook her. I took the bowl out of her hands, placed it on the night stand, where it wouldn't be staring back at us. She leaned back in the bed, her eyes already closed.

"See if you can get some sleep, okay?"

"Okay."

Over the course of the next few days, she seemed to improve slightly. The nausea ended, and she began taking soup once a day. For a brief time, I actually held out the hope that the worst might be over. But there was an irritating voice at the back of my mind that said she wasn't really improving at all, she was simply *adapting* to her cancer.

The days continued to be unusually hot. I had grown accustomed to watching Melanie pace the apartment once the sun had gone down. She rarely slept with me now. I quit asking why, and I quit begging her to let me take her to a doctor. As cold as it might sound, it had become easier to filter out the bitter grounds of what was happening to us and toss them out as if they didn't matter.

The night she died, I woke in a sweat around three-thirty in the morning. I was alone, and for a while, I stared at the grayish-yellow cast of a streetlight across the bedroom ceiling, wishing I could fall back to sleep. Then, from the living room, I heard something that sounded a bit like the rustle of dry autumn leaves.

"Melanie?"

I found her lying on the couch, under a blanket, her eyes closed. The room was dark—except for a sliver of light sneaking in from the bedroom—so I stopped and switched on the lamp.

"Oh dear God."

Her face was a thin scab of flesh pulled taut across the skeletal structure. Flaps of dry, dead skin were peeling from her forehead and her right cheek. Underneath, I could see a thin, crusty layer with a pattern of scales.

"I'm dying," she whispered hoarsely.

"Jesus, Melanie." I knelt beside her, feeling more helpless than ever. My hands were trembling, but I managed to brush the hair back from her dry forehead. "You're burning up."

She grinned from faraway, and I wondered if she was even aware of me. "Dox . . . or . . . u . . . bicin," she said deliriously.

It didn't make any sense, and I didn't have the time to worry about it. "You're too hot, babe. We've got to cool you down." I worked my arms underneath her—one at her shoulders, one at her knees—as gently as I could.

"Bleo . . . my . . . cin."

I had to kick the bathroom door open with one foot, and use my elbow to flip on the light switch. She wasn't heavy—in fact, she was frighteningly light—but it was awkward guiding her through the door and lowering her into the tub. I was haunted by the thought that one of her bones might snap.

"How's that?" I grabbed a towel off the nearby rack, placed it under her head for a pillow. "Is that comfortable?"

She settled back in the tub, her movements slow, her eyes wide and never leaving me.

I ran the tap until the water was cool enough to bring down her fever without making her uncomfortable, then turned on the shower. Melanie smiled. "Oh God, babe, I'm sorry. I should have listened when you told me the cancer was back. I should have trusted you."

"It isn't cancer," she whispered. Her eyes had darkened a bit. "It's the chem . . . i . . . cals."

I brushed the wet hair back from her face. "Shhh . . ."

"The chem . . . icals from the chemo." She reached out and touched my face with the back of her hand. There was still some softness to her touch; the shell-like underpinning was still partially buried. Then she smiled, a pure childlike grin that stretched tautly across the front of her skull. "I love you, Jimmy."

I held her hand against my face, afraid to let go.

"Dox . . . or . . . u . . . bi . . . cin," she said softly. "Doesn't that . . . sound awful?"

She closed her eyes.

"Melanie?"

Cool droplets of water were sliding off her body and lazily

snaking their way down the porcelain tub to the drain. It seemed as if the world had slowed down some. Everything became crystal clear. I stared dully at the way her collar bone and ribs had stretched the skin across her chest. There were places where the scales underneath were showing through now. The water around the drain gradually turned dark from something horrible that was leaking out of her. Her hand slipped out of mine and fell against the side of the tub.

Everything crystal clear.

It's only been a few months now. Melanie never opened her eyes again. I was grateful for that. I wasn't sure I could stand to look at what was behind them. The heat wave hasn't broken. Though it doesn't feel as unbearable as it once did. I keep the windows open at night, welcoming in whatever breeze happens to blow in off the ocean.

The nights seem longer without her. I don't sleep much. When I close my eyes, I see her again, the way she was at the end. And I can hear her struggling with those damnable syllables, trying to recite the names of the chemicals the doctors had used to flush out her cancer. It's an ugly sound. I don't much like listening to it.

The Song of Sister Rain

1

"*Do you smell that, Parker?*"
"*Yes.*"
"*What does it smell like?*"
"*It smells like . . . like autumn, like fallen oak leaves and fresh-turned earth, like thunderstorms and short days.*"
"*Yes, exactly!*"

2

It was there, at the side of the road, just outside the main gate, when Parker came to work that night. He caught only a glimpse of it. Diana was in the other lane, on her way out of the parking lot, and she honked at him. Parker waved, then turned to his rearview mirror and saw the brown clump of fur grow smaller and smaller until it had finally disappeared altogether.

It had looked a little like a dead dog, he thought. Or maybe a coyote, though he couldn't be sure if it had been an animal at all. It might have been an old rug someone had thrown out, the way people sometimes did on this stretch of road when they didn't like the idea of having to haul their junk to the dump on the other side of town. Or it might have been a winter coat. It was getting to be that time of year and it wouldn't be the first time he had spotted misplaced clothing by the side of the road.

Parker thought it might have been any of these things or none of them, then his thoughts went wandering from the weather to . . . the clump of fur to . . . his mother, whom he thought might be able to use a new coat for Christmas, to . . . how well she was adjusting at the nursing home.

Coming to the decision that she could no longer function on her own had been the hardest thing he had ever done. After six weeks, it still carried a sting when he thought about it. Alzheimer's, though, was an ugly beast, and there had been no denying that his mother was no longer the same woman who had raised him.

He pulled into a space near the front entrance of Metallic Wonders and turned off the engine. For a moment, he sat there, watching in his rearview mirror as the last two cars filed out of the company parking lot, reminding himself that tomorrow was Saturday and he wanted to drop by to visit his mother some time in the afternoon.

His black plastic lunch box had taken a tumble off the seat on the trip over. It lay on its side, up against the heater vent. Parker leaned across the seat, picked up the box, and wondered whether or not the Thermos had survived. So many things in life were fragile, he thought as he climbed out of the car.

Metallic Wonders was a strange place to work, made even stranger by the fact that he worked nights as the only security guard. It was a cushy job. Once around the complex every hour on the hour. Check the locks. Make sure everything was quiet and secure.

What made it strange were the sculptures. The Wonders, as the place had come to be known, was an artists' cooperative. They produced mostly commissioned works, the large sculptures you might find outside City Hall or at the entrance to the County Fairgrounds or in a local shopping mall. Others—some commissioned, some not—fell into the hands of private collectors. And still others, well, Parker had no idea where they were likely to end up. These were not your ordinary, run-of-the-mill works. They were, each in its own unique way, horrific. That was the only word he could find to describe them.

Parker locked the door behind him, punched in at the time clock, and made his way to the small office at the back of the building. He dropped his lunch box in the chair next to the door and prepared for his first round of the evening. A couple of months ago some guy from L.A. had come in looking for something he could use as an attraction outside his adult book store. Apparently, he had hid somewhere in the back warehouse where the wire rods and the bronze and the Corten steel were kept. Parker found him in Building Two, buck naked, riding a wire-metal piece called The Whore of Babylon.

You just never knew.

3

Parker slept uneasily the next morning. He had gone to bed reminding himself that he needed to visit his mother that afternoon at the nursing home. But the visit had preyed on his mind and he had drifted in and out of sleep all morning before finally came fully awake, exhausted, at a few minutes after one.

It was late afternoon by the time he arrived at the Happy Valley Nursing Home. His mother was in her room, sitting in a chair, staring out the window. Her hands were folded in her lap, and when he entered, she looked up at him and smiled.

"Hi, Mom. It's Parker."

He never knew when she might or might not recognize him. On occasion she was actually able to call him by name, though such occasions had become less and less the norm the past six months. Even when she was able to recognize him, it was a rare moment when she could share what was going on inside her. The mother Parker had grown up with was locked away now, a prisoner inside her own head.

The dementia—a term he had picked up from the doctors, mostly from hearing it time and time again—had begun so subtlety Parker had at first missed the clues. Of course, they had not been the kinds of lapses that drew attention. She would forget where she had parked the car, or the dentist appointment she had made two weeks ago. Or she would misplace her glasses and spend an hour searching for them before she remembered they were in her purse. Little things like that. The kinds of lapses that Parker, himself, had been guilty of from time to time.

But he had begun to worry about her after she had missed visiting his father's grave on their wedding anniversary. Parker's father had passed away eight years ago after a myocardial infarction —another medical term Parker had picked up from over exposure. It was the man's third myocardial infarction in seven years. He died while fishing on the Sacramento River. Parker's mother had never missed visiting the grave site. Rain or shine, illness or bridge club, she was there every birthday, every wedding and death anniversary, a woman paying her respects to the man she had loved nearly all her life. And then that last anniversary . . .

"What happened?" Parker had asked her.

"I don't know," she said.

"You've never done that before."

"I just forgot, that's all."

"You forgot?"

"I'm sixty-seven years old. I'm allowed to forget once in awhile."

That was certainly true, and Parker hadn't pressed her anymore about it. But then two weeks later he called to invite her out to dinner and she had sounded confused about who he was and what he wanted.

"Mom?"

"You shouldn't be calling here."

"Mom, this is Parker. Are you all right?"

"Shhh. They might hear you."

"Who might hear me?"
"The feeders."
"Who?"
"The feeders."

Try as he might, Parker couldn't seem to get anything else out of her, and the call worried him so much that he went over to make sure she was all right. He found her in the living room, watching television. She looked up and smiled and told him what a pleasant surprise it was to see him. She offered no recollection of the phone call. And she pinched her face at him as if he were crazy when he brought up the feeders.

After that, Parker had started to pay more attention. When they were together, he kept a closer eye on her, and tried not to overlook the little lapses that had seemed so meaningless before. Nothing was meaningless anymore, he had decided. Nothing.

He made the decision to place her in the nursing home after he had gone over to check on her after work one morning and had found her in the garage, dressed in her pajamas. She was sitting in her car, an old Nash Rambler she hadn't driven in ten years.

"What are you doing, Mom?"

"I'm supposed to be somewhere," she said, a troubled expression on her face.

"You have an appointment this morning?"

"An appointment, yes."

"What kind of an appointment, Mom?"

"That's what he said."

"Mom?"

"He said I have an appointment with the feeders."

Parker helped her out of the Rambler and back into the house. She had been sitting out in the garage for a good long time. Her hands were freezing, her lips blue, her breathing shallow. He got her into bed with an extra blanket, and went to make some tea in the kitchen, where he found she had left two of the gas burners on high. The flames were bright yellow, dancing and weaving, having a grand old time. How long they had been burning, he had no way of knowing. Maybe only for the time she had been in the garage. Maybe for days. It didn't matter. The only thing that mattered was that a line had been crossed. She had gone from being harmlessly forgetful to potentially self-endangering.

Hence the nursing home.

"How have you been, Mom?" Parker gave her a kiss on the cheek. She smiled blandly. "Parker ..."

"Yes."

"Parker . . . my boy." She gave his hand a loving pat. "It's so nice to have you here."

It was as lucid as she had been in two months. Parker pulled up a chair and they talked about the Christmas they had spent in Tahoe when he was only eleven; and the time his father had gotten a promotion at the Wal-Mart where he worked and brought home half the store in celebration; and how nice the place on Waterford had been when Parker was growing up; and a hundred other things. She remembered it all, even little things like the birdhouse at Waterford that had blown over during the snow storm in the winter of '76. Parker had forgotten that until she mentioned it.

He took her out for a walk along the river later that afternoon and treated her to dinner at El Papagayo before returning her home again. By then, the inevitable lapses had begun to show themselves again. She sat in her favorite chair and stared out the window, until she finally looked up at him, her expression confused.

"You need anything?" Parker asked.

"They usually come at night," she said.

"Who's that, Mom?"

"The feeders."

"The feeders? You keep bringing them up. Who are the feeders, Mom?"

"They visit, you know. Usually at night, but . . . not always. Not always. Sometimes, they come as your father. Sometimes as you. And sometimes . . . sometimes maybe as a chair or the television or a coat or a pair of shoes or . . . or . . ." Her voice drifted away, taking the thought with it.

Parker sat with her awhile longer, neither of them talking, and by the time he finally got up to leave, she was completely lost again. He

The Song of Sister Rain

kissed her on the forehead. "I'll be back next week. I love you, Mom."

She smiled vacantly.

4

"*Can you feel it, Parker?*"
"*Yes.*"
"*Tell me, then, what does it feel like?*"
"*Like a smile. Like silver tear drops and the first summer jump into the swimming hole. Like the first star at night and vanilla ice cream on a sore throat.*"
"*Yes! Exactly!*"

5

It had been a year now since Parker's sister had died in an automobile accident. She had been on her way home from her boyfriend's apartment. They had just broken up, and she was upset. She had left crying, and it was late out, and it had been raining, and she had tried to take a corner a little faster than she should have. The car lost control. It ended up off the side of the road, wrapped around the trunk of an old oak.

His sister died instantly.

6

The following Monday night when Parker went to work, it was still there on the side of the road, that clump of fur or whatever it was. It was still there, but it had changed in some indefinable way. He passed it going slower this time, straining to get a better look. It seemed as if it might have grown, maybe filled out a bit.

One of the feeders, no doubt, he thought, surprising himself. And where had that come from? He hadn't realized how much his mother's dementia had begun to infiltrate his own thoughts.

The clump of fur, still unidentifiable, disappeared from sight and Parker turned his full attention back to the road. He was running late tonight, and while he didn't need to officially show up at the Wonders before his first round at seven, Parker preferred to get an early start whenever possible.

He clocked in and went to the back office, after his flashlight. The building was empty. It was quiet, the lights dimmed, the air still warm from the day's activity. At his locker, Parker held the Master lock in the palm of his hand, and drew a complete and utter blank. It was the first time it had ever happened to him. He stared at the lock a moment, his mind a blank slate, then dropped it and leaned back on the desk. How long it took before the combination finally came to him, he didn't care to guess. But it came all at once in a rush, and he fingered through the numbers, gave the lock a tug, and . . .

. . . and it opened.

Thank God.

The rest of the night went by uneventfully, except for something that had left Parker feeling strangely uneasy. The sculpture was a wire and sheet-metal monstrosity that had slowly been taking form over several weeks now. He still wasn't sure what final form it was supposed to take. It consisted of two main elements. The central piece, shaped something like a tuning fork with breasts, stood fifteen feet high. The second piece was half that size, a faceless human form that he thought might be female. A bronze placard had been recently added. The work was titled The Feeders.

His last time around, just as sunrise was warming the eastern horizon, Parker stopped and studied The Feeders. He wondered where it had come from—that title, and how his mother had known about it. And he wondered what the sculpture would look like when it was finally complete. And then a strange thought came to him. Maybe it never would be complete. Maybe it was . . .

Maybe it was . . . *becoming.*

Yes.

Becoming.

The Song of Sister Rain

That thought, along with what his mother had said—"*Sometimes they come as your father. Sometimes as you. And sometimes . . . sometimes maybe as a chair or a television or a coat or a pair of shoes.*"—followed Parker home that morning, a nightmare waiting to happen.

7

Parker woke up several days later with only a vague idea of where he was.

He sat up. He wiped the sleep from his eyes. A light, walnut dresser sat against the opposite wall, an RCA portable television on top, pushed into the corner. Next to the bed on the night stand, a digital clock attested to the time: 2:53 p.m. There was a door off to the right, closed, a window off to the left, the blinds drawn. It was at once both familiar and frightening. How had he arrived here at this place, at this time? And where exactly was this place?

Outside, an autumn storm huddled in around the building, the sky low and dark, the limbs of the dogwood stirring in the wind, fashioning shadow puppets across the bedroom walls.

A light rain began to fall.

Parker recalled a similar day from a long, long time ago. He was with his sister, out back of the house at Waterford. It was autumn and a storm swept over the western mountains like a huge wave, bringing down a warm, intoxicating rain. His sister giggled and raised her arms, her lamb's wool sweater dangling loosely as she spun and twirled, a ballerina dancing without an audience, dancing for no one other than herself.

"Isn't it grand, Parker?"

He looked at her, believing she had lost it this time, completely lost it.

"Isn't it?" she repeated.

"What?"

"Life! Isn't it grand? Close your eyes and it's a cool reminder against your face. The world is alive! Take notice! You breathe it in and send it out again, a thousand times a day and never say thank you. But it's all around you, Parker. Everywhere! Just waiting for you to find surprise."

"I've found surprise."

"No, you haven't."

"I have."

"Go on, then! Close your eyes and raise your arms and see if you've ever—"

The phone rang, the sound jarring him out of the memory, nearly jarring him out of bed as well. Parker wiped a hand across his face, and let out a long breath. Outside, a light, steady rain softly tapped its autumn song against the window pane.

The phone rang again, and again once more before he found it on the floor, between the bed and the night stand. He hoisted it to his lap, listened to it ring one more time, then lifted the receiver off the hook. He raised it to his ear.

"Hello?"

"You never did," a voice whispered.

"Never did what?"

"Never found surprise."

And it was true, he realized. Even after that day in the back yard with his sister, he never had found surprise. There were too many things going on, too much to do, too little time to get it all done, and one day passed into another, one week into one month, and so on.

"You're in your bedroom, Parker. At home. It's time to come out and play."

8

That night, the clump by the side of the road was gone.

Parker drove past the spot where it had been, moving at little more than a crawl, straining to make sure he didn't miss it. Going the other way, Diana honked at him and he waved absently. The clump was gone. He drove past the speed limit sign, past the telephone pole with the Child Quest poster stapled eye-level, and the clump should have been there somewhere, but it wasn't. It had disappeared. Someone had picked it up or the wind had blown it away or . . .

It didn't matter, Parker tried to tell himself. It had been a clump, an unidentifiable clump of something, and that's all it had been. He drove past the spot by the side of the road, trying not to glance in his rearview mirror in case he had somehow missed it, and then he glanced anyway, and felt uneasy that he couldn't let it go.

Inside the *Wonders*, he clocked in and made his way to the back office. He dropped his lunch box on the chair next to the door, got his flashlight out of the locker—no trouble with the combination tonight—and started on his rounds.

Building One was where most of the work was done. Parker passed through the maze of torches and anvils, mallets, cutting wheels and shaping tables, and made his way out of one work area and into another. Everything seemed unusually quiet tonight as he crossed to Building Two. The alleyway, all weeds and dry grass, had been overrun with crickets. Sometimes they had raised such a racket he had trouble hearing his own thoughts. Tonight, though, not a sound, not a chirp, as he made his way across.

Building Two was a mammoth brick building that had once served as the assembly wing of an auto plant. Twenty-seven foot high ceiling. Concrete slab floor. Block and tackle hanging from the overhead rafters. Parker moved around the outer perimeter of the building, checking the windows and skylights, trying the doors, shining his light down the long stacks of iron bar and Corten steel. He wasn't alone tonight. Someone or some*thing* was here with him. He could feel it.

That feeling followed him all the way to the far back corner of the building, like a nagging ache, and he found himself standing before the last great sculpture. *The Feeders*. He stood in awe, wondering why he hadn't realized before, wondering why he hadn't understood.

"Oh, Parker," his mother cried. She was the second piece in this great work, the faceless human form he had thought might be female. He had been right. All along, he had been right. "We've been waiting so long."

"Mom?"

She reached and took him in her arms, all smiles and warmth and assurance.

"I've missed you, Mom."

"I know," she said softly, lucidly. She smiled again, held him away from her to look him over, then pointed to the center piece, the fifteen-foot shape that he had thought resembled a tuning fork with breasts. "And who's this, Parker?"

"Sis?" She was wearing her lamb's wool sweater, and for the first time, he made the connection. The clump by the side of the road hadn't been a dead animal after all. It had been his sister's sweater, his sister's lamb's wool sweater.

"Yes!" his mother cried.

Parker climbed onto his sister's lap, feeling warm and safe, not in a dream but of a dream, not lost but found, not alone but attended. He raised his face to her sweet smile, and closed his eyes, free of myocardial infarctions and automobile accidents and dementia, just him and his mother, him and his sister, together again.

Can you feel it?

Yes!

9

"Open your eyes, Parker."

He did, and his sister smiled at him, the smile of sweetness and fond memories, of joyous laughter and soft whispers. He raised his face to the rain, feeling the cool touch against his cheeks, the delight of rivulets down his forehead.

"*Taste it,*" *she said.*

He opened his mouth, the water tickling his tongue, filling his cheeks.

"*Tell me.*"

"*Like spring and autumn. Like a breath of fresh air and the song of a flute. Like a kiss.*"

"*I miss it, Parker.*"

"*I know you do.*"

"*And do you know what I am?*"

"*One of the feeders?*"

"And why I'm here?"
"To take me?"
"Yes! Exactly!"

10

Pete Burton, the janitor, came in a little after five the next morning. He turned on the lights and made his way to the back office, half-expecting to bump into Parker, and surprised when he didn't. He made the rounds through Building One, opening windows, emptying trash cans, sweeping metal shavings off the floor, then moved to Building Two, where he continued the same routine.

He found Parker at the far back corner, lying at the base of a huge sculpture called *The Greeters*. The work was still weeks from completion. It was a Buddha-like figure, reaching to the sky, welcoming an understanding of life and death, of mystery and knowledge, of love and hate. At least that had been the way the sculptor had explained it.

Parker opened his eyes, looking lost and vacant.

"Parker? You all right?"

"Shhh. They might hear you."

"Who? Who might hear me?"

"The feeders."

Slipping

1

"*It's hard to tell the difference sometimes. You spend all day and half the night editing the final version of an ad, then you go home, crash for a few hours and start all over again the next morning. Every once in a while I have to remind myself what day it is and where I live. And there's always the danger, I suppose, that if you're not careful, you might drift a little too far from the reality loop. It's happened to some of the best of them."*
Raymond Hewitt

2

For a moment, before he became fully aware of his surroundings, Raymond Hewitt, age 32, didn't know where he was. He had been sitting in the La-Z-Boy in the living room of his apartment, watching

David B. Silva

Nightline, and nibbling at a leftover chicken burrito from last night's dinner. But now, he realized suddenly, he was standing in his bathroom.

The light was on above the mirror. He stared at himself, dressed only in his pajama bottoms, the toothbrush in his hand. There was a thin line of toothpaste sitting on the bristles, and his mouth was dry. He hadn't started to brush yet. But . . .

But what am I doing in here?

A sliver of grayish light slipped through the opened bathroom door. He glanced down the hallway at the living room where the television was off now. There was plate sitting on the end table next to the La-Z-Boy. Even from here, he could see it was empty, except for a fork and a crumpled napkin. The chicken burrito was gone. He had finished it, he supposed, though he couldn't recall having done so.

What happened here, Raymond, my friend?

"I don't know."

He looked again at his reflection in the mirror, at the puzzled expression staring back at him, then brought the toothbrush mechanically to his mouth. What had happened, he decided, was simple: he hadn't been paying attention. He had finished the burrito, turned off the television, and changed into his pajamas without paying attention to what he was doing. It had been like driving on automatic. Entering the on-ramp, thinking about how you're going to get everything done by tomorrow's production meeting, then suddenly finding yourself a block away from home with no recollection of the miles in between.

Either that . . . or he had misplaced a little piece of himself tonight. Stashed it away in the same hollow place where he kept the bitterness of his separation from Sherrie and his every-other-weekend visitations with Robin. Somewhere out of mind, where the memories were kept dull and painless.

One of those, Ray decided as he climbed into bed. He pulled the bedsheets up under his chin and covered his eyes with his left arm.

It would be another twenty minutes before the Sand Man would accompany him down a long, spiral stairway into the pure black peacefulness of slumber. In the morning, he would struggle to pull himself out of that dark, safe sleep, and by the time he was fully awake, the episode of the night before would be long forgotten.

3

"I'm going to miss it," Bev told him late the next night.

Ray switched his briefcase to his other hand, and checked his Rolex. It was five to midnight. A light rain had fallen sometime after dinner, and the streets mirrored the soft shimmer of the surrounding city lights. It seemed later than it was. In fact, Ray told himself, it seemed almost as if the night had settled in to stay. "No you won't. We've got five minutes before the last train leaves."

He took her by the arm, and together they hurried across Fourth Street and started down the tunnel entrance to the Midtown Station. If there had been someone else on the street, they might have been mistaken for a young married couple heading home after a late-night dinner with friends (a late *sup*, as they liked to say on the Hollywood side of the business). But that would have been a mistaken assumption. Bev had hired on with Baylor & Baylor Advertising a little less than a month ago, after a national ad campaign at another agency had won her a Clio, and CEO Chet Baylor had lured her away with an offer of bigger bucks and more creative freedom. She had been lured right into Ray's office, to work on a campaign for a small independent film called *Timescape*. A get-your-toes-wet project while she learned her way around the agency.

At the bottom of the steps, Bev switched her purse from one shoulder to the other, and brushed a wisp of hair back from her forehead. "I still don't understand why they're front-loading this movie. It's not that bad."

"Ours is not to reason why."

"God, you're cynical."

"Not a cynic, a realist," Ray said easily. "It's a horror flick, not *Gone With The Wind*. Two weeks after it opens, it'll close. And two months after that it'll be in every video store across the country. Doesn't matter how good we do our job, we aren't going to make

Timescape into a box-office hit. They know that. As long as we can max the theater gross they'll be happy. Video sales'll take care of the rest."

"Seems like a waste. I've seen Oscar winners that were worse."

As they arrived at the platform, Ray checked his watch again. Midnight, straight up. It had been ten or fifteen minutes since the last train had come through, though it felt as if it might have been days. A cool breeze carried out of the tunnels, howling softly and faraway. The train was running late, and they were the only two people waiting. He couldn't recall that having ever happened before, being alone in the station.

"Why is it so quiet?" Bev asked. "We miss something?"

"Maybe the system's down."

Overhead, the information monitor ran through a blurb for the symphony: The Skylight Center. Saturday night at 8:00 p.m. General admission $15.00. Ray watched until it went into the Arrival/Departure Schedule. "Nope. Looks like it's just a few minutes late."

"Where is everyone?"

He placed his briefcase on the floor between them, and glanced about the empty station. Someone had spray-painted a symbol in day-glow orange across the face of a billboard of a local FM station. It looked a little like an hourglass on its side, with a man buried in the sand to his knees. A sleeve of newspaper swirled out of one of the tunnels. Ray cleared his throat. "It's midnight," he said with a shrug. "There's never much of a crowd this time of night."

She seemed to relax a bit. "You have your daughter this weekend?"

"Supposed to, but Sherrie took her down to Florida on some sort of business trip. They're doing Disney World and Epcot while they're down there."

"So what's your weekend look like?"

"I don't know." He watched the sleeve of newspaper drop back to the tracks. "Maybe I'll spend some time at the office tomorrow."

"Another look at *Timescape*?"

"Yeah, if you don't mind?"

"No, of course not," she said, and he could see she really was comfortable with the idea. "I suppose I should have brought this up earlier, though . . ."

"What's that?"

"I was wondering what you thought of the IMPs."

"For *Timescape*?"

She nodded, a little less comfortably now.

"What about 'em?" He looked past her, down the tunnel beyond the long line of tracks leading off into the darkness, and was struck by the myriad of images they had put together for the ad, each one flashing on then off again, as if its afterimage were burned permanently into his retinas.

"I'm feeling a little uneasy with the pacing."

"Too slow?"

"No, too fast."

He looked at her now, surprised. "We've got to quick-cut it. There isn't a fifteen-second run in the whole damn film we can bring up. What else are we supposed to do with it?"

"No, I understand that. It's just that we've got . . . what? better than forty cuts in the thirty-second lead?"

"Forty-seven."

"It's too fast, Ray."

"Not if you're targeting the MTV crowd. The world's a faster place than when we were kids. People don't have the patience anymore to sit back and wait for us to make our point. They want everything to be a roller coaster ride."

"You know that's not true."

"Truer than you think." He checked his watch again. 12:06 a.m. Except for their conversation, the platform area had fallen into an even deeper hush. But now, approaching by way of the South Tunnel, the sound of the next train came clicking along at a reassuring rhythm.

"About time," Bev said with a smile.

Ray looked at her, thinking how lovely she looked, even under the weak fluorescent lights of a late Friday night. Her outfit was all business: the gray jacket, single-breasted with padded shoulders and dropped-notch lapels; the skirt pleated in the front with angled pockets

and a wide waist-band. All business at a glance. But you couldn't look at her without seeing the woman. She was thin, elegant lines and small breasts. She could smile at you, reflect serious, or throw a tantrum without ever making you feel uneasy about her. And her eyes—they could stare mysteriously in your direction with never a hint of . . .
 (*CUT TO*)
 . . . what was going on behind them.
 "Don't work too hard this weekend," she was saying.
 Ray closed his eyes, then looked again.
 The train had arrived. He had closed his eyes and opened them, and the train had arrived out of the black midnight of the tunnel. Bev was standing just inside the doorway now, holding on to a stainless steel rail with one hand, looking tired from the long day's work but hiding most of the exhaustion behind a polite smile.
 "Bev?"
 "See you Monday, Ray." She brushed the hair back from her eyes, waved, and the doors closed, like a wall coming down between them.
 The subway train began to roll forward, lurching a time or two before it finally found its stride. It skimmed down the short span of rails, making a sound something like the wind swirling around the tops of the skyscrapers, then sailed off into the mouth of the North Tunnel.
 Mystified, Ray watched it disappear. Something strange had just happened. He wasn't sure exactly what it was, but for a moment it had felt as if time had somehow skipped a beat. He checked his watch again. 12:08 a.m. A full two minutes had passed. The train had pulled into the station, the doors had opened, Bev had climbed aboard. All that had somehow happened without him.
 He stood there a moment or two longer, feeling strangely out of place, and finally, after the platform had fallen back into its uneasy silence, he climbed the stairs again. On the street, there was a chill in the late-night air. The rain had stopped. The sky had opened to a spattering of dim stars. He tucked his briefcase under one arm, and walked with both hands jammed into his pants pockets to keep them warm. It seemed unusually peaceful beneath the sparse patches of night sky. He crossed Washington against a red light, only distantly aware of what he was doing.

By the time he arrived at his apartment on Sixty-Second Street, his thoughts—which had never been far from that picture of Bev standing inside the subway train—had drifted back to the night before, when he had suddenly found himself in the bathroom, confused and feeling as if he had just come out of anesthesia.

The lock clicked into place, and he leaned heavily against the inside of the apartment door. The cast of a streetlight seeped through the living room curtains and cut a path across the floor toward the end table next to the La-Z-Boy. The plate was still sitting there, with its fork and its crumpled napkin. The chicken burrito was missing, though.

Because you ate it, don't you remember?

No, he didn't.

And that was the problem, wasn't it?

It seemed lately he had begun to forget a number of things.

4

Bev beat him to the office Monday morning. After checking his messages—there was only one, a panic call from the B. M. Myers folks who were having second thoughts about their new dog food campaign—Ray wandered into the editing room and found her sitting in the dark, running through the *Timescape* ad.

"Morning."

She waved, back-handed, without looking up from the projector. "Just a sec."

"No hurry." He closed the door, and as the room settled instantly back into its comfortable darkness, he was taken back to Friday night again. It was something he had nearly put out of his mind over the weekend, but suddenly he was there again, on the platform, looking down the long dark tunnel, wondering when the train would come in. He had been haunted all that night by a strange, unexplainable sense of detachment, and finally on the edge of sleep, had decided that something precious had begun to slip through his fingers. He had wondered—quite legitimately at the time, he thought—if maybe he hadn't begun to lose a little piece of his mind.

David B. Silva

Which piece would that be, Ray old boy? A couple million neurons, perhaps?

Perhaps, he thought now, solemnly.

Someone had left a conference chair next to the door. Ray pulled it away from the wall and sat down. He stared vacantly at the soft green light emitted by the projector. He found it, along with the rhythmic clicking of the sprockets and the Monday morning chill that had collected in the room over the weekend, momentarily meditative, and allowed his mind to wander off again.

Sherrie had called from Florida Sunday night. They were having a good time, she said. Though Robin was a little cranky from a long day at Epcot. Everything else was doing fine, even the business part of the trip. They still intended to be back the afternoon of the 25th as planned, she said. Then she had put Robin on the line. "Hi, Daddy! We're on the other side of the country. We went to Epcot today and on Tuesday we're spending the whole day at Disney World, and there's a swimming pool where we're staying!"

"Sounds like you're having a pretty good time."

"Yeah. It'd be better if you were here, though," she said matter-of-factly. "But I understand. Most of the time, you and Mommy don't like it when you're around each other."

That's not true, he thought. *At least not entirely. Sometimes we just forget what it was like a long, long time ago.*

Now, as he was sitting in the chair silently watching Bev run through the thirty-second tape, four, maybe five times altogether, he realized he had forgotten most of the bad times. The happiest times— when they had first met and started dating, and in the early years of their marriage—those were the times he recalled most clearly now. How had he ever lost sight of those?

The rat-tat-tat of the sprockets ended abruptly and the silence brought Ray back from his thoughts. He looked across the room at Bev as she swung her chair around. In the faint green light her face was half-hidden in shadow, but it appeared as if she were lost in thoughts of her own.

"Okay, no secrets between co-workers," Ray said. "What's eating you about this thing?"

Slipping

"It's too fast," she said evenly. She sounded every bit the woman who had won a Clio, though the degree of concern in her voice surprised him somewhat.

"That's still bothering you?"

"It's still bothering me."

"You're worrying needlessly," he said. He leaned back on the legs of his chair and flipped on the light switch next to the door. The room brightened immediately, and for a reason he could not explain, it seemed as if something nearby had suddenly stopped moving.

"I don't think so. This one is going to crater on us if we're not careful."

"If it craters, it won't be because of the IPMs," he said. He had come across a black-and-white, quick cut Nike spot during a Bears/49ers game over the weekend and that ad had convinced him that they had made the right decision for the *Timescape* campaign. It was a gritty, emotional series of shots that had left him feeling pumped up and powerful, the same kinds of feelings they had set out to convey for *Timescape*.

She turned back to the projector, staring silently at the white screen. "I'm not so sure, Ray."

"It's the perfect vehicle for this movie. We take the thrills and all the action, splice them together in a thirty-second run . . . and as long as we leave viewers feeling excited, it doesn't matter how much of it they absorb. It's the *feeling* we're trying to convey here. That's what'll get them in the theater on Friday night."

"I suppose," she said with a degree of resignation.

"But?"

"But . . . don't you ever feel it?"

"Feel *what*?"

"How fast everything seems to be moving?"

He leaned forward, staring at her, thinking: *You feel it, too? That sense that a tight spring has suddenly let loose and everything's becoming unraveled? You feel that?* But that wasn't what she was talking about. She was talking about the rat race and how fast the days sometimes go and how confusing the world can be with all its changes. And he was talking about something much more personal than that. He

David B. Silva

was talking about closing your eyes while watching *Nightline* and opening them again and finding yourself somewhere else, doing some*thing* else.

"I guess I do," he said.

"Doesn't it ever scare you?"

"I don't think about it much."

She turned back to the projector again, and Ray felt the muscles in his neck relax, as if the air had been let out of them. She seemed momentarily occupied by the screen, then . . .

(*CUT TO*)

. . . placed the menu down on the table and looked up at him. "Sorry I was late," Bev said.

He heard a *clinking* sound and followed it across the room to a middle-aged man who was touching wine glasses with a much younger, and appreciably more attractive woman. They were sitting at a small table in the corner, with a flowered trellis behind them. The woman giggled.

"Chet dropped by. He said you were busy on the phone but he wanted us to know that the company got the Timex account. It's ours for the asking, Ray."

A waiter brushed past him like a breeze, kicking up a swirl of hair on the back of his head. He combed it back, and looked up at the man, who was carrying a silver tray on the palm of one hand. There were three or four other tables in the area, covered in white-laced cloths, centered with candles and fresh bouquets of flowers. Through a latticed divider, he could see the soft glow of sunlight slipping in past a curtained window. It was still daylight out.

"Ray?"

He looked down at the menu in his hands, feeling as if he had just opened his eyes after an accident and was still shaking the cobwebs out of his mind. They were at Fitzgerald's. It said so across the top of the menu. And they were having lunch, he supposed. They often lunched at Fitzgerald's.

"Are you okay?"

"Huh?"

"You look pale."

"No, I'm fine," he lied. Across the room, another waiter appeared from behind a pair of swinging doors. He weaved his way through the maze of tables, half of which were empty, and disappeared through an archway into another room of the restaurant. "What time is it?"

"One-fifteen," Bev said. "We've still got forty-five minutes."

One-fifteen.

My God.

Ray closed his menu, and stared across the table at her. She was wearing a pearl gray, loose-fitting blazer over an attractive silk crepe de chine blouse and a slim, elegant skirt. It was the same day as it had been this morning, he realized. Those were the same clothes she had been wearing in the projection room. Only now . . .

"Are you sure you're all right?"

"Just hungry," he said, looking down at his menu again. "So how much do we get to play with?"

"Pardon?"

"The Timex account."

"Two million for the first go around. If they like what we deliver, five mill a year for a three-year run."

"Sounds good," he said absently. An empty, gurgling sensation had begun to roil in his stomach. Not, surprisingly, out of hunger, as he would have expected—he hadn't eaten breakfast this morning and last night's dinner had been nothing more than a couple of bites from a reheated tuna caserole—but from a slight sense of nausea. He slipped a hand below the table and loosened his belt a notch. "When do we start?"

"There's a meeting this afternoon with Chet and Boswick and the production people."

"What time?"

"Three," Bev said.

"Good," he said. "Look, could you excuse me for a moment?"

"Of course."

"I'll be right back."

In the restroom, he leaned heavily over the sink, both hands braced against the porcelain, head bowed. A light sweat had broken out over his forehead, though the sensation of nausea had passed now. He glanced up at his reflection in the mirror, at the man who was quietly becoming a stranger.

What was happening to him?

5

By the time Ray arrived home that night, the apartment was draped in thick shadow. He dropped his briefcase on the entryway tile, next to the door, and thanked sweet Jesus he had made it through the rest of the day without closing his eyes and suddenly finding himself somewhere else. He moved down the hall, pausing a moment to look at end table next to the La-Z-Boy. It had become an unconscious habit the past several nights, to stop there and reassure himself that the plate and the napkin and the fork had all been put away and everything was in its place now, the way he last remembered it.

On his way past the phone in the kitchen, he slipped the receiver off its cradle, then pulled a chair out from the table, sat down, and began to dial the push-button with the thumb of one hand. It rang four times before she answered it.

"Mom?"

"Raymond," she said delightfully. "What a wonderful surprise."

"How are you, Mom?"

"I'm fine, of course."

"And Dad?"

"Your father's watching his football game. He's in heaven. You want to talk to him?"

"No, that's all right. I forgot it was Monday night." He had spent much of the afternoon retracing the last few days of his life, and when they had led him nowhere in particular, he had traced the days back even further, all the way back to his childhood, in fact. Thirty-two years of days, all behind him now, and . . . and they were beginning to pass even faster now, he had decided.

"Mom?"

"What is it, Raymond?"

"I know this is going to sound like a strange question, but . . . what's it like . . . growing old?"

There was a thoughtful silence on the other end of the line. Then, in that soft voice that someone who didn't know her might mistake for fraility, she said, "It sneaks up on you, Raymond. Like an early winter. One day it's autumn and you're picking wild berries and baking pies, the next day it's snowing and picking berries seems like something you used to do a long, long time ago."

"Is it true, that old wife's tale about time going by faster the older you get?"

"It certainly feels like it."

Yes, he thought unhappily, *it certainly does.* He ran a hand through his hair, and by the time he hung up the phone, the words on the other end had become distant and unimportant. He had heard what he had called to hear. However distasteful it felt.

It was getting late.

Later than you think, my friend.

He glanced down the hallway again, at the pale-gray light slipping in through the curtains, and thought about trying to reach Sherrie in Florida. He wasn't even sure where she was staying, but she had given him a number, he thought, and he had written it down somewhere.

But then what was he going to say?

You better hurry back if you ever want to see me again. I'm not sure I'll be here much longer.

No. Not that. This: *Stay where you are, Sherrie. You and Robin stay right there in Florida. I won't be able to see you, but as long as you're there and not here, I'll know I haven't lost anything more than week. I'll know that much.*

No. Better not to call at all, he decided, burying his head . . .

(*CUT TO*)

. . . in his hands.

"A hard night?"

He heard her voice, and knew immediately it was a voice that shouldn't be there, not in his apartment at this time of night, uninvited. It was almost more than he could do, but he forced his hands away from his face. Bev was sitting across from him on the other side of the . . .

desk. They were sitting in his office at Baylor & Baylor. She smiled cautiously, with a look of mild concern.

"Ray?"

"What time is it?" he asked, though the exact time didn't matter, did it? There was sunlight pouring in through the window behind him, and that was all he needed to know. It was daylight out.

"A quarter to ten."

Twelve hours, or nearly that much.

My God.

He stared down at the coat sleeves of his business suit, and realized he had changed clothes since a moment ago—or last night, or a week ago, or however long it had been. And he had shaved and washed up, spent a night alone in bed and climbed out of that bed early, had breakfast and hurried into the office, all of that, and maybe not just once, maybe half-a-dozen times by now.

"What day is it?"

"Tuesday."

"Thank God."

"Are you all right?"

"I don't know. I've been . . ."

"What?"

Losing time, he was tempted to say, but it was an easier thing to think than speak. Therefore, instead, he asked a question he thought might lead into something he had been kicking around recently: "Did you ever see the movie *Sybil*?"

"Sally Fields? About the woman with all those different personalities?"

"Yes."

"It was a good movie."

"Yes. But remember what happened when another personality had stepped in? She couldn't remember things. It was as if she had gone to sleep in the middle of making dinner and then suddenly she would wake up again and she would be somewhere else—at work, maybe—and it would be a different day and she would be wearing different clothes."

"But she thought that's the way it was for everyone? I remember that. It was creepy."

Slipping

Not as creepy as the real thing.

He couldn't ask his next question while looking at her, so he swung his chair around, and stared out the window at the mirror-glassed high-rise across the avenue from his office. The sun was above the building, shining in his face at an odd angle; otherwise he wouldn't have been surprised if he had actually been able to see himself on the otherside. It had happened before, on a clear winter day, in the early afternoon hours. Not this time, though, and he supposed that was all for the best because it might have been too much, seeing himself where he knew he shouldn't be.

"Have you ever noticed anything unusual about me, Bev? Times when I wasn't myself? Not just bad days, but days—or maybe only hours—when I seemed like someone you hardly knew?"

At first, she let loose with a barely-audible giggle, no more than that, then followed it with something that sounded vaguely like an attempt to swallow the rest of her laughter. It had occurred to her, no doubt, in that short mini-second of a moment, that the question had been a serious one. "Ray, you're one of the most consistent men I've ever met."

"Consistent?"

"I've only known you for a few weeks, but yes, I'd say consistent. I know what to expect when we work together. I don't have to worry about temper tantrums or sudden outbreaks of egomania from you. We can differ on things and still respect each other's opinions — no hurt feelings."

Wrong straw, he thought. *You're grasping at the wrong straw. No Sybil here. This isn't about multiple personalities, it's about one personality. One badly frightened personality quickly losing touch with himself.*

"Ray, about the IPMs on *Timescape* . . ."

"You were right," he said in a whisper. "I think I'm beginning to understand that now. The world's spinning faster than when we were kids, when all you needed to sell breakfast cereal was some animated kid saying, `I want my Malt-O-Meal.' Now . . . well, things are a little more complicated, aren't they?"

"They don't have to be."

255

"Don't they? I wonder how we slow them down, make them . . . (*CUT TO*)
". . . comprehendible?"
Oh Christ.

6

The room was pitch-black here and it took a moment for his eyes to adjust to the sudden darkness. Out of the shadows came a sound, a *clickety-clicking* that he recognized as the sound of a projector, and he slowly put it together in his mind. He . . . *they* were in the projection room now.

"What did you say?" Bev asked.

"Uh . . . nothing."

"It works better now, don't you think?"

"What does?"

She glanced over her shoulder, her expression partially masked by the shadows, but even in the dark he could see the trace of a smile as if she thought he were joking with her. "Hey, I know you didn't want to do this, at least not initially."

The Timescape *spot. She's talking about the* Timescape *spot.*

"But you were right," he said calmly. He sat forward in the chair, feeling an arhythmic hammering in his chest. He wondered if his heart were beating faster, trying to keep up with the seconds, minutes, hours that were flashing by. And it felt as if just by wondering, his heart skipped another half-beat. "It does work better now."

"I'm glad you think so."

"Bev?"

"What?"

"I need to tell you something. It's going to sound insane, absolutely Atascadero out-of-my-mind insane. But I need you to listen, because I'm not even sure how much of it I'm going to get out." And he told her about the first time it had happened in his apartment late at night, and the second time in the subway station, and the third time when he had suddenly been at the restaurant with her, and it all seemed to blur together like a grayish-black nightmare that had only just begun. "Five minutes ago," he said finally, "we were in my office, and I was staring out the window wondering what you meant by *consistent*."

Except for a soft intake of air, she was perfectly motionless in the darkness, not saying a word, not giving off a hint of what thoughts were going through her mind at that moment.

"Bev?"

"I don't know what to say."

"You think I'm crazy, don't you?"

"No, of course not." She had draped an arm over the back of her chair as he had shared his story with her, and now she swung the chair all the way around, face-to-face with him, as if she wanted to be able to read his expression in the dull, greenish-white glow of the projector. "Do you know what time it is now?"

"No."

"It's nearly five o'clock. The conversation we had in your office was this morning, almost seven hours ago."

"Oh sweet Jesus."

"Ray, we had a quick lunch at Mattie's, spent two or three hours in a head-banger over what to do to placate the folks at B.M. Myers, did a conference call with Jim Mathews at Timex, and have been hiding out in here for at least a couple of hours now. We've been together the whole time."

"But I don't remember any of that."

"Not a minute?"

"Not since this morning when you told me things don't have to be complicated." He leaned back to flip on the light switch, because it was *her* face that was hidden in shadow now and he didn't like the idea of not knowing what she might be hiding. Instantly, the room went from dark to . . .

(*CUT TO*)

. . . light, and he found himself back at his apartment again, sitting in the kitchen. A slight tremor waffled through his body. He closed his eyes, took a deep breath, and tried to hold himself together. How long was this going to go on?

"Ray?"

The sound of the woman's voice swam up from somewhere nearby. He opened his eyes again, feeling the muscles in the back of his neck tighten. The telephone was off the hook and lying in his lap. He raised it to his ear, listened.

"Ray?"

It was Sherrie's voice.

"Are you still there?"

"Sherrie?" He felt his throat narrow ever so slightly, and fought back a sob that was trying to force its way out. "Don't hang up! Please, for God's sake, don't hang up on me."

"I'm not hanging up; I just got on. Are you all right?"

"Yes. No . . . not really. Hell, I don't know anymore." He sank back in the chair until his body felt as if it had melted into the soft, padded leather. "Where are you?"

"At home. We got in about an hour ago. There was a delay taking off from Orlando, almost three hours. I thought if you didn't mind . . ."

Home?

". . . I'd keep Robin until tomorrow."

"What day is it?" he asked.

"Saturday."

He stared down the hallway toward the living room. The curtains were drawn, but he could tell it was dark out. If the sun were up there would be a soft, golden-yellow glow washing in around the edges. Instead, he could barely make out the dark lines of the La-Z-Boy and the couch.

"What time is it?"

"A little after ten. Ray, did I wake you?"

"No, no, you didn't wake me. But I want you to . . ."

(*CUT TO*)

". . . come over as soon as you—"

Too late.

The receiver was gone.

He stared numbly at his empty hand, first curling it into a fist, then prying it open again, grateful that he could *feel* the mechanics of the motion. But the phone . . . it was gone now. So was the table, where he had been sitting. And the refrigerator, the stove, the plastic simulated

Slipping

wood-grained cannister set on the counter. All of it was gone. Across the room from him, in its place, he found the familiar face of a newscaster on the television screen, and the couch up against the wall, and the ceiling-to-floor curtains open. He was in the living room now.

Through the window, he could see where an orange-brown haze had settled over the cityscape. It was evening, he decided. City colors were always muddier in the evening.

That was something he had never noticed before his separation from Sherrie two short months ago. But the day he had moved his last box of clothes out of the house, he had come here, and standing in the entryway he had looked out this same window. The world had been a dirty place that day. Dirtier than he had ever imagined it could be. It hadn't gotten any cleaner since then.

Sherrie, he thought. *I was on the telephone, talking to Sherrie.*

And what he had to do now was get her back on the phone again, get her to come over so she could stand right next to him, maybe even hold onto his hand when he closed his eyes and woke up somewhere else, some*time* else. Maybe then she could tell him what had happened, if he were crazy, or if (as he had come to fear) the world had suddenly begun to spin a little faster while he was busy looking back at their marriage—hoping, praying, *needing* things to be the way they used to be. *There is no going back. There's only going forward.*

He pulled himself out of the La-Z-Boy, all his weight on the arms, and before he had fully balanced himself, there was a knock at the front door.

"Ray, are you in there?"

It was Bev.

He felt his way along the hallway, his legs unexplicably weary. It was not an easy task to keep himself balanced. *That's because your gravity's changing,* he thought crazily. He pulled open the door, and leaned heavily against its edge.

Bev stared at him in silence, her eyes bright with surprise. "Jesus, Ray, what's the matter with you? You look awful."

He glanced down and was madly amused to find himself dressed in a bathrobe and socks. The robe was open. He had an old pair of boxer shorts on underneath and a tee-shirt with a stain that looked like dried egg. "I'm sorry," he said as he closed the robe and tightened the sash around his waist.

"Are you okay?"

"I . . . I . . . don't know."

"You haven't been in all week. I've been trying to get you on the phone. Don't you ever answer the damn thing?"

"I do . . . I was . . ." He turned, and pointed weakly toward the kitchen. "I was just talking to Sherrie a minute ago."

"Has she been to see you lately?"

Lately? He realized he wanted to ask her what time it was, but hours didn't matter anymore. It was days and weeks and maybe even months that concerned him now. *Lately? When was that?* "I'm . . . not sure. What day is it?"

"You keep asking me that. Every time I talk to you, you ask me what day it is."

"Well?"

"Thursday, Ray. It's Thursday."

His body slumped heavily against the door . . .

(*CUT TO*)

. . . and he heard the phone ringing.

Wherever he was, it was dark now. There was the luminescent glow of a clock face nearby—9:56 P.M.—and a sliver of light coming from somewhere behind him. It divided the darkness into two uneven sections: one on his right, which seemed to exist only a foot or two beyond him; the other, which seemed to stretch across an open area, through a doorway and beyond. He pulled himself up to one elbow, realizing suddenly that this was his bedroom and he had been sleeping.

The phone rang again.

He found the receiver and brought it to his ear without a word.

"Ray?"

"Yeah."

"It's Sherrie."

He closed his eyes, and in the complete darkness could feel his hands trembling, as if they belonged to a boy about to pin his first corsage to the bosom of a girl's dress. The last time he had seen her had been just before she had left for Florida with Robin. They had

Slipping

met for lunch in a little cafe off Market Street called Demercurio's, and talked about how things were going, her in her life, him in his. They had always been on good speaking terms, even as the strain of their two careers had sometimes raised their voices. It had been a pleasant conversation that time out, and yes—though he hadn't said so at the time—he had allowed himself the vague hope that some time down the road he would be able to move his things back home again. It was a hope he wanted to share with her even now, but he couldn't seem to get it clear in his head just how he should go about saying so.

"Ray?"

She had changed her hair style since their separation, cut it short in the front and brushed it away from her face, bringing out the soft slender contours of her cheeks, the bright innocent hazel of her eyes. She had changed other things as well. Started wearing bigger, bolder earrings like the pair with the black onyx stones. And she had used her own credit card to pay for their lunch at Demercurio's. But the thing that hurt the most was this: she had changed from an unhappy woman to a happy woman. He had watched it happen.

"We're never getting back together again, are we?" he asked hoarsely.

"You need help, Ray. You can't keep locking out the world."

"*Are* we?"

There was a pause—he had to give her that—a moment of consideration before she actually answered him. Then she said it: "No."

He closed his eyes . . .

(*CUT TO*)

. . . and began to cry.

"Don't cry, Daddy."

I have to cry. It's started now and I don't think it's ever going to stop.

He took his hands away from his face, and she was there, standing in front of him . . . his little girl.

"Robin?"

"I didn't mean to make you sad," she said. Sherrie was standing directly behind her, with her hands on Robin's shoulders as if she were

261

trying to make certain his daughter didn't get too close. For her own protection, no doubt. Daddy hadn't been himself lately.

He became aware of the tall ceiling overhead, of the three rows of tables, of another small group of people huddled together at the other end of the room. This was a place he had never been before.

"Where are we?"

"It's called Oak Ridge," Sherrie said. "It's a treatment facility."

"Oak Ridge." He liked the sound it made. "Ooo—ak—rrr—idge."

On the table in front of him, he noticed the cafeteria trays. Sherrie and Robin apparently hadn't been hungry. They had hardly touched their food: a little milk from an open carton, half a serving of apple sauce gone, and a few bites out of a hamburger that must have been Robin's. His own tray was empty, though he couldn't remember what he had had to eat. Then he started to cry again.

"We've got to leave now, Ray."

"You just got here."

"We've been here all afternoon," Sherrie said. She had a look in her eye, as if her heart were breaking, and he thought she might join him in his tears, but she didn't. "We'll come back again next Sunday. I promise."

"Promise?"

"Yes."

"I love . . ."

(*CUT TO*)

". . . you," he said. Though he was somewhere else by the time he had finished the words. It was a small room. Two beds. A stale, unventilated smell in the air. He glanced around . . .

(*CUT TO*)

. . . him.

A different place.

Robin was there now, holding his hand.

"You haven't been shaving, Daddy."

He stared at her. God, she was beautiful.

"You should shave."

"I'm . . ."

(*CUT TO*)

". . . sorry," he said.

Somewhere new—no, the cafeteria this time—and Bev was there. She was wearing the saddest face he had ever seen her wear. "*Timescape* opened with a weekend take of nearly seven million," she was saying. "They're happy folks at the production company."

"*Time* . . ."

(*CUT TO*)

". . . *scape*?" he asked, and found himself sitting in a wheelchair outside on a flagstone patio, overlooking a grassy knoll.

Sherrie was with him, holding his hand the same way Robin had held it, as if she were afraid she might lose him completely if she let go.

"It's a beautiful day, isn't it?" she said.

"Please don't go away . . ."

(*CUT TO*)

7

"*I've got to talk fast because I don't know how long I might be here. A few seconds? A minute? Maybe an hour? Sometimes it's hard to tell the difference between here and that* other *place. They can fool you if you don't watch them. One's right. One's wrong. It's confusing. Every once in a while I have to remind myself what day it is and where I live. And there's always the danger, I suppose, that if I'm not careful, I might drift a little too far from the reality loop. It's happened, I've heard, to some of the best of them.*"

Raymond Hewitt